The Actor

The Actor

Bibhuti Bhushan Pradhan

Translated by
Dr Tapan K Panda

BLACK EAGLE BOOKS
2021

 BLACK EAGLE BOOKS

USA address:
7464 Wisdom Lane
Dublin, OH 43016

India address:
E/312, Trident Galaxy, Kalinga Nagar,
Bhubaneswar-751003, Odisha, India

E-mail: info@blackeaglebooks.org
Website: www.blackeaglebooks.org

First International Edition Published by
BLACK EAGLE BOOKS, 2021

THE ACTOR
by **Bibhuti Bhushan Pradhan**
Translated by **Dr Tapan K Panda**

Original Copyright © **Author's Family**
Translation Copyright © **Dr Tapan K Panda**

Cover & Interior Design: Ezy's Publication

ISBN- 978-1-64560-198-2 (Paperback)
Library of Congress Control Number: 2021942602

Printed in United States of America

Foreword

Reclusive Bibhuti Bhushan

Literature is an analogous history of society. While history deliberates on the ascension of kings and rules, war, victory, and defeats, literature speaks about the common man's life and livelihood, dreams, and their broken hope. If the creator of such literature is as sensitive and capable as Bibhuti Bhushan (1957-2016), then those creations touch the quota of being germane.

Bibhuti Bhushan came into the literature arena very late and as if he was occupied, and left us untimely. He passed away at a time when he was crafting very memorable and soul touching stories and novels. This was unfortunate news for Odia literature. Add onto this, he was highly self-respecting and averse to publicity – from that standpoint, not much could be published during his lifetime. Probably he didn't receive any institutional awards other than 'Katha Award' for his novel. After reading the stories from his collections, the readers can realize how worthless were all these matters compared to his enlightened creativity.

Bibhuti Bhsuhan's vocabulary and wordage are exemplary. He was privy to the very rural, colloquial in-country language as well as to the sophisticated, elitist language of the modern, corporate world. He supplemented his stories with visual imageries like a painter who illustrates his imagination on a piece of canvas. His readers experienced and comprehended his stories without difficulty. Stories of Bibhuti Bhsuhan have the uncanny ability to reach to the core of his reader's heart. Many of his stories including *Prajapati'ra ghara* (Butterfly's House), *Khet Aara Paari Gaon* (Village on the other side of the Field) and *Adharatira Gapa* (Midnight Stories) stand testimony to this reality.

As an individual, Bibhuti Bhushan was idealistic and had immense faith in deeply rooted Indian values. He knew that the world around him in which he lived was not what he had imagined or wished for. He didn't accept a world where empathy, compassion, and sensibilities were receding and chicanery, deceitfulness, and ego were on a constant rise.

He was mapping an alternative world through his stories and novels. His story about a little girl Manu who wanted to draw a picture of a house for a butterfly- who was unwilling to return home (in the story 'Butterfly's House') came to an end, with the despair and expiration of millions of orphans.

Bibhuti Bhushan's dexterity in mapping helplessness and the life of rural people is exemplary. While reading his stories, the readers think- Alas! Could the writer have been kind to the characters? They shouldn't have suffered so much! At this moment, my memories transcend to Nobel prize winning author Ernest Hemmingway's words on the writer and his characters. Hemmingway has said- relationship between the writer and his characters is like a fair- going father son duo. They begin their journey from home with a condition that the son will follow his father but after a while the scenario changes and wherever the son wants, the father follows. But at that moment, the alert father has to assert his role or else it will be the end of the night and they can't return from the fair. Similarly, if the characters in the stories of Bibhuti Bhushan are sad and lamenting, he never made an effort to make the characters happy. Had he tried the same in his stories, he would have failed miserably like the father who entrusted the duties of visiting the fair in the hands of his son. If in the story, 'Butterfly's House' the step mother could have cared a bit more about Manu, the story would have lost the existing depth of pathos.

Bibhuti Bhushan's dexterity is not confined to subject identification alone, rather it extends to his vivid expressions. His other competency is style and character building (texturing). We can take the 'midnight story' as an example. The story created a huge furore among the readers when published in Katha for the first time. The main protagonist of the story is an ambitious, selfish, narrow minded, person centric, and greedy Odia housewife. To project her vices, the writer didn't introduce any other characters in the story. The story is crafted in such a way that the reader starts assuming that the protagonist was talking to her childhood friend 'Naaba'. Simply and lucidly, without any inhabitation, the village dame is describing the household chores, children, and her success and failures. It's in the concluding sentence of the story, the reader experiences that there was no friend Nabaa who was listening to the protagonist but she was voicing her thoughts. A single sentence in the story turns it from an ordinary to a classic one when she says- Ehe! I am just blabbering after seeing a vague dream.

Each story of Bibhuti Bhushan is heart touching. Normally, the excellence of a story is judged by two metrics- its readability and memorability. A story is great when it can be read with ease and effortlessly. Similarly, if the impact of a story lingers in the reader's memory for a long time, we can designate the same as a 'great story'. Bibhuti Bhushan's stories have already excelled in these two dimensions time and again.

I am sure that the English translation of his novel 'Nata' by Dr Tapan K Panda will bring more audiences to the magical world of Late Bibhuti Bhushan's creations.

Gourahari Das

Anubhab
378, Village Baramunda
Bhubaneswar-751003

Nata and My Father

It was a sheer thrill in the mundane lives of the villagers. An escape from the monotony of day to day life...

Along with the fragrance of mango blossoms; sweet scented jasmines; enchanting smell of *fagu*; the banyan and peepal tree near our house laden with new baby leaves; the hide and seek game we children played behind the stacked paddy in the barn yards; having no particular work in hand (for the harvest season being already over and there is still time for the preparation for new crops), people idling away their time in playing cards and with the idols of *Radha-Krishna* in the village temple being prepared for their annual expedition in the *vimana(s)*, came the Spring into our village.

And every year, along with the spring came this splendid event, to unfold itself in all its hue to make the spring festival more colorful and to stir ripples of excitement in the otherwise stagnant village life. This grand event was the annual *Jatra* performance during the *Dola utsav* (Holi festival). It was truly an important and much awaited event for the villagers. Since most of the villagers had no access to TV or cinemas (except some affluent families), *the Ramlila, Chaiti Ghoda nacha, Sakhi kandhei nacha* and *Pala* etc. were the only and limited sources of entertainment for them. But no other event was on par with the *jatra* in creating so much enthusiasm (and providing some real entertainment).

After much serious discussions and many meetings among the village elders, every year before holi, one party would be selected and contacted (by the *jatra* committee members). And when the party was booked, posters would be printed and pasted on the walls of almost all the houses and other important places of the village and nearby villages, announcing the upcoming event. Now when I think of those posters, they were not at all fanciful or artistic. But those black and white posters were enough in themselves to provoke the exhilaration among all of us.

Now the countdown begins...

The only topic of discussions would be the upcoming *jatra* (theatre) and only *jatra*. Whether the artists of the concerned party are good or not, how good-looking the heroine or hero is, etc. etc. Anklets and necklaces would be scrubbed and cleaned. Much treasured naphthalene-scented sarees would be brought out of the boxes and put out in the sun. And the women folk of the village would become busier in their annual makeover. And with the perspective of the makeshift bazaar that came along with the *jatra* (theatre) party, we children would be happy (because we would get the chance to buy some toys or enjoy some tasty snacks like *baraa, piaji* and *jalebi* etc.)

Then one day, bringing an end to our waiting, the *jatra* party would arrive in the village. At first two to three big lorries, loaded with the props of the party would arrive at the UP school premises of the village (where arrangements were made for their stay). Then the artists would arrive in a bus. We would be eagerly waiting for them and look at them with wonder-stricken eyes, when they arrived. They were welcomed into the village, with *hulahuli* (a sound made with the tricky use of tongue by women, common in Odisha and WestBengal on different auspicious occasions) and the *shankha* (conch sound).

Now, my father's role in the picture. *Bapa* (my father Bibhuti Bhusan Pradhan), along with some other youths of the village were like the volunteers in charge during the entire period of the *jatra* performance. Beginning from the responsibility of the comfortable stay of the party members, their eating arrangements to the printing of the tickets to their sales, sitting arrangements for the audience; Bapa and his friends would actively involve themselves in the smooth management of the event.

After the arrival of the party, stage (built of soil, which remained unused for the rest of the year) preparation was done. And on an auspicious day there would be the *Bahi puja* (ritual of offering of the drama scripts to the Gods and Goddesses for their smooth enactment and success). Before each play, stage rehearsals would be performed during the day and an auto rickshaw with a *jatra* party member would roam around nearby areas, announcing (through microphone) about the play that was going to be performed.

It was almost like a ritual to perform mythological dramas, such as Bhakta Prahallada, Prahllada- the devotee), Abhimanyu baddha (Murder of Abhimanyu) etc. on the first day. Then there would be historical plays and dramas related to social issues also. Though I could not understand the contents fully, that didn't hamper my spirit of watching and enjoying the dramas with keen interest. And I would always prefer a front seat for that. Everyday, the performance would begin with a *Nrutya natika* (it is like a musical performance, mainly consisting of the *Basanta Rasa* of Radha-Krishna (The romance in the spring of Krishna and Radha). And after that the actual play would begin. At regular intervals, there would be some hilarious acts, called duets too, to ease the moods of the audience.

Since the *jatra* (theatre) artists stayed in the school premises (*jatra* was performed on a pandal (open stage), built near the school) and our house was quite nearer to it, I had uninterrupted access into their camp. And the child artists would be my favourite playmates during that time. I still remember two of their names- Babuli and Kalia and their faces drenched in sweat in fading makeup in the morning. Being invited by my father some of the senior artists would also come to our house at times for a cuppa. In short, we father-daughter duo were deeply connected to the *jatra* artists, in almost every way, during their stay in the village.

I think this is where the seeds of 'Nata' were planted in my father's mind and remained hidden for years in his heart till it was written. Since my father came in close proximity with the *jatra* party members, and got the chance to observe them closely and with keen interest, I think Nata must have taken shape in his subconscious mind from that time. And it was only waiting for the right time (to come into light).

After the *jatra* ended and the artists were gone, the silence became unbearable. For days, we would miss the loud music and the sound of announcements made through mike in the evenings. The abandoned stage, the broken signboards, worn out pieces of papers and any other such remnants of the *jatra* would fill our hearts with sadness. The reader can understand this very feeling while reading 'Nata' (Sandhya belaku ei padia ......dhoi neba adinia barsha).

I have witnessed all these events (though I was just a kid at that time and after that I did not get any chance to watch *jatra* on an open pandal) and have seen my bapa's love for *jatra*. Perhaps that is why all the characters of this novel seem so real to me. While reading 'Nata' one can easily feel that each and every character has got his or her share of importance in it. Starting from the protagonist Binod to Dashabhuja party owner Bini madam, from emotional Bicha to Benu Ustad, from Malini to Munna Panda, everyone has been given justice by the author. Even the unknown village woman, who used to draw *alpanas* in evenings (from whom Binod seeks farewell, silently from distance and is remembered by him frequently) and the banyan tree in the university campus (which is personified as *'Dhyani Buddha'*) are equally treated, as the main characters. Without them, the novel would seem incomplete.

While Bicha, being the announcer of the party fascinates the reader with his quick-witted rhapsodies (*dhaga* or *aashu kabita (Spot poems)* in Odia), Benu Ustad (a former famous artist, but now has no particular work) draws sympathy from the reader for being neglected and ignored by manager Bholi babu and insulted from time to time by some ill-mannered party members. While *jatra* writer Shankar Bhola makes one laugh with his madness for fame but having no knowledge in his craft; womanizer and drunkard Jitu Mohanty compels the reader to hate him for his shrewd tricks of negative publicity, he uses to create demand for his plays. Come to director Kamal Mishra, the reader may get confused by his contradictory personality. At times, he seems just like an ordinary drama director, who is only concerned about the success of his plays, but at times, he is also quite philosophical in his behaviour and attitude.

While Malini, though not deserving of her current position in the party, can go to any extent to earn money and popularity, her husband Charan Das isn't less avarice. He uses her to enhance his social and monetary status. Similarly by hook or by crook Munna Panda wants to raise his value as a popular villain in the field of *jatra*. Bishnu babu's character is quite similar to the character of Benu Ustad, who used to play popular roles like King Puru to Sehensaah Bahadur Shah Zafar in the past. But at present, it has almost nothing to do with the party.

In spite of this he cannot just detach himself from *jatra*. So he comes back to the camp again and again. And here, the reader can feel the helplessness of his daughter Lata, who still has not got the status of a regular artist and is paid with a small allowance. Characters like Suna Bhauja, Suresh Bhanja, comedian Babana Biswal, Tanushree, Saudamini and Dhira Babu are worth mentioning. They have influenced Binod's life in various ways. Sometimes they amaze him with their kindness, friendship, love and respect towards him and sometimes they disappoint him with their immature actions (like Saudamini, when she plays the role of Rizia Begum in *Nila Shaila*).

But the character, whom Binod remembers with reverence at almost every step of his life is Professor Samsuddin. He is not only his university professor but also like his friend, guide and philosopher. He never ever underestimates Binod for being a *jatra* artist. Rather he always remains there for him as a silent inspiration.

Now I am coming to Binod. Most of the time, I meet my father in this character of his novel. Binod's deep love and devotion for *Lord Jagannath* (*Dura hoi bi se nikatatama....apahancha hoi bi antaranga* (being farthest he is the closest, being unfathomable he is the intimate), his attraction towards Puri, his love for writer Surendra Mohanty and his novel 'Nila Shaila (The Blue Mountain)', his revolution against hypocrisy and hierarchical system inside the party, his soft nature, his hankering for true love and affection, almost at every step he is like my father.

And as per Bini madam, I think she is like an idealistic

character. She is perhaps the reflection of my father's imagination, that a *jatra* party owner should be like this: educated, graceful, thoughtful and having respect for the artists and love for art. Yet who can be strict, when it is needed.

While reading 'Nata', the reader would feel an urge to think about the nature of the relationship between Binod and Bini madam for sure. Is it the relationship of an employer and an employee? Is it friendship? Or is it a relationship between a lover and his beloved? But isn't it better to leave some relationships unnamed?

I have read 'Nata' several times. Each time I read it, I felt amazed at the intricacy of the way the writer has presented the story. Not only because it is my father's novel, but as an unbiased reader, I can say that 'Nata' is one of the best literary works I have ever read.

I would like to thank Tapan sir for taking this painstaking task of translating my father's novel. As per me, translation is perhaps the most difficult section of literature. Bringing another person's work to the readers in a different language while remaining true to its originality (both in purpose and in theme) is such a humongous task (though we get to read many great works of different languages because of the generous efforts of the writers who translate others' works). That's why, I am more than thankful to Tapan sir for bringing my father's work to a global platform. I do not have enough words to express my gratitude towards him. If my father would have been still with us, he would have felt so happy to see his work being translated in English.

Now, while writing about 'Nata', I am expecting this miracle with all the sincerity of my heart:

"The stage is still dark... The play has not begun yet... I am sitting in the front row, anticipating a great show ahead...

Suddenly the stage becomes illuminated with the announcement of the first scene...

And what am I seeing!

From there, here comes Bapa towards me with a smiling face!..."

- Preeti Prajna Pradhan

Bhubaneswar,
Odisha, India

(Preeti Prajna is the eldest daughter of Late Sri Bibhuti Bhushan Pradhan and herself an upcoming and yet powerful writer who carries the brilliance of her father in scripting stories and emoting issues on letters- Dr Tapan K Panda)

Connecting with Late Writer
Sri Bibhuti Bhushan Pradhan

By the time I met the writings of Late Sri Bibhuti Bhushan Pradhan, he had left for heavenly abode as if he was in a hurry to leave this world for a better place. Death waits for none and when death decided to befriend Late Sri Bibhuti Bhushan Pradhan, he left jolly well without giving a notice to anyone- family, friends and millions of fans who liked his writing. But for Shri Bibhuti Bhusan- there was no waiting for others; he was as adamant as his writings and left us all in a sudden. If one reads his stories and novels, can realize how much pain he builds into the characters and sometimes as a reader you will feel as if the author could have been kinder to them. It is my misfortune that I never met Late Sri Bibhuti Bhushan Pradhan in person. A part of this can be attributed to my absence from Odisha for more than two decades..

Then trustees of Tapasya Foundation decided to broaden the scope and include promotion of Odia literature as one of the key goals of the foundation. The awards were established in 2016 but they could only materialize in late 2017. As the founding member of Tapasya Foundation I had to surrender my wishes to eminent jurists for selection of worthy contributors to Odia literature. In the very first award event, the jury chair suggested the writings of Late Shri Bibhuti Bhushan Pradhan for 'Tapasya Saswata Purashkar'. I got photocopies of majority of his work collected from magazines and couple of books just one day before my travel to University of Bordeaux- where I was heading for an international teaching assignment, It was my good fortune that I was in my favorite place teaching only 90 minutes a day to a bunch of students drawn from various parts of the world and plenty of time for myself. I used these long hours of solitude reading his writings (along with the copy of Jambu loka by Sri Bhima Prusty). I was thankful to the jury members for both the recommendations for the awards. Now I can count those few weeks as one of the best times of life reading two of the powerful writers of my time.

I fell in love with his writing the way he would situate the plot, introduce and build the characters, develop parallel tracks and then suddenly make them meet and move forward. For a reader, these were magical moments. Tapasya Foundation decided to publish all his stories through Paschima Publications as an anthology of short stories. I came across Late Sri Bibhuti Bhushan's elder daughter Preeti Prajna Pradhan during this period. My sporadic interactions with her made me understand what kind of a person he was, his choices, skill sets and his mastery in using country (deshaja) language to ornament the stories and novels. As a translator, it is important to not only know the author's writing style but also the author himself - that's what the creative writing professor taught me at University of Houston in my audit course. I could meet writer Shri Bibhuti Bhushan through my interactions with Preeti.

Nata (The Actor) is my fifth translation in recent past. I

started with **Asati** (Sri Prashant Patanaik) followed by **From 1909** (Autobiography of Queen Ratna Prava Devi); **Bahni Balaya** (Late Sri Madan Mohan Mishra) and Ramaku Maaribaara Panchoti Upaya (Sri Devadas Chhotray). Majority of these works are published through an arrangement with Black Eagle Books, USA. Tapasya Foundation has a vision to take Odia literature to a global audience including the millennial kids who hardly study Odia in schools these days..Here is my homage to one of the powerful writers of contemporary Indian literature.

Noted columnist, academy award winning author Sri Gourahari Das has written the foreword for the book along with a memoir from Preeti Prajna. I sincerely thank Sri Das for his kind gesture. I am also obliged to the family of Late Sri Bibhuti Bhushan Pradhan for permitting me to translate this masterpiece. My sincere gratitude to Sri Satya Pattanaik and Sri Ashok Parida of Black Eagle Books for their effort in bringing this master piece of Late Shri Bibhuti Bhushan Pradhan in the current form for English readers.

Happy Reading

Dr Tapan K Panda

15th June 2021
Hyderabad, India

GLOSSARY

- Bapa - Father
- Gana Natya- Theatre group
- Krishnachura- Peacock flower(Gulmohar)
- Raja- The festival is essentially the celebration if the earth's womanhood
- Rasa- Especially the emotional or aesthetic impression of a work of art
- Chita- A watery mixture prepared with rice grain
- Gamha Purnima-(Rakhi Purnima- a full moon night where cows are worshipped)
- Kalash- Urn
- Bhai (Brother)
- Bhauja- Sister-in-law (Elder Brother's wife)
- Pithau- White rice paste
- Alata- A dye used by ladies on their feet which is red in colour
- Kastandi- A feathery ,long stalked, broom like blossom normally found on river beds
- Mudra- Symbolic gesture
- Baula- Bullet wood is an evergreen tree
- Nahak- Surname
- Sandha- Bull
- Mahakala- Beyond time
- Bada Osha- The "Festival of Fasting" celebrated in the month of Kartik in Odisha
- Pakhala- An Odiya term used for an Indian food

consisting of cooked rice washed or fermented in water.

- Gomutra- Cow's urine
- Nirmalya- Is the dried rice Mahaprasad of Puri Jagannath temple
- Bada Danda- Grand road on which the deities make their way to their aunt's place
- Shodasha Upchar- Is a complete process to do the rituals of a pooja
- Sathiyae Pauti Bhoga- Food items offered to Lord Jagannath in the holy temple of Puri
- Chhena Poda- A sweet made from cheese
- Arisa Pitha- A sweet made with jaggery and rice flour
- Chitau Pitha-Rice pancake
- Daru Brahma- Daru means wood. Brahma is the mystic expression of the Lord
- Devadasi-A female artist who was dedicated to worship and serve a deity or a temple for the rest of her life.
- Nabakalebar-The word Nabakalebar is a Sanskrit word, that is "Naba" means new, "Kalebar" means body
- Dayana - Also named as Indian Worm wood, Fleabane. Aromatic smell of Dayana keeps the insect away; this is the reason in Puri Jagannath temple Dayana leaves are used on wooden Lord worship
- Panchuka- It falls in the month of Kartik. It is a practice among Odias to give up non-vegetarian food during the entire month of Kartika. Those who cannot do so, shun non-vegetarian food for the last five days or Panchuka
- Baise Pahacha- Twenty two steps in Puri Jagannath temple

- Devdasi- A female artist who was dedicated to worship and serve a deity or a temple
- Dahuka- A person who controls the movement of the chariot
- Ratna Bedi - The throne of Lord Jagannath
- Hulahuli -Ululatus- A kind of inarticulate sound, uttered by women on joyful occasions
- Nandighosa - Chariot of Lord Jagannath
- Ghosayatra- Chariot festival
- Koili Baikuntha - A place in Puri Jagannath temple where old images are buried during Nava Kalebara
- *Chera Panhara* -Customary sweeping of the chariot floor by the Puri king before Ratha Yatra

1

The moon was rising from the profoundness of the meadow.

Why is the ascendant, so exasperated? The azure of the month of Ashwin is in travail. In the moonlit night, the meadow looks like the very picture of an ocean, vast, and immense and amid is the silhouette of an assembled multitude. People from the nearby villages have come to watch an opera. The flashlight in their hands sometimes gleams and gets extinguished like a witch's cauldron.

Today Bitchaa is playing the same annoying song on the record player. It's not a musical song, but arid jubilation and cheeky chime. A concoction of sarcous and reecho.

He had told many times to Bitchaa to throw away those cassettes. But what's the value of his desire and wish here?' Dasabhuja Theatrical Company' is governed by the instruction of the manager Bholi Babu.

How old is Bholi babu? Is he fifty or sixty years old? He has a son, a daughter- in- law, a daughter and son- in- law. Every day as a ritual he unzips his torn leather bag and distributes money in the morning and evening to the people in the opera party to have snacks and screams - Bitcha when will you play the music cassette?

Bitcha said-'I returned just now after carrying out the announcement in the public. It was a tough day and my body is aching.' Wiping his face in the towel Bitcha said Bholi babu,' Give me my money. I will go and have some tea'.

-Bholi babu said,' You have to go immediately and play the record '.

This is an everyday affair of Dasabhuja *Gananatya*. The senior artists like Binodh don't fall into line every day to get the money from Bholi babu for morning and evening snacks but when he sees old artists like Benu Ustad and Raghu babu spreading their hands in front of Bholi babu to have mercy on them and to give them money for the snacks Binodh revolts in anger. Sometimes Bholi babu on the pretext of not having change deducts their money.

Benu Ustad and Raghu babu are now old- fashioned people in the theatre but once upon a time they enacted in many plays and had name and fame. Time is ruthless and unpredictable.

A sour burp made Binod uncomfortable. He has been suffering from gastroenteritis a year after he joined the opera. He takes antacid syrup every day or chews Digen tablets and lies down on a folding cot in the evening .Sometimes Tanushree , Malini, Benu Ustad, and Raghu babu come to meet him. But today no one has come to meet him. He could only hear that cheeky chime in the loudspeaker.

The azure in travail is now serene and restful. The moon is far up the horizon. Binod all of a sudden remembered few lines from Sachi Routray's poem' *Sadya prasuti janha uthichi,bidari matara kumara yoni*' (The sun rose like a new bornchild from the womb of a mother). Oh! It's not only a poem; it's just like a sharp knife! It pierces the heart and makes it bled.

Professor Samsuddin while teaching imagery and

metaphor gave many such examples from Odia poems. His reasoning was- Imagery is like a meteor, diverged from its orbit which touches the soul. It ignites the consciousness for a moment and then gets extinguished. In this regard , the example from English Literature and English poems is mere erudition which doesn't have an impact on a student's mind.

Professor Samsuddin was awesome.

He motivated him in the university campus under the *Krishnachura* tree. Binod often thinks about those momentous evenings of his life. Many of them thought it as a wastage of time but for him the feeling it arouses was everlasting. He might not have realized the true meaning of life if he wouldn't have met professor Samsuddin. Professor Samsuddin said - 'Literature is like a flame .If you are unable to make the students understand its true sense, you can never quench their thirst, and it's futile. There are many connotations for the word 'Futile' in the dictionary and stack of books in the library but when you become a teacher....'

Binod could neither become a teacher nor an officer. He couldn't even become a bank clerk and finally became an actor in the opera. He is just a medium to manifest the playwright's expression to the audience that too with the director's gauged direction.

There are so many regrets in life and the teaching profession is one of them. If he could have adjusted to the situation, he could have easily become a lecturer of a non-aided college.

What would have happened if he would have become a lecturer? He would have opened a coaching center like Madhu Samal or like a school teacher would have given tuition classes to a group of children during morning and evening or would have published a word-meaning book as an experienced teacher. Rather than that the life of a nomadic theater artist is better. Every time a new place and a new experience, a different play, and different character. At least at this place there is no intellectual theft. Acting is limited to the main stage and the second stage. After the opera is over with the ringing of the last bell the world is limited to Malini Baral's makeup- less face, Benu Ustad's snore, and Bholi babu's spiting the beetle nut juice.

Maybe Bitcha is changing the record player cassette. As soon as the microphone was muted a pack of stray dogs started barking.

Benu Ustad called Nanda in his rough and coarse voice and said-'Why are they barking at this hour? They aren't letting people take rest peacefully. Nanda beat them and chase them away'. Maybe Benu Ustad wasn't in deep sleep and was trying to sleep for some more time. Bholi babu came out of his tent and said' Even if a bullock cart runs over you, you won't get up from your sleep. How can the barking dogs disturb your sleep?'

Benu Ustad didn't give a reply to him. He shouted and said' Ustad are you sleeping again?' Benu Ustad woke up hesitatingly. Bholi babu inspected the tent and said-'When will the chairs be arranged? It's already late night. Don't you have the time sense? It's Bholi babu's habit to trouble others.

-Where did Nanda and Bagula go? Is it my work to arrange the chairs? Benu Ustand answered in an annoying voice. Before leaving Bholi babu commented sarcastically- 'No you only eat and sleep. Why will you take the pain of arranging the chairs?

Benu Ustad was an old actor. He played the role of Shree Krishna in the play 'Gopi Ballabha'. His red lips smeared with Alta and the mysterious gentle smile had once created a fantasy in the young minds of the village girls and women. Now the words uttered by him are more raucous. At present, he teaches only Odishi or the folk dance in 'Dasabhuja'. That is required in few plays for chord scenes otherwise he sits at the back of the musicians and plays Gini or Dilruba. The director Kamal Mishra sometimes encourages him and says, 'Your time will come back again Ustad'. The era of tangy play is coming to an end. Again the sound of Bigul and flute will be heard. The audience will detest the record dance and will demand Gotipua dance or plays like Gopal Ballbaha which is the classical depiction of Rasleela and at that time electric guitar and synthesizer will be worthless. Behala's highest-pitched will be filled in the atmosphere.

Benu Ustad's eyes were filled with thousands of memories and dreams. He has been waiting for that moment and is in Dasbhuja despite Bholi babu's rebuke. Bholi babu often gives him instructions either to arrange the chairs or to supervise in the kitchen.

Benu Ustad tied a red towel and placed the sacred thread on his ear and went towards the open ground.

2

Binod babu! Binod babu!

Binod woke up with Shankar Bhola's sharp and shrill voice. He looked at him angrily and dug his face on the pillow. He is another terror in Dasabhuja and appears suddenly from nowhere after every ten to fifteen days. Twenty years back he was a lecture in a newly opened college for six months and was working there without salary. Since then he considers himself as a lecturer and mentions it before his name as honor from the king. Playwright-alias-director was also mentioned after his name.

Hopeless! He couldn't understand the difference between 'Or' and 'Alias' even after being explained. Rather he grins and says, Binod babu , you can't understand. Playwright means a litterateur, a classical entity. Director means..... Means... Ha! Ha!. Bhola doesn't find words to explain.

Means what? Binod gets irritated and asks.

Means... means.. What else? It means professional. A director is bound to be commercial. There is a controversy between them and it's there. If there is no controversy then is there life in the play? Ha! Ha! Ha!. Bhola laughs and shows his teeth like a monkey. When the pamphlets for the advertisement for the play 'Radha hajigala Gopa Dandarae' were sent to the press, Bhola wrote- Composition:- Lecturer Shankar Bhola (Sabysachi) Playwright ,and Director.

Kamal Mishra asked what's the meaning of Sabysachi within the bracket?

Binod smiled and said- Arjuna the third Pandava who could use both his left and right hand to use his bow and arrow and could aim at the target was called Sabysachi. Bhola writes plays and also gives direction skillfully maybe be because of that Kamal Mishra laughed loudly and struck off the mentioned designation and wrote, Shankar Bhola, Opera play writer

What do you mean by Opera play writer? Why wouldn't the playwright be mentioned? Shankar Bhola asked controlling his anger.

Kamal Mishra answered in a heavy voice- You are a Brahmin but your thread ceremony hasn't been performed, go and wear the sacred thread so that you will be wise enough to understand.

Shankar Bhola got up from there and while leaving he said sarcastically,' Why are the opera groups not prospering?'

Shankar Bhola has a goatee beard and a sharp jaw line with unkempt hair. A Shantiniketan shoulder bag hanging from the shoulder, khadi kurta , and pyjama is the professional attire of Bhola. Malini doesn't like him and says that his body gives stringent smell like a Billy goat.

Muna Panda asks – Does a Billy goat smells stringent?

Wiping her face Malini answered sarcastically- 'No he smells sweet like Mogra flower!'

-How did you know?

Malini could understand the meaning of the question very late. She pulled the saree pallu towards her chest and widened her eyes and said-'Idiot'.

Shankar Bhola has again come today with a script of a new play. He has been saying for a long time that he is writing a sensational story for the opera party.

Bholi babu after distributing the money for the snacks

had taken bath and was sitting for doing the puja. He has much belief and has many gods and goddesses. Apart from the main deity of Dasabhuja's there are photographs of many more gods and goddesses. As the politicians change their party in a similar way he changes the photographs of the gods and goddesses in a year or two. Sometimes, the photo of Anukula Chandra and sometimes Saibaba's photo. Like the tent and chairs of the theatrical company the gods and goddesses are also loaded in a truck and carried to different places. There are boxes allocated for setting, dress, light, and sound system. Similarly there is a box for carrying the photos of gods and goddesses. It is included in the main list of Dasabhuja Theatrical Company. When the camp is winded up at that time Bholi babu looks at the list and shouts- Baga! Are the god and goddesses photos loaded?

While describing the glory of the god he becomes fervent. He tries to make his tone normal and says-'Everything is his resplendence'. We are just materialistic! Can anything be done by man? If God wouldn't have favored then this theatrical company would have been in debt because of madam's childish nature and actions'. Binod thinks that gods and goddesses are only denotational. Bholi babu wants to convey that it's only because of him the theatrical company still exists. It also reflects his concern for madam when he criticizes her for her childish behavior that's why he could become a manager of such a big party.

Bholi babu was ringing the small bell and was reciting Durga Stotra or Bishnu Sahasra Nama. When he saw Shankar Bhola there was a reflection of discontent on his face. Bhola was sitting on a box, was taking out a crumpled cigarette from his kurta's pocket, and was shouting- Nanda; bring the matchstick. Bagula ran towards him holding a wood fire in a tong from the kitchen. The youngsters at the party always listened to Bhola and do his work. They thought-If Bhola wants then they can get a small role in the play. Once they start acting on the stage then why will they arrange the chairs, set the tent, or work in the kitchen as helpers?

Bholi babu stopped reciting Durga Stotra and said-'That is a cash box, how can you sit on that keeping your legs? Bagula was dusting a tin chair to make a place for Bhola to sit. Bholi babu screamed-'I called you so many times to bring a little fire to light the censer. Are you deaf? Bagula explained – 'Dhadia nana(The cook) has pain in his back and I am busy in the kitchen. Am I sitting idle without doing the work?'

-'Is Dahadiya again suffering from back pain? It is my ill fate that all the lazy people are here. I have done a mistake by giving that dope head advance salary for two months. Whom will I blame now?'

Nanda entered with a cup of tea for Bhola. Bholi babu stared at him and asked- 'Did you finish arranging the chairs? Listen Nanda, I am warning you, if this time a single chair breaks, I will deduct your two months' salary.'

Nanda said, 'I have already folded the chairs. You are simply getting angry without knowing anything.'

-'What did you say? When will you learn to speak respectfully with me? Are you not always ready to shout at me?' Poor Nanda left the place silently. Bholi babu closed his eyes and started reciting the prayer.

Maybe Malini was going to take bath with a toothbrush in her mouth. Suddenly she looked at Bhola and said- 'Who is that?'

Bhola said- 'The camp has been set here for a long time. I hope if the play based on the new book could be staged here but before that, there are certain things like book puja, party selection and many more things to do.'

Bholi babu finished his prayer and said- 'Show the book to madam. Check if she likes the content or not.'

-'Bholi babu, have you ever seen me doing work which

isn't up to the mark? Won't anyone like Shankar Bhola's play? Wait and watch how this book becomes a sensation.'

Bholi babu said –'You are always boastful. Were you not boasting for the play 'Radha hajigala Gopa dandarae?'

-' That was an experimental play. It is necessary to change the taste of the audience'.

- 'Change! Useless! If this type of plays is staged then the owner has to sell the theatrical company and open a vegetable godown'.

- 'Why are blaming me unnecessarily? I wrote the play keeping someone in mind but you couldn't stop that person from leaving the party. It was a matter of only Rs 10000 and that has become a big issue for you.'

- 'What did you say? Do you think we would have given her whatever she asked for?'

- 'Was it more to pay one lakh ten thousand rupees for an artist like Saudamini Sen? It's only because of her you have collected two to three lakhs in each camp.'

- ' You may go after her. Who is stopping you?' Bholi babu said in an irritable tone and went outside.

Bhola kept quiet at that moment. Now a day's people are crazy for Saudamini Sen. Tickets are sold in a jiffy in her name. It's only because of her 'Indradhanu Theatrical Company' is prospering at present. They are doing a lot of publicity and it has created a sensation in Bengal, Odisha and Bihar. Just a few years back Indradhanu Theatrical Company's owner was searching for a prospective buyer to sell the company as it wasn't doing well.

3

Outside the green room, at a dark place, Binod was waiting for an odious scene. It will be staged after two more scenes. Malini was changing her dress in the greenroom for that scene. Whenever Binod remembers that scene he becomes obnoxious. He feels as if a serpent is crawling over his leg.

Malini jumps from the riser and embraces him in the center of the stage. The stage becomes dark when Binod comes closer to her to kiss her. After that one could hear the continuous clapping which resonates in the audience gallery. 'Mina, don't switch on the lights till the clapping and whistling aren't over.' Kamal Mishra gives strict instructions to the light operators. After the lights are switched on one could see the lipstick mark of Malini on his cheek like a lifeless symbol. Mina in order to highlight it focuses the spotlight on his face. Binod smears the lipstick on his cheek all over his face like a stupid person and looks like a monkey. The audience gallery again resonates with the clapping sound.

Kamal Mishra said-' Binod babu, I have roped the gist of the whole play in a sequence of only two minutes! It's a symbolic envisage. It has created an impression in the heart of the audience.' Kamal Mishra uses words like symbolic, impression, and effect regularly. Dasabhuja's comedian Baban Biswal could never understand the meaning of these words and says mockingly- 'Mishra Sir, you can write new connotations. We elderly people aren't able to understand what you say.'

Every time when the lights are switched off, Malini bites and sucks his cheek like sucking a ripe mango. Binod feels as if he is entering into the mouth of a hungry python. Why is Malini so passionate? Is it only acting? Binod could never believe it. Malini is married. Her husband Charan Das plays table in Dasabhuja. Sometimes Tanushree in order to tease him says, 'Brother' Malini sister has bitten the cheek of Bina sir so badly and there is a mark on his cheek. Why don't you tell her anything? Charan Das shows his teeth shamelessly and says –'What is so serious about it?' That's simply acting. Your sister knows very well how to depict a romantic scene and that's why she is famous.' Malini's annual payment is one lakh fifty thousand rupees. Other than Soudamini Sen no other theatre actress has received more than eighty thousand rupees as salary. Charan Das takes the advantage of Malini and gets fifty thousand rupees. There are many institutions in every nook and corner of the city in the name of Kalakunja and Sangeet Academy to teach tabla and harmonium. In a meager pay of rupees thousand people are ready to play tabla. There is no scarcity of people to do this job. But in order to keep Malini the owner is bound to pay Charan Das fifty thousand rupees. If Malini wouldn't have been there who would have bothered about Charan Das? Charan Das knows this very well. He also has understood that Malini is growing old and is losing her vigor and vitality. In the next few years, she will get the role of a mother or an abandoned woman. In this regard to earn money if she ties her saree below the belly button or doesn't cover up her chest properly with the saree to attract the audience then what is her fault?

-'Bin! Do you have a cigarette?' Binod became conscious

and was out of his thoughts as Bishu Rath called him. He is another insane person. He has become old and waiting for Biswa Janani theatre to succeed. It is surprising- If he is called as Bishu the insane man, he becomes angry but if he is called as insane Bishu he becomes happy. Bishu was the uncrowned king of the theatre. His lively acting as the defeated King Puru in the play 'Alexander', his role as Sahajahan or in 'Pitrubhakta Kunal's' emperor Ashoka, and many more roles as a king has made him a historic actor. People use to say' because a man plays a king well superbly doesn't mean that he is a king ...' He had physic like a king. At present, one could see his everlasting aristocracy among the rags. But how did to form Biswa Janani Theatrical Company,to bring reformation in the society, to protect the heritage ....etc entered his mind, no one knows. In order to form Biswa Janani Theatrical Company, he sold his property for a meager price. He bought the property from his income from the theatre. But before 'Biswa Janani Theatrical Company came into being, Odisha's theatrical companies stopped staging mythological, historical, and imaginary plays. The aftermath of this was terrible. His wife is now selling flowers in a temple near her father's house. To make living, his daughter Lata has joined Dasabhuja.

Bishnu Rath travelled with the party from one camp to another camp. Bholi babu either told him to sell the tickets or to stand as a gatekeeper near the gate. But when Bini madam came to know about this, she said-' Bishnu babu is a historical personality in the world of Odisha's Opera. Why are you making him to stand as a gate keeper?

Bholi babu spoke like a businessman and said- 'We are managing is expenditure.'

Bini madam said-'This isn't the way to keep the art alive, rather it's an insult to modesty of art. It's better if you tell him to go back home.

What will Bishu babu do in the empty house? He has spent his youth in colorful zari embellished clothes, the trumpet sound of war, the clip-clop sound of the hoof of the horse, and in displaying the warfare technique upstage. Whatever he may be but he isn't a person who will embrace an abandoned life. He goes away here and there for few days and again comes back to Dasabhuja. Lata feels embarrassed as she didn't get a role in any play and thinks of herself as a burden for the party. Other than that she had problems with her insane father. As she didn't get any role in the play so Bholi babu gives her three rupees for her morning and evening snacks and her father also shares with her. He behaves like a small kid and says- 'Lata,won't you give me money to have tea?' Whenever he has money he orders special tea and says to the shopkeeper- Add more cream. After all the money is spent he argues with the shopkeeper and says-'For twenty-five paisa only one sip of tea?' The day he leaves the camp ,Lata from her monthly salary of thousand rupees takes out fifty or hundred rupees and gives it to her old father and looks at the path in which he left very sadly.

If Lata could get a role then her salary will increase to five thousand or seven thousand rupees. The snacks amount will be twenty rupees. At least she could help her old father who has dreams in his eyes to survive. But all of them have an eye on Malini Baral. Kamal Mishra says-' Lata couldn't get rid of her shyness ;how will I take her in the play to earn a bad reputation for myself?

Bishnu babu was ready to leave after smoking. Binod asked-'Were you sleeping? Why didn't you come to the mess in the evening?'

-' My name is Bishnu. Have you not seen Bishnu sleeping in Anantasayana and looking after the world? Why are you asking me about sleeping?' He said this and left somewhere through the backside of the greenroom. Though he is insane sometimes he speaks like a philosopher. Binod thinks that Kamal Mishra's symbolic representation of the scene couldn't represent the deep secret of life which gets enlightened in the broad daylight by the nutty Bishnu Rath's imaginary babbles.

Malini came outside the green room and stood near him and asked-'Sir, Does this saree suit me?'

Binod saw that Malini wore an imitation silk saree which was delivered last week and was standing very close to him.

-Usually, a woman drapes a red silk saree for her marriage or for her nuptial night. Why will someone drape a red silk saree for impressing a man or for going to a park?

He didn't have time to notice Malini's expression to his answer. When the lights were switched off for the interval he walked towards the stage for the next scene.

4

'Murder-rape-gang rape' is Shankar Bhola's new play. Bhola has been telling it for the past three days that it will create a sensation as a seasonal play. Bhola saw everyone sitting quietly and said, 'There was such a big sex scandal in the state. Did any playwright open their mouth?'

Bhola's sounded a little concerned as he wrote the play ' Murder- rape- gang rape' and has worked for the deliverance of the state. Then what is first, is it murder or rape? Rape or gang rape? Which one is first? There is no point to make a foolish person like Bhola understand this. He only understands scams or scandals .

Kamal Mishra spread his leg on a wooden box and said,' What is the value of these seasonal plays? It is very difficult to stage a play. It involves thought process and a lot of hard work so it should be staged for a year or two.'

The cinema halls become empty after one month irrespective of the spicy stuffed by Mahesh Bhatt and Subhash Ghai. Bhola asked- 'What do you say about the progress Mishra babu?'

Binod remembered professor Samsuddin when they were arguing. Professor Mishra brought a cheap script for the departmental play. Professor Samsuddin looked at the book and said- Professor Mishra, did you bring this script for English Department's annual play ? Is it a play or a farce?' Professor Mishra argued on that day and said- 'The taste of the audience is based on the human psychology. He wants whatever he couldn't do because of the values, heritage, ideal, and social norms so the actors and actress should perform that on the stage. Today's play is based on human desire, intention, and longing. Can you deny the truth of human psychology professor Samsuddin?'

-'Where is the end to this satiation? Have you ever thought about what will be the result of this? For the contentment of the audience if we open the door the audience will look for something new every day. To fulfill that a playwright and the audience will forget the academicism and will look for new techniques to draw the character of the actress. But, after that?'

Professor Mishra couldn't give an appropriate answer to this question. Binod also couldn't get an answer to this question though he has spent so many years in the theatre. But what's the point of making the foolish Bhola understand this? In one way he is right. For many years the parties are sustaining on these seasonal plays.

What was Kamal Mishra thinking so deeply? As a director of the play, he has got a good hold. Till now not a single play of him has flopped. During ' Radha hajigala Gopa Dandarae' he strictly gave negative feedback. His point of argument was- 'This play won't be a success.' According to Hinduism, and human psychology Shri Krishna is the most loving man. Radha is devoted to this eternal love. The audience won't accept an unethical play in their name. Why will I take a risk and earn a bad reputation?' Kamal Mishra is farsighted. He thinks and analyses every scene much before the rehearsal. He even calculates and measures the movement of the characters on the stage like: the length, breadth, and direction of movement. He makes the actor and actress understand this and sits quietly and smokes. Binod sometimes couldn't understand his strategy and for Malini Baral, and Muna Panda it is beyond their comprehension. The triangles, and circles that Kamal Mishra draws on the stage look like a sphere puzzle to him but the play goes on well. But today he is sitting quietly for a long time . Bhola cautiously said,' Murder- rape-gang rape' by listening to the name of the play, Pinaki and Rudrani are ready to purchase the book for a very high price. I came here because of you people. Kamal Mishra still didn't say anything. Bhola looked at Binod and said ,'I have kept Binod babu in mind and wrote this play.'

-'Baban Biswal said- 'There is always someone in your mind. Sometimes Binod babu and sometimes Saudamini Sen. What's new in that?'

In the afternoon instead of taking a nap, the actors and actress of Dasabhuja came to listen to the story. Kamal Mishra was silent and Shankar Bhola was babbling. Most of them couldn't understand anything. In the meantime Benu Ustad comfortably kept his head on a wooden box, he was in deep sleep and was snoring. The beetle juice from his mouth had stained his vest. Malini in order to show Tanushree that scene pinched her thigh hardly and Tanushree gave a loud scream which startled others; they looked at her thinking that something happened. All of them burst into laughter looking at his weird face. Ustad woke up from his sleep. What did he understand from the situation isn't know but he jabbered and said- 'I am insisting on staging a devotional play for a long time. No one is listening to me.'

-'Grandfather! Are you again interested in playing the flute at this age? But your two front teeth are shaking. Won't the air pass through it?' Malini giggled and asked.

Muna Panda said- 'Yes! Grandfather how long will you

play the role of Krishna? You can play the role of Chandrasena. Radha will go to Kelikunja every day without your knowledge. Grandfather like a halfwit will stand on the stage with wide-opened eyes. The spotlight will be focused on his face and in the second stage; Krishna will take away the clothes of Radha... Ha! Ha! Ha!'

Muna Panda's vulgar laugh took away everyone's slothful afternoon sleep. The place became lively with laughter, chit chat, and arguments. Bhola had gathered them all after a lot of effort but because of Benu Ustad the environment became lighter and he was annoyed. He showed his annoyance for Benu Ustad and said-'Now a days there are two murder scenes and three rape scenes in a play otherwise the play doesn't become successful. Why are you searching for devotional play Ustad?'

-Oh! that's why you wrote about murder and rape. Don't you have shame at all?

Before Shankar Bhola could reply to anything Muna Panda said-'The person who is doing this act doesn't have shame then why is it shameful to depict this in the play?'

Muna Panda is the villain in Dasabhuja. He came in search of a job at the theatrical company with the experience of few village dramas. Benu Ustad was working in ' Bhubaneswari Opera' at that time. He was impressed by Muna Panda and requested the owner to give him a job. In the meantime, Muna Panda has made a place for himself in this field as a villain. But the way he made fun of Benu Ustad and laughed in a vulgar way made Benu Ustad sorrowful. He sat there silently. Looking at his speechless and dumb face Binod thought that with the passage of time, prestige, ability, and valor fades. To him, Gopi Pin Payodhar, Lubdha Nayak, Benu Ustad were looking like a discolored stone covered with moss in Dasabhuja's murder and rape controversy. Maybe in his cataract eyes, he would have imagined Radha and Gopis in Kelikunja. With Kamal Mishra's assurance, those memories sprung up from the depth of the reminiscence. Benu Ustad knows very well that, if any mythological play is going to be staged, no one will offer him the role of Krishna. But he will get an opportunity to teach classical dance to the learners in the party. Bholi babu will no more tell him to arrange the chairs and to look after the kitchen in the mess. He will not regret taking the salary without doing any work. Binod became emotional and was sympathetic towards Benu Ustad. Muna Panda took the advantage of his silence and to tease him said- 'Now a day's mythological plays aren't appreciated, grandfather. Rather you....'

Benu Ustad suddenly shouted and said-'How are the mythological serials like Ramayana, Mahabharata, and others are broadcast on TV? It's only you who says that mythological play isn't appreciated.'

His argument was also genuine. Binod couldn't understand where the mistake is. Day by day the number of audience on the small screen is going on increasing for mythological serials then why is it not appreciated in theatre and is becoming extinct? Is it a combined conspiracy of the owner, director, and playwright?

Malini was a little bit irritated as she couldn't take a rest in the afternoon. After listening to the argument between Muna Panda and Benu Ustad she said in a displeasing way-' If you people haven't planned anything before then why did you call us?'

Tanushree said-' This year is ill-fated. Four new books have flopped.

Malini said-' That's why I didn't want to come.'

Tanushree said- 'How did I know this will happen? Trouble came before the begging.'

Tanushree always plays the role of sister- in- law or a

friend of the leading actress. The leading role is done by Malini or Babita. After listening about three heroines in the play ' Murder – rape – gang rape' she became restless and didn't take an afternoon nap and came there. Addressing Shankar Bhola she said-' Master,Why don't you narrate the plot ?'

Shankar Bhola was turning the pages of the manuscript as if he was searching for something. In order to answer Tanushree he said, 'Let me go and discuss this with madam first. If Mishra babu won't agree then I will give direction for this play myself.' Tanushree looked at Binod and said-' You may ask our Bina sir who is here. Will Madam disagree with what Sir says? What is the necessity to go so far?'

' Binod babu, you have heard everything. Please say something. 'Shankar Bhola looked at him eagerly.

Not only Tanushree, but manager Bholi babu also have a similar notion- without asking Binod about the selection of the play madam wouldn't decide anything. Binod doesn't know how did this notion come into being. He knows very well that his relationship with madam is like a relationship of an employer and employee. If he tries to give his own view here like the university seminar then that relationship will be shattered. Madam is also a strange human being. What she thinks isn't known.

-' Binod babu , why are you not saying anything? What is the point of sitting like this?' Bhola asked restlessly.

-'You may go and ask madam at least once. No one will contradict.'

Binod said this and left the place.

5

'The collection was less than thirty thousand. Bholi babu is groaning like a wounded tiger. Hey!, Hey!, Hey! Shankar Bhola said.

Today is Binod's off day. He was thinking to spend the night lying on the folding cot behind the tent. He feels suffocated inside the tent. After joining the theatrical company it has become a habit for him not to sleep at night. After *Raja*, he gets few days of holidays but couldn't sleep in the house at night. All the theatre artists are habituated to this pattern. But every time he thinks that he will sleep and spend the night. Today when he was feeling a little sleepy, Bhola appeared from somewhere. He will now keep on babbling for two hours. How did Bhola come to know that he is sleeping here?

Without you, I know what the worth of Dasabhuja. You are also amazing!. Why are you here for one and a half lakh rupees? If you want to join, Pinaki and Rudrani will offer you two lakhs rupees Can women folk ever manage parties well? Experienced and inexperienced are all same here. Muna Panda is taking one lakh thirty thousand and they give you only one and a half lakh? Bholi babu must have understood it from today's collection. Why is he not saying, madam? Shankar Bhola would have continued saying something more. Sometimes

I feel good to listen to his babble while sleeping and sometimes I feel like hitting him on his face to stop him from babbling. Bholi babu called him in between and he left.

-Neja Khan doesn't have the role to play today. Why will someone pay rupees thirty and buy a ticket? People were discussing among themselves. In Dasabhuja, according to Bini madam's new rule, there is one day off for every senior artist. Her argument is, if a person gets one day's holiday in a week he will work hard for the other six days. Now a days party's expenditure is more so if the collection per day is less than fifty thousand then the party will incur a loss. Binod is not much interested in an off night. The night is spent sleepless and it's too boring. If he could act in two to three scenes and the party can get more fifty to sixty thousand then what's the problem? But he couldn't say this to Bini madam or Bholi babu. May be it will be taken in the sense of showing sympathy or pride. Kamal Mishra says, 'Now a days the audience pays only for two fundamental qualities or the *Rasa* of a play. One is conjugal love (Adi Rasa) and humour(Hasya Rasa).' But Binod knows that these are false. Now a days people give importance to only one Rasa and that is the Odious (Bibhatsa Rasa). Other than showing unpleasant and offensive things to the audience, does Nija Khan has any other magic wand to attract the audience? After more than two hundred performances the audience is still discontented. Rather they think that Nija Khan should be crueler. He should be more offensive and ruthless in his behavior. Kamal Mishra , to make that more offensive searches for new techniques. Sometimes during his movement is heard the raspy, drawn-out hissing sound of the vulture or sometimes his ruthless laughter accompanied by the tiger's snarl.

Nija Khan ,Binod laughed to himself. Nija Khan has lost his true identity for a long time.

No one other than Kamal Mishra, Shankar Bhol ,and

Bholi babu address him as Binod babu in the party. All of them addresses him as 'Sir'. How did they begin addressing him as sir that he doesn't remember. Why do they address him like this? Does he have a different place because he has done his MA? Is it because he could speak English fluently on stage? Is it because he keeps quiet after listening to everything? Still, he gets immense pleasure when he is addressed in this way. He feels that he hasn't lost his true identity even though he is a theatre artist. He is different from others in the theatre party.

But who recognizes Binod Das today? The theatre company's cassette has made Nija Khan popular in every nook and corner of Odisha. In Kantabanchi station, in Govindapali square, in Badambadi bus stand, and even in a remote village like Balighai's tea stall he has heard Nija Khan's dialogue. One of the company in Cuttack has bought the audio rights of the play 'Kancha Maunsa' by paying three lakhs. On behalf of Dasbhuja Bholi babu signed the bond and gave the information to madam as if he has won a war. Madam instead of being happy was rather annoyed and said- ' Bholi babu, can you sell your identity for money? '

But after the audio cassette of ' Kancha Maunsa'(Raw Flesh- The name of a play) was sold in the market the popularity for the play increased. In a night three lakhs or three lakh fifty thousand was collected for the play. Sometimes after the repeated show, the audience insisted on the same play to be performed for another two or three nights. 'Kancha Maunsa's' playwright Sanat Hota became the number one playwright. Malini's salary was hiked from eighty thousand to one lakh thirty thousand. She became a star, the superstar of Opera Empire. Whenever there is a camp in Cuttack or Bhubaneswar, the college-going students come to take her autograph. He has heard people taking autographs from actors, actresses, and politicians but he had never imagined anyone coming to a theatre artist to take an autograph. If this topic is raised then Kamal Mishra argues and says- 'Are theatre artists not actors? In the field of acting the contribution and excellence of the theatre artist is more appreciable. In cinema, there are thousands of takes and retakes and then - OK. In theatre, the acting is performed only once that too in front of thousands of audience. There is no way to rectify any mistake. Only one scene changes the life and fate of a theatre artist.'

That's true. 'Kancha Maunsa's' only one scene had changed his fate. He became a superstar. He transformed from Binod Das to Nija Khan. When he remembers about that night he gets astonished.

6

Is the lady drawing the *Chita*? From a distance, it looks like a wave of mountains and beneath that the twilight. After dusk when the village becomes desolate she comes out holding the batter bowl in her left hand and opens the front door. She covers her head with the saree and calmly draws the Chita till late evening. Sometimes she bends down or sometimes she stands forming a posture like a question mark or sometimes like a Madhumalati creeper which swings with the gentle wind leans on the wall and gives a shape to the intricacies of her art in her imagination.

Right from childhood Binod likes to watch the Chita being drawn. The mud walls and floors are decorated with murals in white rice paste or *pithau* .With a piece of small cloth or the finger tip ladies take white rice paste and draw beautiful designs in no time. For each occasion, a specific motif is drawn on the floor or the wall. For instance, in Lakshmipuja a stack of paddy or rice sheaves structured like a pyramid is drawn along with, Lakshmi feet, and lotus. For *Gamha Purnima* on the walls of the stable, they draw plow, bullock ,and furrow swing .It looks like a piece of tribal art. During Janmastami there are big designs drawn on walls which have a *Kalash* with a coronet of mango leaves, flowers, and a coconut. Binod couldn't understand the significance of these and asked Professor Samsuddin.

He said-' Yes, I have also noticed those designs that the ladies draw from a distance. I feel they are more symbolic than modern poetry. I have never thought to analyze those things. The intricacies of the design are its identity.'

The smile on Professor Samsuddin's lips seems to be more mysterious than the designs of the Chita. To make the things clear he said-' Binod, Is art a crime?' Is it necessary to analyze it every time? Analysis sometimes destroys the significance of art. You may be aware of the critical analysis of 'Old man and the Sea'.

Suresh Bhanja says- 'Chita designs are a medium to showcase the creativity of the womenfolk. They are not allowed to do many things. How will their imagination, anxiety, displeasure, and remorse get lightened? That's why they sit and draw the designs.'

Suresh Bhanja's work is related to the conscious and subconscious mind. His subject was Psychology. He tries to come up with a different meaning for everything. He can also find an irrational mind under the crumpled bed sheet of a cot and can find cumulated sorrow in the pile of old newspaper under the cot. Sometimes he isn't able to understand his own psychology and asks-' Binod, What has happened to me now a days ? I feel like breaking everything. I want to ruin everything. I want to break the flower pots in the balcony, the branches of the mango tree laden with flowers, the four walls of the house, university campus wall-everything.'

Suresh Bhanja was staying along with one of his distant relatives, his cousin Bira bhai(Brother). Bira bhai purchased a piece of land in Bhubaneswar and constructed a house but he was transferred to Bombay. Sailashree Vihar was like a jungle at that time. Nearby there were no more houses. He kept Suresh Bhanja in his house to take care of his house and his wife Suna *bhauja*. Suresh Bhanja also could save his hostel expenditure. Bira Bhai had taken a month leave and had come home. Suna Bhauja was spending her time with her husband. Sometimes when she comes to Suresh's room, Bira bhai calls her in a loud voice-'Suna, Suna? Suna bhauja tries to make him understand through her eyes- Yes, it's a matter of only one month. Let him go...'

Suresh Bhaja sometimes says in an irritated voice- 'Bina, let's go for the second show cinema. I am not feeling comfortable.'

Suna bhauja didn't have any children. According to the medical report, the problem was with Bira bhai or Suna bhauja no one knows that . Binod thought that maybe Suna bhauja wants to be away from her husband. But, Suresh says, Bira bhai knowingly took a transfer to Bombay.

Bira bhai was handsome. He was six feet tall. No one can doubt his masculinity from his looks. Of course, Binod didn't know about their married life but he has heard many times Suna bhauja saying – 'All that glitters isn't gold.' When asked about this to Suresh Bhanja he gives a mysterious smile and says-'English students are always busy with Daffodils and Night queen. How will they know about the bitterness of bitter gourd and its flower?'

Suna bhauja looks at the innocent face of Binod and laughs. Then she presses his cheek and says-' Bina don't you know how many petals does bitter gourd flower has?' Then she pulls her two plaits on her chest and asks-'Tell me how many strands are there in my plait?' Suna bhauja's hair makes Bina's power of imagination intense.

Bina had noticed that chirpy Suna bhauja becomes very silent in the darkness of the night, she stands on the balcony and looks at the twinkling star for a long time. By that time the bedroom is filled with the snoring sound of Bira bhai. Bira bhai's snore sounds like a bursting of balloons .Suna bhauja also draws Chita every Wednesday night. Like the sound of the raindrops her glass bangles also make a jingling sound till late at night. He is engrossed in the music there is a conflict in his mind - Is it the song to welcome Maa Lakshmi or an imagination of a dreamy mind. He feels sleepy in Suresh Bhanja's room.

What is he looking at till now?

Is it the artistic Chita or her saree ?

He had imagined many times- Whoever will become his bride, in the courtyard under the shadow of Ashoka tree and Madhumalati creeper will lit the evening lamp and till late night will draw Lakshmi feet and lotus in various colors and designs. After the village becomes quiet he will listen to the jingling sound of her bangles. He will passionately look at the feet of his beloved smeared with *alata* and his eyes will be filled with thousand dreamy fancies. Passionately he will walk stealthily towards her, hold her feet and blow thousands of kisses. She will move her feet shyly and will lean on his chest like a ray of moonlight.

-'You don't know sister in law how painful it has become to walk bare fit in this mud house which is wiped with cow dung water. Kalyani was complaining over the phone to her sister in law. Why do they apply cow dung water on the floor of the porch every day? Oh! What a terrible smell.

After listening to Kalyani's complaint, Binod's dreams were shattered. There was an explosion of emotion within him.

Kalyani says- 'Those are useless sentiments.'

The western sky was changing its color into red. In the river plateau are the barren plants of *Kastandi*, the bloom of autumn from which the flowers have fallen. It's the memory of the passing autumn and the river flows on the other side of the plateau.

Binod felt as if the body of a woman is like an impeccable

and unending poem. The poet amazingly expresses and portrays many images in each line of his poem but still couldn't satisfy himself. Chanda, Suna bhauja, Kalyani , Tanushree, Malini, and Lata each of them is a romantic ardor of those indescribable chapters.

Binod left the outskirts of the village and took the riverside road. Before joining the theatrical company he has come here many times and has spent the evening here. Now a days he isn't getting a chance to come. He is busy in the evening either in rehearsal or in teaching the newly joined actors and actresses about dialogue modulation but, today as he was free he went out.

He could hear the honking of the horn of a car which was at the back so he moved aside. The car stopped near him and Bini madam peeped outside and called him-'Binod'!.The driver opened the door.

7

Malini is sulking. Sometimes she behaves in this way. Maybe she has some inferiority complex. She feels offended by small things.

Malini Baral has got a good name for record dance. But she could never perform classical dance properly. In a particular proportion she turns her head and eyes, keeps her fingers in the shape of a beetle leaf or twists her hand like a lotus stem to learn Odissi, Benu Ustad stands in front of her in a classical *mudra* like a stone statue. But Malini isn't able to learn the mudra despite Benu Ustad's continuous effort. Rather she looks at the face of Benu Ustad which looks like a crab burrow and laughs a loud boisterous laugh. Benu Ustad stops teaching her dance, squirms and leaves the place immediately.

Yesterday evening Benu Ustad sat with the harmonium to teach dance to Malini. The dance was a part of a scene of the play where the hero will be sleeping in the second stage and weaving his dreams.

Shankar Bhola proposes- The main stage will be dark as it is a symbolic representation of reality. There will be complete darkness. Like the magician recites the mantras in a similar way Shankar Bhola in a heavy voice narrates the substance of the play.

There will be a faint bluish light on the second stage and the hero will be engrossed in his dreams. Globe light will rotate slowly creating a puzzle of shadow and light and the heroine will enter. In the light, she will be appearing and dissipating like a statue of a motion picture show.

Guest choreographer Babu Rao incorporated a record dance with the amalgamation of dance and acting. In the background was playing the song Hai! Hai!

Binod made a mockery and asked what is this Hai! Hai! Mr. Rao? I have seen the tribal ladies beating their chest and saying Hai! Hai! when someone dies. But why will the beloved who is eager to meet her companion in the closed room sadly say Hai! Hai!?

Babu Rao is simply a useless person. He was teaching duet in some other theatrical company and when the trend of duet stopped in the theatrical company to search for a job he was roaming here and there and suddenly his fate signed as Pandora's magical box. He managed to arrange a certificate of Diploma in dance and at present, he is an eminent choreographer in Odisha. Dasabhuja theatrical company displays his name in big letters through the overhead projector. Dance coordination- Babu Rao(Cinema and Doordarshan). The audience doesn't want to know Babu Rao has given dance direction in which TV channel or cinema. They are happy with what is mentioned within the bracket; Cinema, and Doordarshan.

Babu Rao laughed as if he knows everything and replied- Is it a film Binod babu? This is a theatre- Public theatre. Why are you bothered? If this Hai! Hai! , and Bye! Bye! wouldn't have been there then people wouldn't have spent fifty rupees to purchase a ticket for a play rather they would have paid five rupees and would have purchased a ticket for an Art film

Shankar Bhola supported Babu Rao and said-' Rao Sir is saying the truth Binod babu. In the name of realism, the Art film producers are depicting the scenes which we have experienced in the real life. Why will people pay the money and see it again? They come here to watch the play and buy the dreams. To sell the dreams to the people is our business. Theater is purely a business of dreams.'

Bhola babu revealed the essence of theatre as if he has done a lot of research on it. But, Binod doesn't appreciate the dancers tying a piece of cloth on their waist and forehead and saying Hai! Hai!. They look like scary ghosts. He feels as if ghosts are dancing. Though he felt uncomfortable he couldn't oppose. Babu Rao has gained a reputation in the field of Odia theatre. The day Bini madam didn't like the play and entrusted the work on Kamal Mishra to make the necessary changes , Shankar Bhola argued and opposed. To make him silent madam said-' Bhola babu, there is a certain limit to commercialism . In the name of dreams to expose the body of a woman isn't art at all, not even business. Rather stark naked immorality.

- ' But madam; What about the play's future....', Bhola wanted to say something.

-' No more discussion.' Madam said in a firm voice to make him silent. I haven't established a theatrical party to earn money and there are so many different ways to earn money. If the play isn't appreciated as the dance isn't shown then let it be. Then she looked at Kamal Mishra and instructed him- In the next camp replace this dance with classical dance. You may discuss this with Binod babu.

Kamal Mishra's imagination revolved around the same old conventional Hindi film scene. The hero will be in the second stage and will be in his dream world. Malini Baral, the heroine will stand on the riser with an expression of shyness. The hero will be transformed into her supreme beloved, Shri Krishna. When the smoke will recede he will step down on the stage with a flute in his hand. It is the depiction of the scene of Kelikunja , the immortal love.

Binod didn't object to this scene. In every man, there is a thirst to act as the supreme beloved Shri Krishna. Despite Benu Ustad's continuous effort, Malini neither could learn dance nor could give that perfect expression on her face. Yesterday evening while teaching dance, Malini looked at the shrunken cheeks of Benu Ustad and laughed loudly, Benu Ustad was annoyed and said- If all the dogs will go to Varanasi, who will lick the soiled plates?' Is it Babu Rao's twist dance?

After that, it wasn't possible to control Malini Baral. She walked towards Benu Ustad and screamed and said-' What did you say Ustad?' Am I a dog and you are a god? In annoyance, she left the place. Bhola and Bholi babu requested her so many times come back and do the rehearsal but she was rigid. Binod thought-In this situation if Lata could get that role...!

He has imagined Lata in Malini Baral's place in the play but he couldn't say anyone anything.

It has been a long time since Lata joined Dasabhuja. She could have got a role if a new play would have started. As she didn't get any role so she stays in the place where other lady artists stay. Sometimes she sits next to the music party during the play. Binod has noticed that her eyes are deeply filled with sorrow. No one is thinking about her. All have an eye on Malini Baral.

Bholi babu said Benu Ustad – 'If you beg for pardon is there anything you are going to lose?Why are you creating unnecessary a scene here?'.

-' Am I creating a scene?'

-' Then is it so that the outsiders came and created this nuisance? Why did you say her a Bitcha?'

-' When did I say her a Bitcha?'

-'It's the same thing. You said the thing indirectly.'

-' Why was she looking at me and was laughing like a

transgender?' Muna Panda appeared from somewhere and said-
' Are you again babbling Ustad?'

Benu Ustad roared- 'Are you trying to overpower me? Will you hit me? While teaching us to dance our Ustad use to beat us hard. If I say something good she can't digest it.'

Bholi babu to make Benu Ustad understand said in a low-pitched voice,' Time has changed Ustad. If you could speak just a line of apology the whole the problem will be solved.'

-' Why should I apologize to her? Does she feed me?

-' Let me see how will you not apologize.' Muna Panda said firmly.

Bini madam was going towards her car. She heard the noise and asked-' Bholi babu ,what is this farce going on since past two days?'

Bholi babu to make her understand the situation stood up.

Bini madam didn't let him speak and said-' If Malini isn't able to perform Odissi dance then look for a substitute. At any cost next time in that scene Odissi dance should be added.'

Bini madam got inside the car. She always takes quick decisions.

The hope which was dying in Binod's mind again brightened up.

8

Today the camp will shift from here. The tent, chairs, light, and mike men had already left in the morning. Other artists had left by bus or truck. Binod is waiting for the car along with Muna Panda, and Malini Baral. They are the main attraction of Dasabhuja so it is better to keep them away from people. The far, the better. If the distance is maintained from the general public then their curiosity will increase. If they travel by bus or in the carrier of the truck like ordinary artists then why will people purchase tickets paying fifty rupees to see them?

Muna Panda was sitting with Malini Baral and was playing Ludo in the classroom of a school. With one roll of the die value of Muna Panda , Malini's token which was near the finishing square returned to its owner's yard. Muna Panda laughed like a villain. Malini pinched his thigh and said-'You are always a villain'.

Rubbing the thigh Muna Panda said,' There is a different type of happiness in sending the finishing token back to home. A new player runs after the first token .Am I a new player?'

Binod woke up as they were talking loudly. He was lying down on the bed and was watching Malini's activities. This is the reason why people think of them as theatre artists and look at them with hatred. How cheap can be a woman be! Malini was sitting very close to Muna Panda and was saying something in a very low voice. Maybe knowingly or unknowingly her saree was falling from her chest. Muna Panda with his lustful eyes was looking at Malini's chest and Malini tried to interject what Muna Panda said last and she said-' Malini isn't a new player'. Then she pressed Muna Panda's cheek, closed the Ludo board and got up from that place.

-' How can it be? Does an old player leave the game halfway?' Muna Panda said snatching the Ludo board from Malini's hand.

In the scuffle Malini's saree pallu fell from her chest and touched the ground. The upper portion of her body was visible.

Binod went outside as he was irritated.

The ground outside was looking empty.

Binod feels very touchy looking at the emptiness which is created after the completion of the play. He felt the emptiness when the stage was dismantled in the college, university, and in the auditorium after the performance. He felt as if the sky was covered with untimely dark clouds. He became restless and went to the nearby village.

The ground was covered with torn papers, polythene, burst balloon, groundnut shells, and ashes from the fireplace of the shops which sell tea and snacks. The wind has scattered them all around. The empty ground was looking like a graveyard. Binod was walking there as a lonely traveler and was searching for someone. But whom? Why is he searching?

Binod asked the question to himself and laughed. In the meantime a woman came out with a bowl with white rice paste to draw Chita but why is she not seen today? Is she late purposely? Maybe after a little while, the car will arrive and he will leave the place and go to another camp. He may not be able to return to this village again. There is no certainty in the life of a theatre artist. He could have seen the lady for the last time if she would have come. He would have bid her goodbye in silence. Sometimes a lot of attraction develops for unknown people but why? Why does the heart become so restless?

In the evening this ground will be empty and only the skeleton structure will be left. The wind will blow away the rest of the memory of the theatre- torn paper, polythene, the shells of groundnut, and ashes of the fireplace. Whatever will be left out will be wiped away by the unseasonal rain.

When will the lady come here; during dusk or in the moonlit night? Maybe along with her the ladies who have come will say- 'During the opera the ground was noisy. Here was constructed the second stage…. , the man who was performing the role of Nija Khan had a broad chest. His eyes were revolving like the potter's wheel. Have you seen?

Who knows what will be the answer of the lady.

Did she come to watch the play?

But would anyone understand that under the disguise of Nija Khan there was a hidden soul of a man which eagerly and breathlessly waited to see the chita drawn by that lady.

No, no one will come to know that. Neither this ground, nor that lady. Maybe the day she comes, Binod will be disguising himself as Nija Khan in some other tent in some other ground or maybe sleeping and watching the late moonrise of an unknown Vedic lunar day. Slowly the memories of the lady will be covered with a layer of dust or if remembers he will feel- 'Oh! it was a meaningless emotion.'

But today the memory is fresh and deep. I feel it's the most precious wealth.

Other things seem to be very faint and dull.

Binod had noticed earlier that on one side of the field there was a long bed of Done flower and on the other side palm trees were planted in a row. At the backside of the palm grove were long stretched fields. The rice field with ripe crop looked yellow. He got the opportunity to see these for many days.

-Sir ,whom are you searching for? An old man sitting on a porch asked Binod. He had already reached the outskirts of the village engaged in his thoughts. In the middle of the road, there was a *Baula* tree. On the other side of it was the house. There was a high, stoned porch. The mud walls were also in a good height. There were two big windows. In between was a door that was intricately crafted. It looked like the house of a wealthy man. On the other side of the road, on a porch was sitting an old man. Next to him was kept a water jug, tea glass, beetle nut case, and a cane stick. He looked as if he belonged to a prosperous family. Binod gave an explanation and said-'No, I am not searching for anyone. We will leave today that's why I thought to visit your village.'

-'Ha; You have done the right thing. But what is there in the village to see? '

-' Why what happened?

- ' Just see! After the theatre got over the two parties in the village are arguing over the profit money. Old people in the village say - Nilakantheswar temple is half-constructed and the God is kept outside in the heat and rain so the temple will be constructed but the youth folk says- the roof of the Jubasangha room will be constructed'

-' It is the same issue in all the villages. It's not the olden days.

-' Why are you standing there outside on the road, son? Please come here. Then the old man looked at the house and called out- O! *Nahaka*'s daughter, send a mat to sit through someone. Where did your mother in law go? Tell her to make some tea.

-' No, no tea isn't necessary. I came just like that to visit the village.'

-' It's not a big issue son. It's a big thing that you have come to my house.'

Binod couldn't remember anyone speaking to him so affectionately. He is just an ordinary human being. All of them address him as a 'boy'. On the university campus friends said- The boy is introvert so what- he is talented. The teachers said- The boy got spoiled being with Professor Samsuddin. After his marriage also he was like a child in front of his mother. His mother use to say very often- What type of boy you are?

Kalyani always complained-'It was not necessary for a person like you to get married.'

That episode of life is very small like the chord scene of the play but very much heart- wrenching. While explaining Shakespeare, Professor Samsuddin said, Shakespeare in his play depicts many characters and scenes whom if you sideline will not cause any harm to the play. Maybe for him Kalyani is like an unnecessary character. An unrhythmical song in life.

-'Anyways you are born with Gandharvakala(the art of the Gandharvas). All of them can't do that work, son! The old man was speaking continuously.

Binod felt good listening to his appreciation. Thoughtfully he looked at the stone porch. The windows were open but, there was no light inside. Nothing could be seen.

By that time many children had already gathered around the porch. Few ladies with their half- covered face in the veil were looking curiously at him. Maybe the lady who was an artist and draws chita was among them. A seven to eight years old boy climbed the stairs and said-' Nija Khan is here!.

' Then he climbed down the stairs and shouted-'Nahaka's daughter?'

The girl was standing near the window and was speaking very softly- Nuabou, nuabou(Sister in law)?' Without the notice of the old man, Binod looked at the window but could only see the darkness inside.

A middle-aged lady with a veil on her head brought two cups of tea and a few beetles on a glass plate and kept it and left. The old man asked- 'Didn't your mother in law get up? Why is she sleeping for such a long time ?'

-'Grandmother was watching the theatre for seven nights. Was she sleeping like you in the house?' A boy standing near the porch said.

-' Oh! Theatre! It's useless. The ladies in the theatre are dancing half-naked. Can anyone see all these sitting with the family?'

-' Do you think that those who are watching theatre are all of them fool?' The boy asked humorously.

' The old man had forgotten the presence of Binod. He suddenly remembered about his presence and asked in a very uncomfortable way-' Did you feel bad, son?'

-' No ,no now a days it happens. Why will I feel bad?' Binod replied to make the old man comfortable.

-' Why are you not doing a play on mythology?' Bhakta Parikshya' and 'Shiva Tandav' dance is awesome.

The old man would have said something more. A boy ran towards them and informed- 'The car has arrived and the people of the theater company are calling you. The village children ran towards the school building to see the car.

Binod took a deep breath, thanked him, and left. The door on the other side of the road was still closed.

9

The market was crowded and noisy. The shade of the Suadhara mountain was overshadowing the marketplace like a woman in the veil. Binod's consciousness was still lingering with the thoughts of the lady who was drawing the chita but it burst like a bubble.

'Uncle said nephew
Let us see the theatre.'
Bitcha was announcing in the loudspeaker
'The grandfather is calling the grandson,
To watch the theatre at night.'

His technique of advertisement is good. Before he joined Dasbhuja the technique of advertisement of Dasabudha was different.

-'Today's play… today's play…. today's play… Bagha Hendaluchi… Bagha Hendaluchi(The tiger is roaring) the voice wasn't clear . The advertisement jeep was moving around in the summer afternoon.

' Sister in law, sister in law,
Let us go to see the theatre at night,
Wear the anklets and Alta.'

Bitcha was composing the words of the doggerel amazingly. How does he get an idea to compose these? The advertising jeep was coming nearer. Binod went inside a tea stall in a hurry otherwise people would have recognized him in the marketplace. Bitcha is the only person in Dasbhuja with whom he is a little bit attached.

There is only one day in his hand to roam around. Today no one knows him here. From tomorrow onwards he will be known as a theatre artist. People of all age groups will look at him with curious eyes. Why are people so curious to see a theatre artist outside the theatre?

'The drum is empty from inside
Today night there will be a play
In the old Bilasuni's cave.'

People have gathered near the advertising jeep. Bitcha is busy distributing the pamphlets. Bitcha is a poet. If he wouldn't have entered the theatrical company then definitely he would have become a nonsense poem writer. Many people make him write doggerel for the marriage ceremony to be given as a gift to the guests. See! How he has composed the doggerel before reaching the old Bilasuni cave.

While drinking tea Binod asked a person sitting next to him- 'Are there few old stone statues found in the nearby areas?

The man looked at his face and said 'yes'. Next to him was sitting a man who looked like a leader. He spoke with a little enthusiasm and said-'Why are you looking so surprised? Sir is asking about the Baruali statue of Suadhar mountain. Did you come from any college?

People think that lecturers from the archeological college and university are interested in this and the irony is a History teacher like Nila Mohanty is busy writing the question-answer book.

In the meantime, the shopkeeper was frying vada. He washed his hands and arranged the vadas on the skimmer said in an indifferent voice-' Many people come here every day. Sir has come to watch the play near the old Bilasuni cave. Of course when he has travelled such a long distance what will be the problem to see the statues at Baruali?

-' Baruali?' asked Binod as he couldn't understand.

-' If not Baruali what is it? Is it the statue of the god and goddesses? A man who looked like a leader said and laughed.

Binod felt that his laughter was meaningless.

There was a man who was sitting there and looking at them as a fool. After some time he understood what were they saying and laughed with his toothless mouth. Then he pointed at the mountain on his left and said-' Sir, look at that banyan tree on the mountain. Beneath that the statues are kept.'

Binod looked at the banyan tree with the hanging aerial roots on the mountain. It looked like the figure of Buddha in meditation.

Binod had another cup of tea and left the place.

The shopkeeper said-'If you want to go there then you should return soon. The actual enjoyment lies in Bilasuni fair in the evening. If you are late then you mayn't get the ticket to watch the play. People are ready to watch the play for a month because of the reputation of Dasabhuja theatrical company.

-' Which play are they going to stage today'? asked the man who looked like a leader.

-' Sendha matichi gaa rae'(The furious bull in the village), replied one of them.

The man laughed loudly and said-It's not sendha.. it's sandha..*sandha*.Hey! What type of man are you? You are speaking like a stupid person and pronouncing it as-sendha.

To cover up his mistake the other man said- It means the same. If the bull has to become furious, it will. Let it be sendha or sandha.

The shopkeeper asked- Why did the group come here now? Belasuni fair is in the month of January. This is the harvesting time. Will the fair be joyful?

Why are you asking the fair will be joyful or not? Are you asking it knowingly or unknowingly?

Shankar Bhola is farsighted. He understands the psychology of people before naming a play. Binod was ready to have another cup of tea.

After he left the market ground and was walking down the lane, Bini madam's car stopped near him. She was driving the car herself and was going somewhere. She rolled the window glass down and asked-' Where are you going Binod?' Before Binod could reply anything she opened the door and said-' In the mountain range few stone statues were found. Come, let's go and have a look.'

Binod sat in the car and was about to close the door when he heard Bitcha saying the doggerel.

'Sister in law is calling her brother in law
Brother in law said-'O'
The theatre artist is winking
What will I do so?'

Bini madam looked at Binod's face and smiled. Binod felt an unknown sensation within him.

Bini madam is very beautiful. Like whom? Is she like Mama Mishra or like Kalyani or like Suna bhauja? Or has she taken the features from all three and is made like a wax statue?

Bini madam noticed him staring at her. She felt shy and looked at the road. Binod felt a little uncomfortable. To manage the situation Bini madam said-' The boy is very talented. What is his name?'

-'Bitcha. Binod answered in short. He knew that it was just an excuse to avoid the situation which was created just a few minutes back when they exchanged their looks.

Bini madam changed the gear and pushed the accelerator. The car moved forward in that stony road. Small stones and sand were scattered on the way. In a few place, there were heaps of sand which were brought down by the rainwater.

Bini madam was driving the car very carefully. The car started climbing on the mountainous road.

Binod had climbed the mountain many times during NCC camp, study tour, and picnic. But the experience of climbing the mountain was different this time. Earlier he had climbed the mountain on foot which was difficult but this time he is travelling by car and it's not difficult. Earlier the process of climbing was very slow and he couldn't understand that he was climbing up. The scenery outside was changing rapidly. The villages which were looking like a silhouette aren't seen anymore. The bushes on either side of the road were becoming deeper and deeper. From a distance was heard the noise made by the axe of the stone breaker. There was a sharp curve under a neem tree. Bini madam couldn't change the gear immediately. The engine screeched and the car stopped and after that, it started rolling down slowly. Binod could see the deep gorge which was next to the tree. Bini madam pressed the brake and shouted-Binod !. Binod kept his leg on the clutch and changed the gear and the car started moving up. He took over the driving seat and madam went to the backseat. Many things happened in a moment.

There was a sense of adventitious, fear, and anxiety. This experience had left Binod aghast. There was some other feeling which was mixed with it but he couldn't understand. The same was in the case of Bini madam.

Both of them were calm and quiet like the mountain road.

-' If you wouldn't have been there what would have happened? Bini madam came close to him and asked him after some time. Binod was driving the car smoothly. What answer would he give to madam's question?

10

In the past few days, Binod has heard some gossips at the party. No one could dare to speak in front of him. But he had noticed that Malini Baral gossiping with Muna Panda. Shankar Bhola says, 'He goes in madam's car!' He speaks in such an accent that one can make out that it's a criticism. Even, the manager Bholi babu says,' I know that if you say then madam will never disagree.' He didn't give much importance to this matter in the beginning. It's a very common thing in a theatrical company. It's their habit to gossip about others. After working throughout the night as they don't have any other work in the morning- they gossip. After spending four years in the theatrical company it has become a part of his life. But last evening he felt, day by day they are crossing their limits. If he doesn't stop them now then the matter will reach madam with sugar and spice. Maybe at that time, she will think that Binod is responsible for this and is knowingly trying to propagate the rumor and must have told about her to someone with sugar and spice as there will be no smoke without fire. That's why yesterday he was extremely annoyed with Srikant Prusty .

Srikat Prusty is an artist in Dasabhuja. He acts as the hero's friend or the heroine's brother. He is after Kamal Mishra and Muna Panda to get the role of side villain but his physic doesn't match with the physic of a villain. Srikant gives voice-over for the imaginary characters like the narrator or *Mahakala* which has become a fashion in the play at present.

Suddenly he got an idea to become a playwright. He has many Bengali play scripts. Binod remembers that on their visit to Calcutta almost two years back, Srikant took two months' salary in advance from Bholi babu and bought few many Bengali books from the footpath and old book stalls. Now a days other than performing his role in the play he writes play and reads Bengali plays. He is sometimes found sitting under a tree or on someone's porch and writing something. After writing two to three pages he runs after Shankar Bhola to rectify the mistakes or bribes someone, in the party with a beetle and cigarette to listen to his story.

He worked for one and half years and completed writing a play and now he is after Binod to speak to madam regarding his play. Maybe yesterday evening he wanted to remind the same thing and came to Binod. Why is Srikant so docile and timid? He washes the clothes of Shankar Bhola to get his script edited by him, to get the side role as a villain he takes care of Kamal Mishra. He treats Muna Panda with tea and cigarette and polishes his shoes to learn how to act as a villain. What play will he write?

Binod woke up from sleep as Srikant called.

'Brother, don't you know sir gets annoyed when disturbed during odd hours?' Bitcha cautioned Srikant.

Srikanth was about to leave the place and at that moment Shankar Bhola and Muna Panda arrived. Shankar Bhola asked Srikant ,'Did sir like the book?'

Shankar Bhola uttered the word 'Sir' in a slow and painful voice. Shankar Bhola envies the word 'Sir'. All of them in the party address him as 'Master'; in a similar way how people address others by their surname. Otherwise, they address him as –'Bhola Master'. Usually, a name is always followed by the caste or the position in the society. Bhola feels very uncomfortable when he is addressed in this way. Sometimes he gets irritated and says angrily- Why are you all calling me Master?

Bhola didn't get any reply from Srikant and again asked- ' Is Sir not awake?'

Malini appeared from somewhere and said-' Sir won't wake up now. By the time he wakes up, it will be evening.'

-'Yes. Now a days sir goes around in madam's car! How will it be justified if he doesn't show the attitude of the rich people?' Muna Panda gave a very derogatory and sarcastic remark. Binod was listening to the conversation silently and felt like giving a slap on Muna Panda's face.

Srikant said in a very polite voice-' If you can go through the script before sir wakes up it will be helpful for me.'

Shankar Bhola said-'Srikant, You are speaking unnecessary things. Do I have any value in the presence of 'Sir'? What is my knowledge? I have spent twenty years in this theatrical company but have you ever seen madam seeking my opinion? I think I don't have the age to give you any suggestion.'

Muna Panda scoffed-' Colour your hair. Is there any scarcity of colour here?

-Malini asked,' What about the beard?' Master's beard is half grey.

Muna Panda laughed and said sarcastically-'You are right'.

Stupid! Malini said and joined him in the laughter. After they stopped laughing, Shankar Bhola said-'Yes, why won't you laugh at me? I look as I am. Shankar Bhola huffed and said- Rudrani and Satrupa are waiting for my new play . I am here because of Bholi babu as I have a very old association with him.

Malini said-' Bholi babu doesn't have the hold anymore.'

Muna Panda endorsed Malini's views and said-'Yes, we have come to know this as Baligotha camp was postponed.' For the past three years, the theatre party was visiting Baligotha and the organizers of Baligotha had printed the pamphlets but everything went in vain.'

Baligotha Yatra is on the next day of *Bada Osha*. This year a competition is going to be held in Bali Yatra ground on the same day. All the theatrical companies of Odisha like Rudrani, Satrupa, Navajyoti Meghasan, etc will participate in the Bali Yatra Gananatya competition. Even if it is said that theatre is the reflection of our culture but still the educated people of Odisha have never accepted it and also don't have a good opinion about it. It's not fair to just include the theatrical companies as business establishments. It is also necessary to draw the attention of the educated people towards it. Bali Yatra is the apt place that will give such an opportunity. Bali Yatra which exhibits Odisha's culture and heritage will give a platform to enhance this art. That's why he suggested madam to postpone Baligotha camp for ten days. How will these narrow-minded people understand it? All the efforts to make them understand will go in vain.

Is the Baligotha camp postponed? Malini asked sadly.

Muna Panda mocked and said-' This year you can't eat dry fish.'

Every year during Balighotha camp, Malini brings twenty to twenty fives kilos of dry fish from her so-called brother's house. She sends some of those to her parent's house and wraps the rest in a piece of cloth and keeps it along with her to have it along with *Pakhala* in the morning. In this way, she and her husband Charan Das were able to save the amount which was given to them for breakfast. She was able to purchase a house at Bhubaneswar by saving money. After leaving the theatre company she may open a business over there.

-' Party wouldn't go to Baligotha this year.' What will you do?' Muna Panda said Malini Baral mockingly. Malini Baral giggled and said-' Why are you so much bothered about my dry fish? Were you not eating those? Many times Binod had seen Muna Panda and Malini Baral eating together from the same bowl. Muna Panda doesn't have a good sense of taste. He snatches the half-eaten dry fish from Malini's hand and eats it like a craving cat. Maybe it's one of his inferiority complexes.

Shankar Bhola wasn't interested in these unnecessary talks. He said-' Panda babu ,you were supposed to leave, isn't it?' Isn't Manikagada too far?

Malini said-' Why was I not told about going to Manikagada?'

-Muna Panda said-' Do you want to go?'

- Malin said-' What do you mean by want to go? Wait for me; I will change my saree and come.'

After Malini left, Shankar Bhola said-'You will never mend your ways, Panda babu.' Who knows when will Malini come? Sit and wait for her.

Muna Panda said-' Is it so that there are bare Baruali statues in Mankigada?' We will have great fun going there with Malini.

-' Take Benu Usdad along with you. He will teach Malini the classical mudras there.

- Do you think I am not capable of that?

-' Will you come with us Srikant? You will get ample plots for your new play there and by the time we come back sir will wake up. ' Shankar Bhola said mockingly.

Srikant wasn't willing to go. After Muna Panda and Shankar Bhola left, Srikant again called in a feeble voice-'Sir, Sir'! Binod couldn't control his anger and shouted-'Who is that bloody hell?'

11

When Binod reached hotel Madhulika he could see Muna Panda there. He was surprised to see him there because he didn't expect Muna Panda to be there.

A room was booked for Jitu Mohanty and it was sponsored by the party. His writing style is different. He writes only four plays in a year. Before he starts writing he discusses it with the party in the camp. He makes the placement of all the actors and actress on the stage and also analyze their performance in the play they are acting at that time and then asks the owner- ' Do you want a spicy play or a seasonal one?' In the beginning, Binod wasn't aware of all these formalities but now he can understand it. He charges different a amount for different types of play. The honorarium for the play is paid according to his demand. It can be said that he charges like the doctors and lawyers. But in Bholi babu's words, it's –'Salary.'

Jitu Mohanty's fooding and lodging, travel, phone bill, and other ancillary expenditure are born by the party. The playwright conceives and writes the play in anonymity and after a month he is ready with a new play. It's not only a play but a sensation in the world of theatre. He incorporates a few scenes or dialogues in the play which creates a sensation as soon as it is staged. It raises the eyebrow of the critics and the case is filed in the public interest and then all the tickets get sold out within half an hour.

Binod has heard that Jitu Mohanty failed in his intermediate exam and then took a loan from the bank for a chicken farm. He also had a novelty store in front of the farm but at present, he drives an AC car from his earning as a playwright.

This is called fate. An auspicious moment in one's life can open the doors to success in theatre and cinema. Maybe because of that the artists in cinema and theatre believe in good luck.

As soon as Jitu Mohanty saw Binod he said loudly-' Binod babu, Please come and listen to the script of the new play'.

Binod noticed that there were many Bengali and Hindi , sex and crime magazines scattered on the floor. On the bed were two empty whisky bottles and the ice pot was kept open on the table. The lid and the spatula were thrown into a corner of the room. The room was in helter-skelter. There was a half-lit cigarette on the ashtray. The spiral shape of the fume rising from the cigarette looked like the fumes of the funeral pyre. Jitu Mohanty was sitting on the bed which wasn't arranged properly and was looking at Binod with his rolling eyes. Muna Panda filled the glass with beer and went to get the spatula which was thrown in a corner of the room to put ice cubes in it . Muna Panda asked-' You were supposed to come tomorrow, isn't it?'

Binod didn't answer his question and asked him-' What are you doing here?' Muna Panda gave the beer glass to Jitu Mohanty and said-' I came to Bhubaneswar and thought of meeting sir'.

Jitu Mohanty mocked Muna Panda and said-'Where did you get this beer from? Is it beer or *Gomutra*?'

Muna Panda was startled and said-' This is from the military canteen. My brother in law gets it for me from the military canteen.'

-' Didn't I tell you to get two Old Monk or Mc Dowell bottles? Henceforth you will get the military type of dialogues in the play and don't crib about it later on.'

-' Sir ,I will get it next time....'

-' Leave it. You are all of the same. Unruly folks! Do you ever keep your promise? Go and get two packets of Red wills.'

Muna Panda immediately left the room to get the cigarette packets as if he is following the command of the King. Jitu Mohanty looked at him and cracked up. He stopped laughing and commented- Stupid fool! He runs after Malini Baral like a dog and needs the dialogues like Gabbar Singh's dialogue. Rascal! I will make you an agender this time... Jitu Mohanty gave a loud hearty laugh. He wasn't able to hold his breath as he was laughing continuously. He got up from the bed, lied down on the floor, and gazed at the ceiling perplexed. There was utter silence in the room. Only the ticking sound of the watch could be heard. Jitu Mohanty suddenly remembered something. He got up from the floor, went towards the bed, sat on it, and started singing like a drunkard- ' Tick, tick, tick the clock runs... Ha! ha! The clock runs....

Jitu Mohanty stopped in between and said-' Rascal! The manager of Madhulika hotel is useless.' He can never do things in the right way. I have told that Rascal in the evening.... Jitu Mohanty became silent for a moment, he looked at Binod with his empty eyes and said-' Binod babu, What's the name of the new girl who has joined your party?'

The dark mystery of the theatre was revealing slowly in front of Binod like a new dawn. Srikant Prusty was telling the truth. He had said-' You will see sir, when my play becomes a hit, Muna Panda will run after me to get few good dialogues.'

Binod was silent. Jitu Mohanty asked-'How is that girl,

Muna Panda? It seems her father sold all his property to become the king and finally became a beggar. What for did she join the party? Is it to become the queen or the empress?

Muna Panda had returned after purchasing the cigarettes. To impress him he said-' Sir, what to say about her? She is perfect. I swear sir, I have never seen such a girl in a theatrical company but she is very shy.'

-' What is shyness, Panda? The two directors of Dasabhuja are glutinous.'

- Sir, you......'

-' Wait Panda. I have got a new idea. Open the bottle.

Jitu Mohanty didn't have the patience to wait till Muna Panda opened the bottle. He snatched the hal -opened bottle from Muna Panda's hand and opened the cap with his teeth and gulped the beer from the bottle till it was empty.

-' Panda?'

-' Sir.'

-' The villain made the heroine stand on the riser and had tied her hands.. Heroine... What's her name? I can't feel the fun in the idea if I say heroine, heroine.'

-' Lata.' Muna Panda replied in a fearful voice.

-' Yes, Lata...' Jitu Mohanty said-It's a good name. You will pull her saree with your teeth similar to how the dog pulls the flesh from the corpse but at that time you will walk like an animal with your feet and hands on the stage. Did you understand? Why are you standing like a statue? Show me how you will walk.

Muna Panda bent down and started walking like an animal. Jitu Mohanty kicked him and screamed-'Did anyone in your family ever acted as a villain? Is this the way a villain acts?'

Muna Panda asked in a feeble tone as if he didn't understand-' Sir'? Jitu Mohanty opened another bottle and pushed it into the mouth of Muna Panda and said-'Drink rascal, drink. First of all drink and you will automatically become a villain.'

Jitu Mohanty's hands were shaking and half of the bottle got spilled. Jitu Mohanty kicked Muna Panda and said-'Lick it rascal!. Lick like a dog and clean it.'

Like an animal Muna Panda licked the wet floor and said-'I will not only pull Lata Mishra's saree, I will disrobe her and make her naked.'

-' Great ! Muna Panda,Great! How is the idea Binod babu?

Binod wasn't there to answer to Jitu Mohanty's question.

12

Binod left hotel Madhulika and ran towards the road madly. He was breathless by the time he reached the road. He felt , though he wasn't drunk still was in intoxication. Lata Mishra's sad and empty looks lingered in front of his eyes.

What will he do now? Bini madam will come in the evening. He thought that he will reach Bhubaneswar in a day and will discuss with Jitu Mohanty about the play. If required he will advise him to make necessary changes. But Jitu Mohanty is a devil. He has gained name and fame in these four years in the field of theatre and plays this has made him mad with ego and vanity. Why will he listen to Binod's advice?

Bini madam heard this and said-'He is paid for it. We are paying him to write a play for us. Do you think that a person like Jitu Mohanty has got any ethics? All his ideas are plagiarized. He puts those ideas into proper sequence. That is only his credit. We have to spend a lot on that. Jitu Mohanty isn't a specialist; he is just an ordinary writer. His job is to fulfill the needs and requirements of the owner.'

The way Bini madam narrated the things, Binod felt as if he has equal rights to advice for the benefit of Dasabhuja theatrical company. According to that, there is no harm in giving the correct advice to Jitu Mohanty other than that he tried to avoid any type of controversy by contradicting Bini madam. Maybe it is because of the owner and servant relationship which prevails. That's why he quietly agreed to come to Bhubaneswar. But, in hotel Madhulika he met Jitu Mohanty who behaved indecently, and because of that his heart revolted not only against Jitu Mohanty but against the entire theatrical world. How does Bini madam tolerate these people? Shankar Bhola is a thousand times better than him.

What will he do now? How will he spend such a long time in Bhubaneswar?

He knows Bhubaneswar city very well. He has spent three years in this city while doing his MA but now he feels as if the city is unknown to him. In just five years the city has changed a lot! The place where the hotel Madhulika stands was a place full of thorny bushes and now Bhubaneswar is expanding rapidly and the land is cleared for its expansion. Nothing is left from the past. It seems this city is hungrier than Muna Panda. He doesn't feel ashamed of licking from the ground. In front of Binod's eyes was dancing the beauty and bounty of Lata Mishra.

Ah! Binod felt as if he is getting suffocated. He sat in an auto and said-' Gyanaloka'.

Gyanaloka has changed a lot. There are no more cabins or betel shops near the main gate. There is a statue of Gopabandhu near the main gate. The authority has demolished a small temple which was on the left side. He had spent many evenings sitting on the porch of the temple and looking at the people and vehicles passing by.

What work does he have in Gyanaloka now? Why did he come here? Who will recognize him here?

If Professor Samsuddin would have been there, he could have spent his night easily in his house. During the difficult situation in his life, he was the only one who could give him the right suggestions and would have showed him the right path. But he has already left the campus. Where did he go after completing his post Doctorate from JNU? As he was leading a nomadic life of a theatre artist he couldn't to be in touch with Professor Samsuddin. He was the only well wisher who never made a hue and cry about his life as a theatre artist rather he encouraged him and said that each and every profession has its importance. No profession is big or small, it's necessary to realize the ethics of that profession. Every day, everything was new, like a new place, new audience, a new play, a new character, and new experience. Oh! Great! Binod, there is a thrill in the nomadic life which you will not get in any other profession. In the glamorous world, what is the difference between a TV, cinema, or theatre artist? What is necessary is to make yourself glamorous. 'Oh! Professor Samsuddin why did you give this initiation?

He entered the campus after crossing the main gate. But, where will he go? It would have been better if he would have gone to a hotel.

Many people are known to him who stay at Bhubaneswar. His cousin Uma bhai's house is nearby. His uncle stays in Baramunda. Hari Mahapatra's quarter is nearer to AG square. But wherever he goes all will ask him the same question- 'Are you going to spend your life in the theatre company? A talented man like you...' These questions are intolerable. It's not easy for Binod to keep quiet and listen to these. He feels as if his personality and identity are disgraced.

He sends money to his home regularly and visits his family every two to three months. Those who show off and make hue and cry don't do anything for their family but his fault is –he works for a theatrical company and it's a degraded identity, he can't escape from it throughout his life.

The life of a theatre artist is quirky. Unknown people show their eagerness to meet him. The cassettes are sold in his name from Govindpalli till Kantabanji but his own near and dear ones make a hue and cry thinking that has spoiled his life.

Talent? Which talent? The talent which isn't capable of providing you food to satisfy your hunger will that be called talent? If he wouldn't have joined the theatre then he would have given a donation to a college, worked there without salary and would have taught Shakespeare and Wordsworth. Who would have bothered for him? Who would have said- If you don't have money to pay the rent, don't worry I am there. Who would have given the solace- Don't worry about money. Tell me how much money do you want?

Binod knew very well that not a single person would have bothered about him. Now he is a theatre artist. Is it so that he lost his talent? Bloody Hell! It's the near and dear ones who criticize and deceive. The unknown people are far better than them. They never shed crocodile tears in the name of giving assurance and comfort.

On the left side is the university office and on the other side is the hostel. Which way will he take? Who will recognize him? Who will say- He is Binod Das, he was staying in Kabisurya hostel in room no 203 and was very talented. He remembered that he had spent his evenings with Professor Samsuddin in the college ground and the library. When he was in the library he forgot about the time and was engrossed in the American novels. He gave speeches, watched movies, acted in the plays, and also wrote love letters to the girls.

Today no one will recognize him here. Neither in the name of Binod Das nor in the name of Nija Khan. University students don't watch theatre.

What will he do? Will he return to the party camp? Will the bus be available at night? The banyan tree on the square looks dark. All the banyan trees look similar to Binod just like Budha in meditation. They don't have any relationship with the happiness and sadness of this world. It is only deep meditation that is their life. The other day when he saw the banyan tree in Manikgada Mountain it seemed to him as if the tree is much older than the statues excavated. The artist has given his sweat, blood, and imagination to engrave these statues under the tree. Those statues were buried underground with the passage of time unknown and undesired. Again they woke up from the deep slumber to see the sunrise of modern civilization. The old banyan tree of Manikgarh is a silent witness of the twist and turn that the civilization took. It doesn't have any relationship with the outside world. It is imperturbable. It is standing alone, rigid, and strong in different weather conditions and natural calamities.

The banyan tree in the university campus is also very old. Every year in the month of July the students who have graduated come and stand beneath it with a lot of dreams in their eyes. In that season the banyan tree is loaded with the new leaves and the dark rainy cloud cover the sky from the east. After completing their two years course, in the month of May and June, they go back with their bag and baggage. In this time period there are so many instances and experiences like the exuberance during campus election, fights, annual drama, and sincerity during the examination, and revolt against the establishment. Boys stand underneath this banyan tree and wait after making a phone call to the ladies hostel. Girls have Panipuri here and people like Professor Samsuddin stand here and look at the night sky and try to measure the depth of life. Many things happen here. Like the banyan tree of Manikgarh, this banyan tree is the witness of many dreams and broken hope.

It has remained as a sweet experience in the heart of people of all ages who have left. The middle- aged teachers write poems, youth weave dreams and regret unsuccessful love, the old and retired remember about the old days and say-' Campus isn't like the campus it was before.' The unemployed youth to break the monotony of boredom sit on the bench of the tea stall and ask-' Do you remember Alka Choudhary?' The girl in the Sociology department with two plaits.' For them, the meaning of campus is a girl with two plaits, Pass Pass, Capstan filter, Bihar chat stall, and the colorful pictures in Debonair magazine.

-' Bin?'

Binod was out of his imaginary world. He felt as if his buried past has popped up from the depth when he heard his name. He turned back to check if it's true or his imagination. Suna bhauja! He took some time to realize it.

Suna bhauja walked towards him and said-' I called out your name but wasn't sure whether it is you or someone else.'

-' Where are you going alone in the evening?'

-' My brother in law has come here for two years in the deputation. I went to their house. I don't know where they have been as there is a lock on the main door. I thought why to go back as I have come from a distant place, it's better to visit the handloom fair. Anyways I met you. Let's go home.

It seemed he landed up in trouble. Binod said- 'Bhauja, some other time.'

-' It's not done. Tell me we met after how many years? Suna bhauja held his hand and dragged him towards the main gate. But why is there so much warmth in Suna bhauja's hand? He has acted with so many women, has embraced them in the play, and has carried many on his shoulders. He has got a lot of experience with the actresses of his plays but he has never felt the warmth of anyone's body.

She called an auto on the road , sat, and said- 'Nirjan Vihar'.

There are so many Vihars and Nagars in Bhubaneswar.

There are so many advertisements in the newspaper regarding the newly constructed apartments and enclaves. Binod couldn't recall where is 'Nirjan Vihar', At present ,we are all searching for peace and tranquility from the hustle and bustle of city life that's why the construction and real estate companies under the advertisement plan draw an arrow and mention in bold letters the distance of their property from a busy and crowded square. The real estate and construction companies are trending ancy words like-Lonely, solitary, solitude etc. Previously they use to mention- In the heart of the city or at the core of the town. Where is this 'Nirjan Vihar' among the lonely and solitude?

Suna bhauja saw him sitting quietly and asked-' Whom did you promise and was waiting for in that square?' It's an old habit of Suna bhauja to call the square near the University's banyan tree the Time Square.

Whom will he give time today? The girls like Mamata Ray, Alka Choudhury, Mama Mishra who were studying along with him must be married by this time and maybe busy with changing the nappies, feeding Cerelac, and applying Johnson baby powder to their children or may have joined any private college and waiting for one- third grant in aid. Suna bhauja pushed him with her elbow and said-' What are you trying to hide? Don't I know the nature of the boys?'

-' How many of them were giving you time?'

- ' Why are you saying were giving? Are they not giving now? Suna bhauja laughed and said.

- 'Who is that Romeo?' Binod asked wittily.

-' You will take the account of the Romeos later on. First of all, calculate how many times your brother has given me time. It is almost two years but he didn't come. He wrote a letter that he will come during Dussehra. Again he has written a letter mentioning that he can't come. Maybe he is having an affair with some Muslim lady.

-' If brother doesn't come then why don't you go there?' Bombay isn't so far.

-' Oh! I think you don't know. Your brother isn't in Bombay. He is in Dubai for the past four years. He visited two years back and we bought the house. He was saying to purchase a piece of land and to construct the house but I didn't approve it. Now a days it's very difficult to deal with the mason and the workers. Who will take the pain and run after them to get the work done?

Suna bhauja has a double storied building' Swapna Mahal' in 'Nirjan Vihar'. The auto stopped in front of it. Suna bhauja took out the purse to pay the fare.

-' What about Sailashree Vihar house?'

- ' It's given on rent.'

Binod noticed that Suna bhauja had put on a little bit of weight. She looks very elegant and attractive. He could smell something very sweet. He was trying to figure out what is that smell. Suna bhauja called him and said-' What are you doing outside?'

13

The experience of following evening and night was exceptional and surprising.

' He sat on Bini madam's car from Nirjan Vihar square and reached a place. He couldn't figure out whether it's a hotel like 'Madhulika' or a house like ' Swapna Mahal' but after arriving there he realized that he had made a mistake. He shouldn't have come there.

Before them, many other people have reached there but they were waiting for someone and were spending their time in chit chat. The atmosphere was similar to the atmosphere of the audience gallery before the first bell of the play.

Binod noticed that as soon as Bini madam entered the hall the people in the hall stood still. She became the center of attraction for all and many cameras light flashed on her. The atmosphere resonated as they addressed her all together like- 'Hello madam', 'Hi ma'am',' Good evening',' How do you do?' Bini madam accepted everyone's wishes with a smile, by raising her hand, nodding her head, and handshakes. Binod was very happy but he couldn't understand the reason of his happiness. He was standing near the door in dilemma. He was giving a second thought whether to go inside or not. He was feeling uncomfortable standing there but he couldn't gather his courage to enter. What will he do there? He doesn't know anyone there. Even if he goes inside he will stand there like a log. But how long he will stand there like a watchman? He thought that madam has completely forgotten about him after entering the hall. Will he go back? But where? Will he go to hotel ' Madhulika' or Suna bhauja's 'Swapna Mahal'? In the meantime, the gateman had already told him twice-'Please go inside sahib'.

Suddenly Bini madam walked towards the center of the hall, took the microphone, and announced in the tone of an announcer-'This evening is only for drinks and dance.' No introduction, no lectures… nothing formal. Drink, dance, and enjoy.'

Someone asked from the crowd-'Anything special?'

-' Nothing special. Everything is extremely casual.'

After she finished her announcement the bright light of the hall was switched off and the hall was lightened with a dim blue light. The waiters in their uniform moved around with Rum, Gin, and Whisky. The tune of Pop music was played in a record player.

-' Sahib?' the gateman called. Binod turned back. He was requesting him to go inside for the third time. Binod walked inside and he closed the door. Binod remembered that in these types of doors it's either written 'Push' or 'Pull'. It's not closed like the door of ' Madhulika' nor restricted like the door of ' Swapna Mahal'.

The Pop music played on the record payer was much more intoxicating than the intoxication of the liquor. But no one here was behaving indecently like Jitu Mohanty. All of them were talking and enjoying but everything was within the limits. They were talking very softly. One can't hear what the other was talking. He couldn't understand whether they were talking, singing with the Pop music, or were just miming. He can never sing. In the play for a scene if he has to sing a song then from the background Ramani babu sings for him. He only mimes on the stage. He couldn't understand the rhythm, tone, and pitch of the song. Even after he stops miming Ramani babu keeps on singing- Neelakai-Ni.. La... ka... Ee. Kamal Mishra says- 'The impression that the song Neelakai has will it be justified if you complete it so soon Binod babu?' Listen to Ramani babu carefully. He sings the song rhythmically. If you stop miming before the song gets over then the situation will be worthless.

Neelakai or rotten mangoes? Malini Barala's mouth gives a very bad smell as she eats dry fish. The smell is much worse than rotten mangoes. He quickly tries to maintain distance.

-' Sahib , madam is calling you.' the gateman informed him. In one of the corners of the hall, madam was talking with three gentlemen dressed in coat and tie. He always hesitates to go in front of unknown people. He staggers and is unable to speak as he feels shy. His face turns red and if forced then tear rolls down from his eyes. During his childhood, if any relative came to the house he hid in the house or went outside through the backdoor to the backyard because of that whenever any relative comes it was sure that he will be scolded. Though he has grown up still he has that shyness. During his college and university days, he could be friendly with hardly a few. The same is in the case of a theatrical company. Muna Panda sometimes comment- ' See! how proud is he because he has done his MA.'

It wasn't at all wise for him to come here. All of them here are dressed in tie and suit. The ladies look like showpieces who have adorned themselves with beautiful sarees and expensive jewelry. Is there anyone here like him who is an ordinary theatre artist? Why did Bini madam bring him here? If he looks at the carpet on the floor he feels uneasy as that is soft and beautiful. It is much softer than a cushion. He looked at his leather sandal and thought that it looks so dirty on this beautiful carpet. He doesn't remember when he polished his sandal after he purchased it. Netra polishes the party shoes every day and maintains those. After the play is over it is taken away . Netra's duty isn't to polish the personal shoes and sandals of the actors and actresses. He has been using this sandal for a long time and travelling from one camp to another camp. He could have polished his sandal before coming here. Why didn't he think about it before? Has he become a parrot by rote learning his dialogues?

His clothes are also looking shabby. None of them present there have folded their shirt sleeves till the elbow. He rolled down the sleeves carefully and buttoned it and thought what else can be done?

Will he go back to Suna bhauja's 'Swapna Mahal 'without informing Bini madam? Suna bhauja was requesting him to stay back. It would have been better if he would have stayed back. He could have returned directly to the camp. But he never knew that madam will bring him to such a place. He thought maybe madam is taking him along with her to discuss with Jitu Mohanty in hotel Madhulika regarding the play. Suna bhauja cooked such delicious food for him and tried to stop him from leaving her place. How is he related to her? He is just a friend of his brother in law. He met her eight years back and it was a very brief introduction.

Are Suna bhauja's eyes are filled with the same sadness which is reflected in Lata's eyes? What is she devoid of? She has a husband who earns a lot. She also has a double storied building in Bhubaneswar, still, she is devoid of something. She said that she has no more interest to have a child. She also said-' Will the children ever take you to heaven? What about the emptiness that reflects in her eyes? Is it the huff of a frustrated soul? Is it a complaint against fate? Is it self deceit? Who knows?

Ah! Suna bhauja is so lonely in that double storied

building of 'Nirjan Vihar'. She feels good when someone known visits her and she tries to hold on to them for a longer time.

Is there a true friend of a human being? If that would have been then why is he so lonely in the midst of the noisy people of the theatrical company? Why is he standing near the hall door unwontedly? Why is Bini madam indulged in this tumult?

The music playing on the record player was about to end. He tried to understand the meaning of the song. He realized that it's not music but a bizarre snivel, a roar of a wild animal. Rather than this Babu Rao's record dance is more polished and agreeable.

The light in the room was gradually becoming dim. In that dimness, the couples were dancing hand in hand. They were changing partners after dancing for some time. Just before some time the lady who was dancing with a man in a maroon outfit is now dancing with a curly-haired young man. The maroon suit man who was dancing with a lady in a red saree has wrapped his hand on her waist and had pulled her towards a dark corner of the room. Another lady isn't concerned about her saree which has slipped from her shoulder and is madly searching for a partner to dance.

Is it dance or a mockery of dance? Binod has read about this in the story and novel. He has heard about the obscene dances that are performed in the hotel in the name of Caba and Cabaret. Today he can see it in person.

Where did Bini madam go? What's her intention? Why did she bring him here? After reaching the hall he realized that Bini madam is the Queen Honeybee of this arrangement. He could understand that he is just a silent spectator of this.

Why is this party arranged? Why did she make the people wait for her and went to ' Nirjan Vihar ' to bring him? These questions were making him restless as soon as he reached the door of the hall. He was curious to know the true identity of Bini madam.

The lights were switched off as soon as the song playing in the record player was about to create turmoil, in the darkness before Binod could understand where to go, he was in somebody's arms. He felt as if the thirsty land was waiting to feel the first drop of rain.

He forgot about the situation and screamed-'Who?'

14

-' Didn't you find anyone at the party?' Bini madam asked him. She had rudeness in her tone like a disciplined teacher.

-' I don't drink.' Binod said bluntly.

-' Why? Are you Gandhiji or Swami Vivekananda? The tone in which Bini madam asked the questions had a touch of irritation. She paused for a while and said-'Does it mean that as you don't drink so you will never drink?'

-' I don't have the habit of drinking from the beginning'.

Bini madam opened the fridge to bring the ice pot. She turned towards Binod and said-' Does anyone learn drinking from the birth?'

What answer can be given to this question? Binod thought for a while. Bini madam came back and sat in front of him. She gave a beer bottle to Binod and said-' Open this. Do you know how to open it?'

There is a charm to open the bottle using the opener. While opening the cool drink bottle Binod takes the opener from the shopkeeper to open it. If he opens the bottle like a layman then the froth comes out from the bottle but if the cap is opened a little and then opened completely it doesn't happen. Binod similarly opened the beer bottle. Bini madam was keenly looking at him as the examiner of a practical examination. As the froth didn't spill from the bottle she said-' Good! You look like a habitual opener. Though you don't drink still you have the habit of opening the bottle. Why were you standing in the party like a circus clown?'

Bini madam's witty remark pierced his heart. He knows very well that they have an owner and servant relationship. Bini madam is the whole and sole owner of Dasabhuja Theatrical Company. He is a mere actor. But today he was feeling embarrassed and that ached his heart. The way madam gave a remark 'Clown' was like adding fuel to fire. Madam knows very well that he is a theatre artist. This is his identity in front of her and it's enough. He has never expected anything more than this. He also doesn't have any interest to get anything more. What's her intention to bring him here and to humiliate him?

He looked at Bini madam and tried to answer her questions. He said-' Those who were in the party today, they have an identity and reputation in the society. I am just a theatre artist.'

Bini madam said-' At least you have that identity. The people whom you saw in the hall don't have that. If they have any identity that is in the police record or the underworld Don gang list.'

-' What's your relationship with these anti-social elements?' Binod asked hesitatingly. Is the question too personal!

Bini madam saw his hesitation and smiled. She said-' Binod,You are asking a very childish question. You are very immature. The anti-social are the most socialized people in the society. The identity of this age is based on the donation and contribution. Whoever has the capability to give more donations and able to contribute more maintains a high status in the society.'

Madam offered him a beer glass and took the other glass. Just before a while, he was curious about knowing the true identity of Bini madam. Now the mystery was unfolding in front of him slowly.

-' Each individual must drink once in his life and should seek for the company of a woman otherwise life isn't complete. He makes himself devoid of many experiences.' Bini madam was talking as if she was giving a lecture. There was no reluctance in her voice and her eyes were sharp. Binod felt as if he has heard this before. Who said this? Is it Professor Samsuddin?

Bini madam came close to him and asked-' Why are sitting with the glass? Don't you want a new experience in life? Will you live like a theatre artist lifelong?'

Binod was startled. He never thought that she looked down at the theatre artists in this way.

-' Why did you make a theatrical company?' he asked

-' Binod, life, and profession isn't the same. Dasabhuja maybe my pathway, I have never seen it as my path. Bini madam's words were sounding like Professor Samsuddin words to Binod. He also said-' Giving lectures in the classroom is my profession, but life isn't limited to lectures. It is also not in Philosophy and Literature. Life is inevitable, an intractable power, as much you try to figure out, it becomes more and more challenging.' Maybe in search of that enigma, he lost himself in JNU campus. Binod took a deep breath. She looked down and asked-' Binod, What are you looking at?'

-' Nothing.' Binod said in an inattentive voice. He was engrossed in deep thought of the past. There was the star-clad sky of April, the blooming of Peacock flower(Krishnachuda), and Professor Samsuddin. Binod was indulged there in the enthusiasm of searching, getting, and losing.

-' Nothing'! Bini madam smiled and repeated Binod's words. There was no complexity in that smile. In the meantime she had already finished her drink. While opening the cap of the bottle she said-' In front of you is sitting a human being made up of flesh and blood who is a healthy and youthful woman but how can you say that you aren't looking at anything?'

She walked towards him and said-' ' Liar'. Then she took Binod's glass and said-'Will you drink or I will finish it?'

Binod drank from the glass at one go and kept it on the table. He felt a burning sensation in his throat and chest. There was a blaze inside him. Binod couldn't understand if that is the blaze of attraction or repulsion. But he realized that the blaze within him has overpowered the burning sensation of his throat and chest.

-' Binod, did you drink liquor of Ganga water? Does anyone drink in this way? It is drunk sip by sip and along with it you lose your consciousness. He felt as if madam has already lost her consciousness. She again refilled Binod's glass. Binod followed what madam said and drank from the glass sip by sip. He felt as if the room has expanded to the horizon. After some time the horizon wasn't visible. The house didn't look like a house. It looked like the dazzling water of the wide-spread ocean whose waves were bouncing. It seemed the moon was rising from the foggy horizon. He remembered the lines from Sachi Routray's poem. He forgot about the place and situation, stood up, and recited the lines from the poem.

-'Bravo! Bravo! Bini madam clapped and said. Binod stopped reciting the poem. He became conscious and thought-Did I do any mistake?'

- Madam said in a normal voice-' Have you ever felt the difference between moonlight and blood stain? I think moon light is more perilous and more frightful than bloodstain. Man is frightened seeing the bloodstain but the moonlight fills the heart with remorse.'

Binod wasn't in a mood to think seriously about what

madam said. He was thinking-' Who is more beautiful?' Is it Bini madam or the moon rising from the horizon like a silver plate? Who is beautiful? He wasn't able to conclude. He asked-'Madam, have you ever seen a moon- lit night in the vast fields, in solitude riverside, or during full moon day?' Madam took a deep breath and said –'No, I never felt so. Today after listening to the poem recited by you I feel like looking at it.'

Binod said-' A moon- lit night is enigmatical. It has got many shapes.'

-' Who has written the poem must have seen the enigma of the moon- lit night. Do you know what my perspective was?'

-' What?'

-' I thought that Odia poets mostly write about the carnal desire or about the girls collecting leaves. Binod, can you show me the moon lit night in the vast fields or near the solitude riverside?'

Binod stood up and said-'Let's go now, at this moment. Bini madam laughed and said-' I think you are intoxicated.' After drinking a little beer how could you see the moon in a dark night?'

Binod's intoxication level came down suddenly as the mercury of the thermometer. He sat down and pulled his hair. Madam asked-' Do you have a headache?'

Binod didn't answer and looked at her face. Madam turned towards his back and started caressing his hair. Binod's eyelids were heavy. He was drowsy. He felt as if the chair, table, wall, clock, and everything present in the room were swirling. The next moment Binod thought-No, he is moving around all these things. Are all of them plotting a conspiracy against him? The ocean which was violent just a few minutes ago has become silent like a stream. Binod apprehended that they will throw him into that stream as per their conspiracy. He tightly caught hold of madam's hand. Madam took his head towards her and said-' In the beginning, you may feel like this. After sometime you will feel better.'

Binod was thirsty. He felt like falling in a gorge and was losing his consciousness. He couldn't open his eyes.

Binod woke up from the slumber with the noise of the raindrops. It was sweet and melodious to listen to the pitter-patter of the raindrops. He wasn't able to understand whether it was raining outside or is if his imagination. He felt as if the rain is flying around like a colorful butterfly and is also taking him along with it. It was difficult for him to open his eyes. What will he get if he opens his eyes? It's better to listen to the melodious sound made by the raindrops. Is there a better experience to feel light- headed and move around like a soft cotton ball? It's a funny game to move from here to there without any destination. There is no aim, no desire, new places, and new experiences. Is there so much excitement in any profession?

Professor Samsuddin! You are a fiery flame. You can only burn. Where did you disappear leaving behind the beautiful world full of colorful butterflies, flowers, and clouds?

-'Binod?' Binod opened his eyes as Bini madam called. Madam was calling him wiping her hair with a towel. Binod couldn't gather his courage to keep his eyes open for a long time. What did he see in front of his eyes? Is it a piece of cloud or the blooming flower? A sky filled with stars or a colorful butterfly?

-' Go and take your bath. I am making the dinner ready. Bini madam said. She had just taken her bath.

Binod was still not in a conscious mind. He closed his eyes.

Bini madam pulled him and made him stand and said-' You are an innocent child.'

Binod entered the bathroom and thought-' Oh! Madam

has left the shower unturned and he was thinking it was raining.'

Madam was cutting the salad on the chopping board which was kept on the dining table. The tomatoes, cucumber, and carrot were looking more colorful to his eyes. He was searching for the description of each color like the color of the onion peel is like the color of madam's thin nightgown.

Yes, still he is in intoxication. He doesn't understand how Jitu Mohanty writes play in an intoxicated state? Nothing seems fixed in this state. Everything seems to slip out of his hand.

Madam kept something on the cooker and came back from the kitchen. The thin nightgown revealed the bounty of her beauty.

Binod was well versed with the curves of a female body. But no lady dares to sit in front of him in a thin night gown. Not even Kalyani. Through the hostel window, with lustful eyes, he has seen the half- bare body of Jaga gardener's wife. There was no bathroom facility in Jaga gardener's single- room house. His wife takes bath under a dense Croton plant where the water pipe was fixed but till Jaga gardener was in the house she hesitated to take bath.

During the afternoon Suna bhauja only wraps a saree and sleeps and when she listens to the footsteps near the door she immediately pulls her saree on her chest and says-' It's so hot.'

In the makeup room when Malini Baral goes to change her saree she shouts at Muna Panda and says-' Go out. How will I change my saree?' Muna Panda shows his teeth like a monkey and says-'OK! I will close my eyes.'

They were all very conscious about their body. They guarded it like a miser. It seemed as if they lose their wealth by the look of a person. Till the end , he couldn't understand the sentiment of Kalyani. Her body was a prohibited area for

Binod. If he tries to look at her body, she says-' You Brute! You are an animal who loves only flesh. Do you know anything other than that?'

When she catches a common cold, she says-'Do you know I am not feeling well for the past two days?' Have you ever tried to look after me?

He had never noticed anyone being so casual about one's body. For Bini madam, it seems the body is a medium to survive like the Dasabhuja Theatrical Company or the thin nightgown where she doesn't exist . It can be inferred from her body language.

Bini madam was cutting salad and suddenly asked him-' Binod, do you remember about Mankigarh's stone statues?'

Binod was distracted. Why did madam suddenly remember about Manikgarh's stone statues? He visualized the bare stone statues of Mankigarh under the banyan tree which were lying on the ground without a care. Those aren't only statues but a depiction of V?tsy?yana's Kamasutra's erotic love.

Madam's next question -' Can you tell me why did someone sculpture that Maithuna mudra on those stones?'

How could have Binod answered that question? Who knows under what mindset, during the rise and fall of morality, twist and turns in life the sculptor had engraved those postures? He had read about it in history. But at that moment he wasn't interested in those intrinsical discussions. He started peeling the onion in an inattentive manner. The onion peels flew and scattered here and there.

-' Binod, why didn't you give any answer?'

Binod started thinking about the answer but he wasn't able to recollect anything. Like the onion peel, the curves and circles of a woman's body were swirling in front of his eye. He was not able to differentiate which one is alive and which one is the stone statue.

-Do you know what do I think Binod? Madam said. After some time she said-' Once they were all alive. A magic spell has made them stone. Have you not heard that human beings can be turned into stones by the magic spell?'

Binod looked at her in surprise. What is madam saying? Madam kept the knife down and laughed. A dimple was created in her chubby cheeks. She asked-' Are you surprised listening to me?' She paused for a while and again said-'Maybe at that time there were not so rigid rules and discipline in the society. There was not so much of modesty and ethos. Maybe they thought coitus as an embarrassing activity.' Madam posed for a moment again, took the hot case towards her and opened the lid, and said- 'Maybe the opposite of what I said is correct. Maybe there were rigid rules, discipline, modesty, and ethos in excess in the society and they revolted against it. You must have read about the fall of Boudha Vihars. They protested and revolted against the rigid rules of the society and were engaged in mass copulation.'

-' Were they involved in mass copulation?' This question resonated within Binod. He felt as if he was falling into a deep gorge of astonishment. What is madam saying?'Is it not too much absurd?' Binod asked unknowingly.

-' Binod, Whom will you say it as absurd?' Is it not absurd which is going on right now about the mutual exchange of partners in the clubs? Would people not have told you that it's absurd if you would have told these twenty to twenty five years back? Binod was trying to understand madam's justifications. But still, some of the justifications were uncomprehended. Is it possible for so many men and women to be naked and indulging in copulation?'

Madam noticed his skepticism and said-' Everything is possible in war and love. There is no fixed rule in war and love. No one follows it and in sex... Madam paused.

After looking at the dance in the hall in the evening Binod

had certain apprehensions in his mind but he didn't gather the courage to discuss about it so openly.

-'Did you notice the men and women dancing in the hall today?'

Binod nodded silently.

-' Did you notice their state after the light was switched on?'

Binod was trying to recollect. He couldn't recollect anything. He was unable to recall the man in the maroon suit, the woman in a red saree or the curly- haired man. He felt as if all of them were playing merry- go- round and was deceiving his thoughts.

-' If there has been a little delay in the lights to be switched on and if someone would have clicked a photo in that darkness then what you would have seen? What...?'

-' Something more fierce than the stone statues of Mankigarh... more exciting, and loathsome postures.' Binod nodded his head in approval. He wasn't able to conceive any argument to deny it.

-' Then why did you say absurd? At every age, every time the greatest attraction for a human being is sex. Time and rituals have adorned it with different getups. If you notice carefully, you will understand that the human mind frame is raw.'

Now Binod didn't have any hesitation to look at Bini madam's unveiled body. He picked up the knife and unnecessarily poked an onion.

15

Puri.

Binod had a lot of attraction for the camp in Puri which was organized once a year. Dasabhuja Theatrical Company sets up its camp on Bada Danda for a week every year. Binod waits eagerly for this camp.

He doesn't go to the temple every day for the darshan of the deity like others. The way Bholi babu prays in the morning and chants Bishnu Sahasra nama or Durga Chalisa and rings the puja bell and in between calls out the name of Nanda and Bagula he doesn't appreciate it neither he appreciates going for darshan every day like others.

Binod doesn't appreciate the people who don't start their day by reading Gita. Is reading Gita is like taking bath, like taking breakfast or signing the office attendance register at 10 O' Clock and going to the market to purchase groceries?

Gita is practiced in the mind. It is accomplished in the heart. Binod doesn't find any reason to make a rule to read Gita every day.

This is the matter of Lord Jagannath. Who is absolute enigmatic and a puzzlement.

Who knows when will he appear and suddenly disappear? Shri Krishna can be understood by giving justification but Lord Jagannath is obscure. Binod left the temple premises with a sigh.

In front of him was Bada Danda. There were so many shops selling different varieties of stuff. At the beginning of the month of Kartik ,there is hustle and bustle.

What do they purchase with so much sincerity and interest? Is it dried *Nirmalya* or the photo of Lord Jagannath, Balabhadra, and Subhadra? Is it utensils made of black marble stone or sandalwood stick or the brass bell, plate, or Puri's cane stick?

All these things aren't made in Puri. Brass bells and plates come from Balipatna, black marble stone utensils and sandalwood sticks come from Nilagiri, Pattachitra from Raghurajpur, and Pipli comes the canopies and bags. The shopkeepers have assembled different things from different places which are found in Puri. These are like the memories in life. There is a lot of attraction to purchase these from Puri's *Bada Danda* and they will keep these as the most precious things in life.

When grandmother was alive she carefully stored Nirmalya in her bag. When it was necessary she took it out very proudly.

He has seen the devotion of a common man towards Lord Jagannath even in Bihar's remote village Rimidega. They kept the photo of Lord Jagannath, Balabhadra ,and Subhadra in a groove on the wall. When there was a party camp in the village a man with a lot of enthusiasm allowed Binod to stay in his house. As he belonged to the state of Lord Jagannath, people took bath, came in the morning, and touched his feet. Binod felt embarrassed.

What is he?

He might have gone to Puri with a lot of hardship from this remote village. He must have walked, might have taken a bus or train, and must have saved money to go to Puri. Don't know whether he could have seen Lord Jagannath to his heart content amidst the chaos created by Puri pandas . In an unknown place in the crowd, he might have bought the photo of Lord Jagannath and has kept it with utmost care in a groove on the wall and worship it with sandal and incense stick.

The people in the village don't know the rituals of *Shodasha Upchar*. They might not have also heard the names of *Sathiyae Pauti Bhoga*. They don't know anything about the rituals, services, and holy chanting. Lord Jagannath is Lord Jagannath for them. All their sins and sadness are wiped out when they bow their head in front of the photo on the wall.' Jay Jagannath' is their Maha Mantra.

Ah! why Binod couldn't be like him. Like the innocent man in the Rimidega village. He could also have offered his prayers to Lord Jagannath with reverence, devotion, and complete submission. He is the ultimate remedy for the entire inner blaze and the conflict.

He stood for hours looking at Lord Jagannath on his Ratna Simhasana. He has tried to bring in his heart the same feeling of reverence and devotion as the innocent villager has but he couldn't.

He feels as if Lord Jagannath is very far, unreachable. He has returned with disappointment.

Long back he bought an idol of Lord Jagannath in Konark Craft Fair. A small idol made up of Neem wood. What was that attraction! When he saw the idol his heart was filled with happiness. He felt as if it is the same Lord Jagannath of his imagination. In the shop, there were many idols of Lord Jagannath in various sizes and different attire. Binod couldn't understand why on that day, that particular idol attracted him. He felt as if that particular idol has brought him here far from the university campus and Professor Samsuddin.

Binod still couldn't understand- Whether he selected the idol or the idol selected him? Was it looking for a person with whom it will stay lifelong in all the happiness and sadness in life?

But was he able to keep it with him?

Is there any certainty in the life of a theatre artist? How could he carry it with him? At the end of the year when he gets holidays and goes home that time he could see the idol.

The idol is a witness to many things in his life like the time that he spent with Professor Samsuddin on the university campus,a time during his unemployment, marriage with Kalyani, and divorce. It has seen everything with its wide-open eyes and also today's nomadic life of a theatre artist.

Though he is not near he seems to be near. Though not reachable, still closer. To purchase attire for the idol Binod searched in the shops on the footpath. He bought a coronet last year but it was small and it was looking like the turban of a Kabuli Wala. The coronate didn't match the smile of Lord Jagannath's idol. It's difficult to understand that smile. If you try to analyze it ,it becomes sombrous and more mysterious. Kalyani said that it's the work of the artist but is the paintbrush of an artist worthy enough to draw a contagious smile like this?

Why is the makeup artist Mohan Singh not able to bring out the feeling of modesty in the eyes of Malini after applying the eyeshade? Despite all the efforts made by Mohan Singh, and the modesty of a woman, Why does her eyes reflect the hunger of a lustful woman?

-'Binod?' There was an end to his imagination as Bini madam called his name. Her car was a little far from the footpath. She was standing near a tea stall and was waiting for him.

-' How are you here?' Binod went closer and asked. Bini madam didn't reply anything but smiled.

-' We were supposed to decide on Jitu Mohanty's play ,isn't it?

Madam sat on a chair and said-' What do you expect new from Jitu Mohanty's play? Everything is the same. Shankar Bhola has written ' Murder- Rape- Gang rape.' Jitu Mohanty has written' Rape and Murder.' If we don't get a good play we have to manage with that.'

-' Then?' Binod pulled a chair and sat on it disappointed.

-'Were you thinking about Bali Yatra competition depending on his play?'

-' Anshupa, Indradhanu, Shibani etc will select their play and will participate in the competition.'

-' Binod,it should be different from other play. Is Bali Yatra Gana Mahotsava Competition is as simple as that? It will be a platform to showcase the heritage of Odisha. Many intellectual people will sit in the audience gallery. It's better not to compete rather than showcasing the play of Jitu Mohanty and Shankar Bhola.

-' But we don't have even a month's time. Where will we get a new play from?'

-' I was thinking about that and couldn't sit peacefully in Bhubaneswar.'

-' There are cane stick, Mahaprasad shops in Puri but I have not seen a readymade play shop . Binod said humorously.

-' It's ok if we don't get a play but the actor is here.' Bini madam gave a reply to Binod's sarcasm craftily but it touched the heart of Binod from within and he could feel the rhythm playing in his heart.

He looked at the temple and thought-'It's right!' It's possible that a play could be written keeping in mind Lord Jagannath as the protagonist. In the life of Odia people, he is Maha Nayak.

Shree Mandir- Neela Chakra- Sudarshana Chakra and on it is the flag which is fluttering in the air slowly with the wind like the victory flag of the warrior. It seems as if the painter has painted the beautiful clear sky.

Binod looked at it enchanted and thought-'Why can't it be the background scene of a play?' Instead of stage decoration, light technique, screen change in the second stage according to Pattachitra style a still picture can be drawn. Neela Chakra and on it Sudarshana Chakra with the fluttering flag. Scene after scene can be acted with the same background. The background painting will remain the same till the end.

-' Binod, what are you thinking? The tea is becoming cold.' Madam asked. Binod said-' Madam, can you see the Neela Chakra and the Neela Neta? Why can't a play be conceived keeping this scene in the background?'

-' Which new play will you do about Lord Jagannath? There are so many TV serials and movies based on him. Of course, the content will be good but will there be something new in that?'

-' Lord Jagannath is a vast puzzlement. I am not saying to do a historical play to propagate his ethereal glory. There will be many people who will be interested to watch this play especially the people from the villages. But there won't be any inventiveness in that.'

-' Then?'

-' Have you read the novel Neel Saila (Blue Hills)? If a play can be written based on ' Neela Saila' novel!'

- Oh! Is it the novel 'Neela Saila' by Surendra Mohanty?'The novel has been praised by many. I have heard that NBT has translated the novel in various Indian languages but I have never got an opportunity to read that novel.' Madam said.

-' It's not only a novel ' Neela Saila' but a generative flame. I have read it many times and every time it has ignited a flame in me. There is no redemption from this.'

-'I have heard that Surendra babu has composed the latter half. Why are you saying that it is never- ending?'

Binod looked at Bini madam as if he is doing a favor.

Bini madam appears as if she has wisdom, self respect ,and is aristocratic. But now her appearance looked very miserable to him.

He said-' It's not possible for any author to conceive the latter part of his artistry. Artistry is like the bubbles in the ocean of art. It gets created and then merges in its individualism. In that particular moment the appeal that it creates, repetition of that is impossible. Not only Odia or Indian literature but in the World Literature also second half and third half has been composed. But they could never be equivalent to the original composition.

-'Is it also for a classic composer like Surendra Mohanty?'

-' I can't make you understand properly.' Surendra babu wrote ' Neela Bijaya' and the next half of 'Neela Chakra'. That novel's mood is different. It is also popular like 'Neela Saila' and many editions of that have been sold in the market. Many critics have the opinion that it is more significant than 'Neela Saila' but ' Neela Saila is after all 'Neela Saila'. It has no other alternative.

-' What do you mean?'

-' One can't understand twirls and turns of art. I feel that 'Neela Saila is like the calm sea line of Chilika Lake and 'Niladri Bijaya' is like the turbulent water of the ocean. The first one is aimless and a wacky saint and the other one is like a warrior with a specific aim.

To make Binod more emotional Bini madam said-' Binod, will you tell me the story?'

There was an end to Binod's emotions. He asked mockingly-'In this tea stall?'

16

Kamal Mishra pardoned himself after listening to the name of the play 'Neela Saila '. He said- 'There is no comparison of 'Neela Saila' as a novel. Binod babu, I have also read that novel many times but to stage it as a play ...,' He stopped in between.

Bini madam asked-' What's the problem?' Wouldn't it be appreciated as a historical play?'

-' No madam, if 'Neela Saila ' is written as a play that won't be only a historical play. That will be a reflection of an anachronistic approach to human life. In that way 'Neela Saila is appropriate but the problem is who will write it as a play? Now days such playwrights don't exist.

-' Is there a scarcity of playwright in Odisha to write it as a play for such excellent content? Gopal Chhotray gave many popular novels the shape of the play. I have heard the radio play conversion of Gopinath Mohanty's 'Paraja'. It was transformed into play and was staged successfully.

Kamal Mishra said- ' I have heard that when Surendra babu was alive a cinema Director wanted to make a film based on this. But he wasn't successful. When there was a trend of historical plays in the theatre, many theatrical companies must have tried it.

-' Is it so that if it couldn't be done in the past, it can't be done in the present? We should at least try it once. There is no need to worry about profit and loss. Don't worry about how the audience will accept it. With the blessings of Lord Jagannath if this can be staged during Bali Yatra Gana Mahotsava that will be Dasabhuja's greatest tribute in the lotus feet of the Lord.'

Benu babu and Raghu babu were listening to the conversation about the play with a lot of hope. Benu Ustad said-' There is a person who can write a play like 'Neela Saila'. It's difficult to catch hold of him. He is a very moody person.

-' Who is he?' Binod asked eagerly.

-'Dhira babu'. Benu Ustad answered calmly.

-' Who is Dhira babu, Ustad? I have never heard his name among the play wrights.' Shankar Bhola asked in a very casual tone.

- He has left writing plays twenty five to thirty years back. He is an expert in writing mythological and historical plays. His plays like' Chandraloka Ra Chadaka', 'Bhina Panipat',' Karubaki', 'Chandrabhaga' etc were once created a sensation in Bihar, Bengal, and Odisha. In Dhira Babu's ' Abhisapta Jagannath ' play, I and Raghu babu played the role of Jagannath and Balbahadra . Amazing script! People sat and watched it silently even though it was too late. The stage resonated with the sound of claps and appreciation. You may ask Raghu babu. It has become a dream to watch such a play now.

Shankar Bhola got irritated and said-' Play, what play? Ustad, Why are you unnecessarily boasting? Tell that it was a farce, a useless farce. I have seen that type of farce during my childhood days.

Binod turned back and asked Bhola babu-' What's the difference between a play and a farce?'

Bhola kept quiet listening to his question. Binod said -' When you are trying to write a play, at least read about Odia

Drama and its progress in literature.' Shankar Bhola tried to digest the insult and his voice became deep in vainglory. He said-' I have been writing the play for the past twenty years. Why will you say me to read the plays?'

-'When did Binod babu tell you to read the play? He suggested you to read the history of drama.' Kamal Mishra laughed and said.

-' The historical plays aren't appreciated. Why read those?

-' Is the history of drama and historical drama are the same thing? You don't understand Bhola babu and unnecessarily getting irritated.

-' Kamal babu, don't try to make me understand. Do you think that I am a fool? Do you think that I can't understand what is said? Why will a person who writes play will go and read the history of drama?'

-' I think you were a lecture in a college. What was your subject?' Bini madam smiled and asked.

-' Why are you asking that madam? I thought that I will worship art and didn't value the job otherwise I would have become a reader and would have been promoted to class one officer category by this time.'

-' It's good. Odisha's education department could escape from a disaster.' Benu Ustad commented.

-' Yes ,why won't you say so? You are on cloud nine after listening about the historical play. But what are you saying it Ustad? I have to listen to all these because of my fate. Anshupa, Satrupa theatrical companies are waiting for my play. I have been running after the party shamelessly for the past one month.'

-' Who has stopped you here? Bini madam said as she wanted to end this unnecessary discussion. She paused for a while and gave her final verdict. She said-'Henceforth, Dasabhuja won't stage such cheap plays neither in Bali Yatra Gana Mahotsava nor in any other place. The decision is final.'

All of them kept quiet listening to her sharp voice. Everyone knows about her nature. She looked at Benu Ustad after taking her final decision and said- 'Can you give me the address of Dhira babu?'

Raghu babu answered-' On the other side of Chitapala river is Phulahata village. After crossing Tarapur Bridge the distance is almost two miles.

-' Binod, shall we go tomorrow?'

-' Sure. Is there anything to ask? Binod replied.

17

Across the river Chitapala, in Phulahata village is Dhira babu's house. He belongs to an affluent family.

There was an old bullet wood tree in front of his house and around it is a stone platform. Next to the stone platform, there is an old armchair on which was sitting Dhira babu who was very weak and his face looked like a barren desert. He was wearing a lungi and a khadi kurta and on it an old jacket. He had tied a muffler on his head like a turban and another muffler around his neck.

At a distance was seen Chitrapal River's 'U' turn and on the other side was the river plateau. Dhira babu was sitting still and was looking at the river plateau with his dusky eyes. His attention wasn't diverted though the car stopped at the gate. Binod thought that maybe he was not able to hear properly.

Benu Ustad went and touched his feet. He looked at him for some time and then smiled. He caressed Benu Ustad and said-'Benu, how come you are here? How did you remember me suddenly?'

Benu Ustad's became sentimental. He said-'When did I forget you? When I didn't forget you how can I remember you suddenly?'

Dhira babu wasn't able to make out how to welcome his old beloved friend. He looked at the house and called out-' Hema's Mother! Look who has come.'

Hema's mother stepped outside the house and stopped. She looked at the unknown people standing there.

Dhira babu looked at her and said-' Can't you recognize him? Can't you recognize Benu?'

Hema's mother was unable to recognize him properly. She covered her head with the saree and stood near the door.

To make the identity clear, Dhira babu said-'He is our Benu. The actor who did the role of Krishna in 'Gopi Balabha' play. Ha! Ha! Ha!

As soon as Dhira babu laughed loudly he was short of breath. He took control over his breath and asked-' Did you recognize him now?'

Hema's mother was able to recognize him now. She said-' A guest sees more in an hour than the host in a year.' How can I recognize him? Did you come here by mistake?

-'Sister- in- law, why are you asking about this at this age? I am waiting for my last breath.'

-' It's not there in the hands of anyone otherwise with this unhealthy body who wants to suffer? Look at me, I have arthritis and I am not able to sit or walk properly. I need support to walk. In winter it becomes more severe. During the night I become breathless and it's difficult to sleep. It's only sufferings, what else!'

-' Will you ask him to sit or will you go on talking like this? There are two more people along with him.' Hema's mother said.'

Dhira babu looked at Binod and Bini madam. He became worried and said-' I have lost my sense. Please send the chairs along with Mayadhara.'

Bini madam said-'Please don't worry. We will sit here.'

She sat on the platform.

Binod understood the health condition of Dhira babu and thought-'It won't be fruitful to come here after traveling such a long distance.'

A middle- aged man came with the chairs. He may be Mayadhara.

He kept the chairs and said-' Why don't you sit in the house? There is mist outside.

-' It's afternoon and you say that there is mist? How long a person will sit in the house? Dhira babu said annoyingly. In his voice was aversion.

Like a guardian Mayadhara said-'Ok. You shouldn't feel breathless at night. The doctor has told you not to step outside, isn't it? Dhira babu ignored his words and said-'Will fish be available in the market now?'

-' In the month of Kartik fish isn't sold in the market so Deja Behera is going around the village to sell fish. Which fish I should bring?'

-' Go and get some good fish. Check if it's fresh or not and also tell Deja Behera if the fish isn't good then I won't pay him money. While returning, bring one kilogram of *Chhena Poda* from Nakhi Sahoo's shop.' Dhira babu took a deep breath. It was difficult for him to speak properly.

-' Sister- in- law has told to remove the coconut from its shell. I will complete that work and go.'

Is this elaborate arrangement is done for them? Binod was worried. They didn't begin the discussion regarding the play. Did Benu babu forget the actual topic of discussion and is ready for the hospitality? Puri is hardly a four to five hours drive from this place. Till Tarpur Bridge the condition of the road isn't good.

Mayadhara came back and kept a center table which was made of fiber. After some time he came back with a brass plate with *Arisa Pitha*. The smell of Arisa was filled in the air. Binod hadn't eaten Arisa for a long time. His mother doesn't prepare it as it's a tedious process. Still, after Raja when he is there in the house for a few days his mother prepares something or the other. Bini madam took a piece of Arisa Pitha and said-' Such a nice smell! Is it fried with pure cow ghee?'

-' Not with cow ghee, it's fried in buffalo ghee. Dhira babu made the necessary correction. He took a deep breath and said-'There are no more cows in the house. People aren't available to take care of them. There are only two cows to fulfill the needs. My son and daughter- in- law are staying outside. It becomes difficult for them to come here for three to four days a year. Whenever they come, they always book the return ticket and come.'

Dhira babu laughed as if he was mocking himself. Binod couldn't make out whether it was a hearty laugh or was it filled with sadness.

Benu Ustad asked-' How many buffalos do you have now?'

-' Who knows?' Dhira babu replied in a disinterested voice. He took breathe and said-' Kirtanpur's Kanu Das has taken the assignment of buffalo ranching. He knows in detail. We are happy with two pots of ghee that we get in a year. Now a day's people use the ghee available in the market in packets to do the holy rituals but your sister- in- law doesn't allow using the outside ghee for the rituals.' Hema's mother came there with tea. She smiled and asked-'Are you discussing about me? Listen! Benu, Your brother will never give up criticizing me. He can't digest his food without doing it. He doesn't have any other work.'

' That is not criticism sister in law. You may feel that he is criticizing you but it's like coaxing Lord Jagannath as 'Kala Sarpa'.

-' Who will supersede you thespians? Said Hema's mother and she left. Suddenly she stopped as if she remembered something, turned back, and said-' Come inside the house after finishing tea. There is mist outside. I am preparing *Chitau Pitha*. Eat it and then talk till I finish cooking.'

-' We will leave in some time sister- in- law. Is there any time for so much hospitality? We are just waiting for brother to give a reply. There is a camp in Puri. It will be late by the time we return.'

-' Are you still there at an opera party? Dhira babu asked. Benu Ustad said-'What will I do sitting at home? The devil enter uninvited when the house stands empty so I will be with the party till I am fit and fine. I will think over it when I become unfit.'

-' Does your body permits you to do so much hard work and to spend sleepless nights?'

-'Is there any other way? What will I do alone at home? At the party I spend my time with my friends and regarding hard work which you asked, I don't have much work. Sometimes if required I teach Odissi or other folk dances. Sometimes I sit with the musicians and play hand cymbals (Manjeera).Otherwise, there nothing else to do. It's because of madam's compassion I can sustain.

Benu Ustad didn't say that Bholi babu tells him to arrange the chairs and to look after the cooking in the mess. Binod couldn't understand the reason. Is it because he doesn't want to trouble Dhira babu or to maintain his self- dignity?

Does Benu Ustad have anyone in the house? Is he going around with the party for friends? No one knows if Bholi babu pays his salary or not. He is there along with them for a long time but he has never asked him about his well- being but what relationship does he have with Dhira babu and Hema's mother that they are so happy to see him? While drinking tea, Bini madam said softly-' Binod, please ask him about the play.'

-' Benu babu you should begin with the conversation.' He said to make Benu babu understand.

Benu Ustad was thinking about how to begin with the conversation. Binod suddenly said-'During Bali Yatra ,in the Bali Yatra ground the cultural festival will begin. A play competition has been arranged. All the prestigious theatrical groups of Odisha are invited to this competition. We are planning to stage 'Neela Saila' instead of the cheap seasonal plays. If you could ....

Dhiru babu asked-'Is it Surendra Mohanty's 'Neela Saila?' He was enthusiastic. Bini madam was excited and she said-'Yes sir, that's why after listening about you from Benu babu we have come to you with a lot of hope.

Dhira babu said-' I think Odia audience don't have interest for a mythological or historical play.

-'It's not correct.' Binod said in an agitating voice. The interest of the audience is like a puzzle. Ramanand Sagar and B.R Chopra made Mega serials with Ramayan and Mahabharata. Color print was taken out for Mugal-E-Ajam film. It's doing well on television and cinema screen. There is no scarcity of TV serials and cinemas in Odia based on historical themes. Is it so that it doesn't work in the case of theatre?

-' But ,in Bali Yatra ground, in a competition, to test...? Dhira babu said with apprehension.

-' Sir, you be assured. The audience of Odisha will accept it. Lord Jagannath isn't only the God of Odisha state; he is the soul of Odia community. The audience of Odisha will watch the play with reverence. The most important thing is the necessity of an actor who will give life to the play. We also need the director and playwright. There is no need to decorate the stage for the play, no need for the second stage or the stage technician. The audience will watch it even if the play is done on an open stage with the Petromax light.' Benu babu interfered in between and said-' Binu babu is an eminent artist of Odisha's theatrical world. People are crazy about his acting.

In his name, a company from Cuttack is earning money in lakhs by selling the audio cassettes of ' Kancha Maunsa'. As he is saying-I feel that ' Neela Saila' play will be appreciated. Please, don't say 'No'. Other than you no one can properly handle the script. I have brought them here with so much hope and expectation. Madam has also come'

-' Benu why do you trust me so much? I am a mere human being and I have left all those twenty five years back. Will I be able to do it?

-' Every creative man has the doubt in his mind. 'While writing 'Waste Land' T.S Eliot had struck off many times what he wrote. It is obvious to have such apprehensions while giving shape to the imagination. Surendra babu also spent his time in expectation, hope, and aspiration before writing 'Neela Saila'. Sir, you can do it. Please! Don't say 'No'. You should have the will for it.

-' Binod ,you are wrong. This isn't a matter of my will. It is the will of the Almighty. You may not be knowing that if he wouldn't have been defeated by few votes then it wouldn't have been possible to write 'Neela Saila' and 'Neela Bijaya'. When Surendra babu was alive it has been tried many times to recreate ' Neela Saila' into a play but it wasn't possible. It was a golden era in the history of the theatrical companies in Odisha as plays like 'Bargi Utakla',' Haldi Ghat', 'Mogul Patan' were staged. At present, I am not interested in interfering in what is done nor dare to do so. I feel as if I have entered a deep forest. I don't know if I will be able to return or not as it is I am not well.'

-' Surendra babu had the same experience while writing 'Neela Saila' like entering a dungeon. Please, don't say 'No.' Binod requested him.

-' Ok ,according to your request I will begin writing 'Neela Saila'. Rest is the wish of Almighty. If I can complete writing the play then I will think that it was the wish of the

Almighty and if I couldn't then I wouldn't worry about it. Surendra babu has also mentioned that Art is incomplete like Life.'

-'In the prelude of 'Neela Saila' novel.' Binod answered.

-' I think you have read many novels of Surendra Mohanty. He was a classic creator.' Dhira babu laughed and said.

-' Binod is a student of English Literature. He has completed his MA in English.' Bini madam said.

Binod interrupted and said-' Is it necessary to mention it? I am what I am. Is this identity isn't enough for me?'

Dhira babu smiled and said-' This identity isn't only a pride for you but also for the world of theatre.'

-' Not true. It's not correct that my MA degree will only bring pride to me and not the world of theater. No one can bring pride to other. Those are only for the sake of saying. It's the matter of earning a livelihood.'

-' Is also staging of 'Neela Saila'? Dhira babu said mockingly. Binod replied-' Sir, Is life only bound to earning a livelohood? It also has insistence and obligation. I feel that there is a continuous tug of war between life and livelihood. Who will be the winner, no one knows.'

-' It's so. Surendra babu was a politician, author, and journalist- Three in one. To judge out of these three which one was his livelihood and which one was his life is difficult. He tried to perceive livelihood in life and has blended life and livelihood.'

-' I think you have also read the novels of Surendra Mohanty.' Binod said.

-' Binod, is it possible to realize what is life if you don't read the novels of Surendra Mohanty?'

Binod took a deep breath and said-'Life is a mystery. The more you try to understand it, the more mysterious it becomes. I have read the books of many classical writers. I am trying to understand what is life according to them. But now I think that it was childish. Life is an unknown mystery, a difficult problem to solve or the darkness of night- The shady river plateau in darkness or like the noiseless stream- Which flows till eternity. '

-' Binod, if a human can explore the mystery of life then what will be left to live? Life is a mystery that's why humans strive to live.'

Hema's mother's call interrupted the conversation. She said-'Will they have food or sit and listen to your stories?'

When Binod heard about this he said-'Sir, we have to leave as soon as possible. Puri is far and it will take four to five hours to reach. We have the show at night.'

In between Benu Ustad went inside the house without their knowledge. He came and said- 'Today is your off day. It doesn't matter if we are a little late. Will you not eat what sister- in- law has cooked for us? She cooks very well it is more wonderful than brother's play. She has prepared prawn with coconut milk and along with that a mixed curry with greens, yam , pumpkin, and fish.'

Bini madam asked-' Sir, how many days will you take to write the play? She paused for a while and said-' We have very little time in hand and that's the reason I asked.'

Dhira babu said-'It depends on when I start writing. If I begin, then it won't take much time. Everything that is written has its life. It's like a blooming lotus which is eager to bloom.'

Dhira babu paused and again said- 'If the Almighty wants then it will take less than one month time. ' Karubaki' play was staged just in a week isn't it Benu?'

Benu Ustad said-' Yes'.

-' Wouldn't you meet our artist at least once before you begin writing? If you say then I will send the vehicle'. Bini madam said.

-' Is this the trend at present?' Dhira babu asked in surprise.

-'Jitu Mohanty and Shankar Bhola do that.'

- ' Why should I meet the artist? My job is to write the play. The director has to work with the artists. Please don't worry. Let me finish writing the play.'

Hema's mother again reminded-' Food is getting cold.'

Binod suddenly said-'Jai Jagannath !.' Benu Ustad folded both his hands in praise of Lord Jagannath.

Bini madam smiled with contentment. All of them were happy.

18

Binod was visualizing a scene of a remote village. Among the sands and thorny bushes, few palm trees standing straight like the guards. At the back were a stretch of Casuarina trees and Kewda plants. In the midst of that was an isolated south-facing small thatched house on the porch of which was sitting Saradei and looking at the vast water of Chilika Lake with her empty eyes.

Saradei! Saradei!

While reading the novel 'Nila Saila', at many times Binod has tried to draw the empty eyes and the sad face Saradei in his imagination. He has tried to analyze how disconsolate and still were those eyes like the water of Chilika Lake.

It is depicted exquisitely in the book 'Neela Saila' which is beyond imagination.

Was that the reason why in the past, the scenes from 'Neela Saila' weren't possible?

If 'Nila Saila' is staged by Dasabhuja then who will do the role of Saradei? Whose eyes can depict the disconsolate, gloomy, and profound look which touches the heart?

It would have been different if Saudamini would have been there.

Now, who will do? Lata?

Binod remembered that for the first time when

he saw Lata he remembered about someone else. But who is she? Binod couldn't recall though he tried.

Saradei's eyes are exactly like Lata's eyes. Brimming..

Lata can only act as Saradei .

But who knows Kamal Mishra will give the role to whom? He will give the direction in 'Neela Saila' play.

Yesterday when Dhira babu promised him that he will write the play, he was a bit relaxed. In that excitement, though it was an off night for him he didn't get sleep. He was lying down outside the tent in the folding cot and was imagining the planning for the next play. When he woke up from sleep he again started planning about the play.

-'Bina bhai'.

Bitcha was calling him. Binod could recognize his voice though he didn't open his eyes. He addresses him as Bina bhai with a lot of love whereas others address him as 'Sir' or 'Bina babu'. He was standing with a water jug and a cup of tea.

On other days, after the play is over he removes the makeup and lays down in the folding cot to take rest. He feels relaxed and tireless. He doesn't like to sleep like others for the whole day. Bitcha wakes him up and gives him water and tea before leaving for the publicity campaign. Bitcha washes his clothes though he doesn't want him to. He arranges his bed and after returning from the publicity campaign he gives him Jaljira and sometimes sits along with him and talks.

Bitcha sometimes ask-' Will you be always there in this theatrical company?'

Binod could understand why he asks this. Still, he pretends as if he didn't understand and says -'Where will I go?'

Bitcha doesn't like his answer and says-'Of course for illiterate people like us there is no other way. Why will you be here as you are literate?'

-'What's wrong in that? Binod asks.

-' If I would have the capability to make you understand what's right and wrong then why I would have been here?'

- 'Don't you like theater?'

-' Why not? But ,where ever people like Malini Baral and Muna Panda are there who will like it? They only know how to criticize and defame others. There was a reflection of abhorrence on his face.

Binod tried to make him understand and said-' Bitcha, isn't people like Malini and Muna Panda everywhere?'

Bitcha didn't contradict and kept quiet. But Binod could understand that Bitcha didn't like what he said.

-' Bitcha, why didn't you study? You can compose so well. You would have become a poet if you would have studied.'

-' It's not difficult to compose. Do you think it's difficult to compose?'

-' Then?'

-' As soon as I hold the microphone, I compose. When there is a crowd around the publicity jeep, the composition comes automatically.'

Bitcha looked like a philosopher at that time. Deep, thoughtful, and detached. He couldn't understand what he said.

Can you write a poem if you try? Professor Samsuddin said. Poetry is the spontaneous overflow of powerful feelings: it takes its origin from emotion recollected in tranquility. If you forcefully write poetry it's equivalent to rape.

As Binod didn't open his eyes, Bitcha kept the water jug and the teacup and left. What will he do if he wakes up so early? It is one of his weaknessess that if he gets involved in something then he sticks to it and isn't able to concentrate on anything else.

Who knows how long Dhira babu will take to write

the play? The decision was taken just two days back. Just before two days, there was nothing in his mind regarding the play 'Neela Saila '. Now he feels as if it is the ultimate decision and he can't be peaceful until the play 'Neela Saila' is staged.

-' Binod babu, Are you still sleeping ?' Kamal Mishra called him. Bitcha has left the water jug and the teacup on the chair so there was no place for Kamal Mishra to sit.

Binod called-'Nanda?'

Kamal Mishra understood his intention and he dragged a chair and sat.

Nanda came and Binod said-' Get two cups of tea.'

Kamal Mishra said- 'Dhira babu is willing to write the play. I heard it from Benu Ustad.'

Binod yawned and said-' Yes,he is willing to.'

After Binod washed his face and came, Kamal Mishra said-' It's good. Lord Jagannath always fulfills everybody's desire. I had a desire to do a historical play but was unable to gather courage. As Lord Jagannath wished for it so the idea came to your mind and that too in Puri's Bada Danda. The wish will be fulfilled. The stage performance of 'Neela Saila' will not only be yours but also my dream project.'

-'But where is the time? We have less than one month.'

-'Who is the personification of supreme joy by his grace even the dumb can become eloquent in speech and lame can cross over the mountains. Once the character and situation for the play are finalized only a fortnight is enough. You don't worry.'

-' Tanu, what are you doing at home at this time? When will you take bath so that we can go to the temple? I am hungry. Malini was screaming at Tanu while going to take bath.

Kamal Mishra stopped the discussion listening to her scream. Malini came and asked-'Sir, you didn't take bath till now? When will you go to the temple? People from distant places come to offer their prayer in the temple during Kartik month. You are in Puri still you didn't take your bath? Malini was wearing a cheap cotton saree which she bought from a hawker. It wasn't cleaned properly so was looking dirty. Through the saree, Malini's belly and chest were looking ugly like the scales of a serpent. She was wearing that small width saree till her knees. Her legs were looking like the legs of the crane. Alltogether she was looking like a distorted image.

Binod was irritated and didn't look at her.

Binod or Kamal Mishra didn't give a reply to her so Malini Baral twisted her waist and again screamed- 'Tanu? Are you still sleeping? Have you become deaf?' Kamal Mishra saw her leaving, took the water jug and gave it to Binod and sang- 'I twisted my waist and the whole world vibrated…' He asked did you hear the song when it's played by Bitcha in the loudspeaker?'

Binod was astonished listening to such an absurd question from Kamal Mishra. Binod looked at his face. Kamal Mishra smiled and said-'Whoever has written the song has kept Malin Barala's twist and walk in mind.'

Binod laughed loudly and said-' Yes, a woman like her think that by looking at their twist and walk all the men in this world will be attracted.'

Binod paused for a while and asked-' Which role will you give to Malini in 'Neela Saila'? Lalita Mahadae or Rajia Begum?

-' Which role would you like me to give her? As revengeful Lalita Mahadae or the lovable Rajia Begum?'

-' Why did we go to Dhira babu to write the play? You can frame excellent dialogues.' Binod laughed and said.

Kamal Mishra said-' But you didn't tell me about your likes and dislikes.'

-' What is there about my likes and dislikes? You are the director. You will do the selection.'

- What is there about likes and dislikes? If not Lalita Mahadae then never Rajia Begum...' Kamal Mishra paused and looked at Binod.

-' Then is it Sardae?' Binod asked anxiously. Kamal Mishra said-' Malini will act as the widow Kantani .'

In front of Binod's eyes danced the image of a woman in an isolated forest who has thrown all her jewelry and clothes, is bare and lustful.

Binod laughed aloud and said-' Then Muna Panda will be assigned the role of Kantha Mekap. Otherwise who will wrap his hand around Malini's waist and touch her chest and say- 'The Ratha(Chariot) which has blue silk cloth wrapped around is Taladhwaja Ratha(Chariot of Lord Jagannath). It has got fourteen wheels.'

Kamal Mishra became serious and said –' Which other role can he do other than Kantha Mekap?'Taki Khan? He again said-' He is also misfit for the role of Kantha Mekap.'

Binod thought that he is right! Muna Panda doesn't have the look of Taki Khan. Who will do the Taki Khan role? Whom will Kamal Mishra chose for that role?'

Nanda brought the tea and kept it. While drinking tea Kamal Mishra was deeply engrossed in his thoughts.

'Neela Saila ' is deep and calm like Chilika Lake. It has ducks and swans as well as whales. Why was he thinking about the role of Saradei? Kamal Mishra has a good knowledge about the direction that's why he is known as a good director. But he has to give the role of Kantani and Kantha Mekap to someone. A skilled playwright like Dhira babu will give importance to these small characters in the play. The beauty of 'Neela Saila' lies in these small characters.' 'Neela Saila' isn't history anymore. It's a skeleton of the history covered with the colors of the present.

Whom will Kamal Mishra give the role of Taki Khan?

He couldn't control his curiosity and asked-' Then, whom will give the role of Taki Khan?'

-' Let the time come. Kamal Mishra answered. He smiled mysteriously and left.

That means he has already finalized the roles. An experienced director like him must have decided to give the role of Saradae to Lata. Is it Saradei or Rajia Begum?

He was again confused. Who is fit for which role?

He doesn't have an insight. Kamal Mishra has that so he is the director. Binod is like a horse who will run according to his instructions.

Professor Samsuddin was correct –'Insight, Binod, to have insight is the greatest thing.'

19

Today is the last day of Puri camp. Tomorrow he will leave Puri.

Again after one year.

This world will change. Many things will happen in life. He will again come to Puri after a year with many new experiences. He has to wait for another year.

What brings more happiness? Is it to get or to wait?

What does he get from the Puri camp? The time passed so soon in Puri. How the good time slips out of the hands is never realized.

Sometimes he thinks to sit and calculate how much sadness and happiness he got in life. When was sadness there in life and when was happiness.

Is the time that he spent with Professor Samsuddin on the university campus was the happiest time?

No, at that time he was occupied with semester examination. There was criticism, competition, envy, and anxiety.

Then ? Are those the days after his marriage with Kalyani?

Will that be called as happiness or attachment? Maybe it was an attraction towards a woman and her body. Otherwise, how did he tolerate Kalyani for such a long time?

On the day of the marriage before leaving her father's house Kalyani cried and complained to her father –' To get rid of my responsibility you did this to me after knowing everything?'

How could you?

Many things were untold in that complaint.

Binod doesn't have a job. They don't have a double storied building like her father, they don't have an oil mill, petrol pump, or they aren't contractors. They don't have anything. Binod is unfit for her.

Her father consoled her at that time and said–' Why are you worried? I am there.'

At that time Binod thought that those are the common things that happen when the girl leaves her maternal house after marriage. She complains about her husband's looks, education, and status.

His village Nakuli Sahu's daughter also cried in a similar way while leaving her maternal house after marriage.

Kalyani is complaining in a similar way.

Binod has never supported Kalyani. It was her father who always supported her. She always boasted about her father's wealth. While watching the old movies by looking at Dilip Kumar or Guru Dutt in the silver screen she remembered her father's childhood face. She compared them with her father. She says that the people in the village have taken a loan from her father as he is rich.

He took a lot of time to free himself from the attraction that he had for Kalyani.

A woman is like a puzzle.

Suna bhauja is like the flowers of Bitter gourd. It gets destroyed if you want to pluck it.

-'Bina?'

Binod turned back. Saudamini was standing at a distance.

Binod was surprised to see Saudamini in Bada Danda. He asked-' Mini, How are you?'

-' We have a camp near Jatani. Today is my off night. I thought of visiting Puri. I think your camp is here.'

-'Yes,it will be over tonight.'

- 'How are you? Who are the new artists those who joined this year?'

-' There is a new girl whose name is Lata.'

-' How is her performance?'

-' A new play hasn't begun so she didn't get any role.'

-' Is Bholi babu paying her salary without work? It seems Golden age (Satya Yuga) has come back.' Saudamini said and laughed.

Binod knows that Bholi babu is annoyed with Saudamini. It was Bholi babu who opposed a lot to increase her salary. It's only for him, Saudamini left Dasabhuja.

Binod laughed.

-' How are the other people?'

-' All are well. The camp is nearby. Come and visit the camp.'

-' What will I do in the camp? Let's go to the seashore.'

-' Won't you go back today?'

-'No, I will go back tomorrow.'

-' Then stay in the camp overnight. You can meet everyone.'

-' I am fade up with this camp life. I have thought to spend the night sitting on the seashore.'

-' Don't you know that there is no through fare in the seashore after 10 pm?'

-' Do you think that I would have spent the whole night on the seashore?'

-' Where will you stay?'

-' I am staying in the hotel 'Sweet Home'. I have kept my

luggage there. Do you think that I have come to visit Puri without any luggage? Saudamini laughed and said.

Saudamini looks very beautiful with a smile. It is one of the characteristics of her face. She doesn't look tensed even in the worst situation.

But, Kalyani?

She feels as if she is carrying the burden of the whole world. A smile on her face is very rare like the electricity service of the state. Binod has never seen her laughing happily or singing a song.

Why is he remembering her today?

After sitting on a rickshaw to go to the seashore Binod remembered about drinking tea. He met Saudamini after so many days but he didn't ask her for a cup of tea for courtesy's sake. What will Saudamini think?

Why are the rickshaws in Puri so narrow? They are a little bit tilted. He told the rickshaw puller to open the hood.

-' Has Malini changed her attitude?'

It was a useless question. Saudamini left the party just a month back. What changes does she expect from Malini'? Binod said in an annoying voice-' Don't ask me about the party and tell me something about you.'

Saudamini's laugh faded. She looked thoughtful and said-' News ! What news? I am trying to cope up.'

Binod was disappointed. He expected that Saudamini will say-' I don't like the new party at all. The hero of the party is not worth to act with.'

Saudamini didn't say anything like that. She sat quietly in the rickshaw and looked at the buildings, the moss- covered walls, small temples, prasad shops, and the Bengali tourists.

What else will Binod ask? Will he say about the play 'Neela Saila'? Will he say that he and Bini madam is very much eager about the play? Will Saudamini be happy to listen about Bini madam?'

If Bini madam wanted she could have increased her salary easily. But was the hike in the salary was the main issue?

No. Binod knew that Saudamini couldn't accept the gap between the owner and the artist like others. Stubbornness is her characteristic. After completing her BA she joined the theatrical company. She belongs to a well to do family and to joining the theatrical company wasn't necessary for her.

She is a good actress but her stubbornness wasn't liked by Bini madam. No one tries to understand the thin line between being stubborn and obstinate. That is the greatest tragedy in the life of a smiling woman. Maybe because of that she didn't get married and isn't able to stick to any party for more than two years.

Was Kalyani so stubborn? No, she was inflexible. She couldn't adjust to the situation. She thought that adjusting is against her ethics. She thought that to adjust is to accept defeat. She wasn't ready to accept that life is a compromise with the universe. She never agreed to it. Her father who had an oil mill, petrol pump, and was a contracted pampered her a lot and brought her up in the artificial surrounding of ego and vanity .This didn't give her an opportunity to understand the reality of life. She thought only about aristocracy which isn't real life. Oh! Kalyani- she is standing on a building which is made of sand. The day the building will collapse, it will be difficult for her to understand the fact.

After the rickshaw stopped in front of the hotel 'Sweet Home' Saudamini opened her purse and gave the money and said-' Come to my room.' I will get freshen up and change my saree. I am not feeling good wearing the same saree throughout the day. I will feel good if I freshen up.

-' Did you go to the temple?' Binod asked.

-' No, I will go tomorrow morning. My train is at 5pm . What will I do sitting alone here? I think you will also leave tomorrow. When will you leave?'

-' You are asking me like an outsider. Is there any stability in the life of a theatre artist?'

Saudamini took a deep breath. Very deep, so deep that he could hear the sound of her breath.

Saudamini has changed a lot in these six months. The smile in her face looks a little sad. It seems she is a little startled.

Suna bhauja has also changed a lot.

He must have also changed. Who knows how much he has changed? Will Alka Mishra and Mama Choudhary recognize him today? Will he be able to recognize them?

In the department, all of them made fun of Mama Mishra. She had the habit of being dissatisfied with everything. Radhe Shyam to tease her imitated her and said-' You are always dissatisfied with everything. You will become the mother of seven children and will be busy wiping their running nose and washing your hand every time.'

Mama Mishra use to say-' Haa! As if I don't have anything else to do.'

Sometimes in his free time, Binod tries to draw a picture in his imagination- A child with a running nose in the arms of Mama Mishra and another child standing next to her holding her hand. The saree has become wet with the saliva dripping from the child's mouth in her arms. The child who is standing is wiping his nose in his mother's saree. She is busy in managing the children and is worked up.

If Kalyani would have got two children like them? She would have committed suicide.

Though Suna bhauja always said she doesn't want a child in front of others but in reality she was restless for a child.

This world is strange and more strange is the nature of a woman.

Saudamini washed her face and came out from the

bathroom. Her fresh look was looking like a bouquet of Rajanigandha. She has a good look. Saudamini is beautiful. There is a thrill in acting with her. When she was there, she played the role of an actress opposite him. Acting with her was comfortable. It wasn't uncomfortable like acting with Malini's with a fat body and bad breathe.

-' Shall I order for snacks? We can have it and leave.'

Binod said-'No. Let's go to the seashore. I will make you taste delicious snacks.'

-' What will you get in the seashore other than peanuts and chickpeas?'

-' You come along with me. Have your snacks and then say.'

Saudamini applied a thin layer of powder on her face and was trying to blend with the skin with the saree palla. She sprayed a mild perfume and came back from the front of the mirror.

She sat on the bed and said-' Did you increase the limit of smoking?'

Which perfume does Saudamini use? Though it has a soothing fragrance, a little erotic.

-'No I haven't. Binod replied as if he was distracted.'

-' Your lips are looking darker than before.'

-' I was roaming around in the sun. Maybe because of that.'

-'I came to know today that lips become dark in the sun.' Saudamini mocked at him.

Saudamini has noticed correctly. He is smoking frequently now. When she was there, sometimes she warned him within her limits. She can't say anything more than that as she knew her limits. The person who had the right to say never said to him about it rather encouraged him to smoke and said-'Those who don't smoke are androgynous as if they don't have the masculine temperament.' The days he spent with Kalyani, he smoked and it has become a habit and he can't get rid of it.

I think the AC isn't working properly or Saudamini has set it in low speed. She is perfect in everything. Let it be her clothes, her behavior, and the way she smiles and talks. Binod is just the opposite. He can't sleep if the table fan isn't at high speed therefore there is a table fan next to his folding cot. It doesn't matter if it's required or not irrespective of the weather condition. Others get annoyed because of this. But what can Binod do? There are many habits of which a person can't get rid of. To turn the fan in full speed, to smoke are his two habits.. What else, he couldn't remember.

Let it happen. Are there any new possibilities in life? He will leave Puri tomorrow so he is going around without a certain aim as if he will carry along with him a memory which will last till next year. He has a headache and wants to sleep for some time. But where? Is it on the lap of the ever smiling and perfectionist woman?

No, it's not possible in this life. Sometimes when he felt like sleeping in Kalyani's lap she use to get angry and say-' Did you see! How you have spoiled my saree? You don't have the facility of dry cleaner here. This saree my father bought from Bombay.

Her father purchases everything from Delhi, Bombay, Calcutta, or Hyderabad. I think he doesn't like to purchase things from Cuttack and Bhubaneswar.

-' Go and freshen up. You will feel fresh. You look pale going around in the hot sun.' Saudamini gave him the towel and said. While washing the face in the washbasin the sweet fragrance deluded Binod.

What is this fragrance? Is it the fragrance of Saudamini's body or the perfume that she uses? Why is he attracted to it?

-' Mini ,get ready soon. If the Aloo dum gets over in the

snacks stall then the fun is over.' Binod said from the bathroom while combing his hair.

Saudamini didn't like the pakoda and Aloo dum of Bihari's food stall. She was eating it very slowly looking at the ocean as if she isn't interested to eat.

-'Didn't you like it?' Asked Binod.

Saudamini didn't reply and turned towards him and asked-' Do you wait eagerly for Puri camp for a yearlong for this pakoda and Aloo dum?

Does Saudamini remember so many things? Binod was surprised. He became a little sentimental.

-' Do you eat so much spicy food? Can you see how much artificial color is added to it? Wouldn't you suffer from acidity?'

Does she remember that I suffer from acidity? To ignore the topic he said' Will it become less if I don't eat?'

Saudamini threw the plate into the paper box which was kept as a dustbin and washed her mouth.

Binod said-' It would have been better if we would have been to a restaurant. You didn't eat anything here.'

Saudamini walked towards a little isolated place on the seashore and said-' I don't like the seashore now. There is no place in the seashore that is isolated and peaceful rather than this Chandrabhaga is better. Last month there was a camp in Chandrabhaga. I sat on the seashore till 9pm.'

-' Alone? Were you not scared?'

-' No. In a little distance was the camp. There was a through fare and the shops weren't closed so early.'

She paused for a while and thought about something and said-' Is it good to be scared in this lonely life?' Isn't there fear everywhere? Isn't it in the camp or at home?

She was looking at the sea fixedly. The darkness of the night has slowly become more intense from that indefinite threshold and the waves were touching the seashore. How beautiful will be the sea beyond this from which originates these waves!

Saudamini asked-' What are you thinking?'

-' Nothing.'

-' Do you know what do I think sometimes?'

Binod looked at her face and said-' What?'

-' Why do these waves originate which makes the sea excited? Can you see with how much emulation they are progressing towards the shore? After a few minutes, they will become quiet.'

-' As it is crushed on the shore it sings yoddles.' Binod pointed at a wave touching the shore and said.

-Isn't life similar?'

-Maybe or may not be. Am I a philosopher? I am a mere theatre artist who is roaming like a vagabond to earn living. How can answer to this question?'

-' Not only you. Maybe no one knows an answer to this question. Life is like Pottasium cyanide, the most dangerous poison in the world. To taste it you get the time but not to speak about its taste. To understand the mystery of life is death.'

-Binod said-' Why is life like Potassium cyanide? Life is like the red Aloo dum of Bihari's shop. It is spicy as well as colorful. Will you be scared of acidity if you want to eat it?'

Saudamini smiled and said-.' Yes, who can defeat you in a debate?'

Her smile was lovely. It was like a distant wave in the sea. Before he could get engrossed in the smile his cell phone rang.

-' Bloody hopeless.' Binod looked at the number displayed and said. He said-'Let's go. Today the play will begin at 11pm.'

Saudamini took a deep breath and said-' You may go. The hotel is nearby. I will go after some time. What will I do alone in the room? Binod pulled her right hand and said-'

How can it be? It's already late. I will leave you in the hotel and go.'

Saudamini followed him silently. After sometime Binod asked-' Why are you so silent?'

Binod turned back as he didn't get a response from Saudamini. Saudamini's eyes were brimming with tears. It looked like a drop of pearl in the sodium light.

Binod said-' Is it right to be so sentimental?

Saudamini said-.' Do you know how do I feel like sometimes…?'

Saudamini's desire was blown away by the wind on the seashore.

Binod wasn't able to know about her desire.

20

-' Dhira Mohanty is in a critical condition. Did you hear that? Muna Panda said in a defeating tone. Binod turned back irritated and said-'Who said?'

Muna Panda replied confidently-'Madam spoke to Bholi babu as your phone was switched off.'

There was excitement in his tone. After informing Binod about the bad news he noticed his reaction and in that his excitement vanished. He sat quietly and smoked waiting for the end of the episode.

In Dasabhuja , out of courtesy, no one smokes in front of Kamal Mishra or Binod but Muna Panda to disgrace him smoked in front of him.

He has never competed with Binod for any role in Dasabhuja. Not even for the role of Nija Khan in the play' Kancha Mausa'. But because of his performance in two or three plays, he thinks that his popularity is also not less than Kamal Mishra or Binod. He has also played a big role in the success of Dasabhuja. Dasabhuja can't thrive without him.

He bribed Jitu Mohanty with liquor bottles and had made arrangements to get a good role in the new play. In the world of Odisha's theatre Murari Panda and Narendra Das are his role models as the villain. Muna Panda purchases their cassettes from the market and listens to those. He always plans to combine their style and different other styles, tries to follow it to create a sensation. He thinks that by watching his acting the audience will be thrilled.

After Jitu Mohanty's proposed play was rejected he was disheartened but still, he had a little hope for Shankar Bhola's play' Murder- Rape- Gang rape' After madam denied Shankar Bhola's proposal and sent him back Muna Panda was annoyed. He wasn't able to tolerate the proposal of staging the play 'Neela Saila' which was appreciated by madam, Binod, and Kamal Mishra. He was very much annoyed with Binod. He said Malini mockingly-'You will do the role of the queen. Why will you think about us?

To make him happy Malini said-'Who will give me the role of the queen? The person who will become the queen is unknown. It seems I wouldn't be able to deliver the dialogues of the queen. Why are you unnecessary teasing and irritating me?

How did they come to know about his meeting with Saudamini? Since that day there was a gossip that Saudamini will again return to Dasabhuja.

To pacify Muna Panda said to Malini -'There are three heroines in that play. Queen is only for the name's sake. The real fun is in the other two roles. Won't you get one of those? Will they give that role to Tanu or Babita in your presence?'

-' Among those roles, there is a role of a widow. She always blows her nose. Will I accept if they give me that role? What will happen to my image? Will I do the role of a widow from now? As if I don't have anything else to do.

She paused for a while, thought about something, and said-' The other role isn't of a queen but the role of a Muslim kept. Who will speak like a Muslim lady? Not possible.

-'Who told you?'

-'Who else will say?' The old monkey who is dancing after listening that the play will be staged told me about it.

- Yes, Hind and English. Binod makes a mockery of it. Now a days unworthy playwrights like Jitu Mohanty and Shankar Bhola are using one or two words or a sentence in a dialogue in English or Hindi in between the play. Those dialogues are the way a retired clerk Patra babu speaks English to impress others. Malini Baral and Muna Panda write those dialogues in Odia, rote them, practice them many times and present it in a loud voice on the stage. The dialogues that they deliver are very harsh to the ears.

After completing the Spoken English Diploma course many Post Graduates are working in the schools for a meager salary of eight hundred to thousand rupees per month and are teaching children the alphabets. They think people will be impressed listening to English spoken by Malini Baral and Muna Panda. All are bloody rubbish ideas.

Who gave them such a weird idea about 'Neela Saila? Is it Benu Ustad?

That's why after knowing about the health condition of Dhira babu, Muna Panda is so happy. But what's the real matter? Where can he find Bholi babu now? He heard in the green room that the collection amount is good today. Bholi babu must be sleeping somewhere with the cash box under his head. The phone is there in the trouser pocket. If he will call madam he will come to know the exact thing.

-'Sir?' Tanushree called.

There was an announcement for the interval and the lights on the stage were switched off. The moment he climbs the second stage the screen will be removed. He climbed the second stage quickly.

It wasn't a matter of surprise for Dhira babu to fall sick as he wasn't in a good health. He is old . Did he get asthma? It's a terrible disease.

Mina is an idiot. Even though he was told not to focus

on the spotlight still he does that. What's so great about this situation?

In the main stage, Muna Panda is pulling and pushing Babita. What is his dialogue?

Jitu Mohanty is a useless fellow. He isn't able to maintain a proper sequence in the dialogue.

-'Sir?'

-' Binod babu?'

Tanushree and Kamal Mishra were calling him desperately.

Binod has to deliver the dialogue and run towards the main stage but he was unable to recall his dialogue.

Kamal Mishra again called-' Binod babu?'

Binod ran towards the main stage like a storm.

The audience gallery reverberated with claps. He slapped Muna Panda very hard. Muna Panda fell on the ground like a chopped tree. Binod lifted him with his hand and threw him outside like the garbage.

Nija Khan-Jindabad! Binod Das-Jindabad!Dasabhuja-Jindabad!

There were nonstop clapping and praise.

That was the end of the scene. Lights were switched off.

Before he could understand the situation, Kamal Mishra shook his hand and said-Well done! Binod babu, Well-done!

He came back to the green room, had a glass of water, and lighted the cigarette. Kamal Mishra said-' The scene should have been like this. Jitu Mohanty has unnecessarily introduced the dialogue there and has spoiled the scene.

Binod didn't pay attention to what he said and asked-' Do you know that Dhira babu isn't well?'

-' Yes. He has been admitted to a nursing home in Cuttack. Kamal Mishra is a strange man. After knowing about the bad news about Dhira babu he isn't perturbed rather he is congratulating him for a mere scene and is happy.

- 'Bina bhai it was a terrific show.' Bitcha got up from the music circle, came near him, and said happily.

-'You are an idiot.'

Bitcha smiled and said-' Is that a new thing?' He returned to the music circle.

He could still hear the claps of the audience from the audience gallery.

How did it happen?

Binod suddenly remembered a scene from 'Kancha Mausa'. This scene has made him a star overnight in the world of theatre. He still can't recollect what happened on that day like today.

Now when he tries to recollect he remembers the desperate call of Tanushree and Kamal Mishra who were behind the screen and after that Kamal Mishra shaking his hand and saying- 'Well done Binod, Well done! '

Whatever happened in between was without his knowledge. He couldn't understand his achievement.

Bholi babu woke up from his sleep and said-' The audience has requested to stage the play again. If you agree, I will commit them.'

Binod said-' I am like an ox. If I wouldn't plow the field, I have to thresh the grains. Why are you asking me?'

-'It's not like that..'

'What does that mean? You are the manager. You will take that decision.' Bholi babu was happy to get such an answer and went back. Binod called him and asked-' Dhira babu is admitted in which hospital in Cuttack?'

-' I don't know which nursing home. Leave that topic. There is no gain if we depend on him.'

-' Why are you always calculating about loss and gain?' Binod told angrily.

Bholi babu wasn't happy and he left the place. Bitcha was coming towards them. Bholi babu saw him and burst with anger and said-' Why are getting up from your place during the show?' Tomorrow the play will be repeated. Declare it on the stage and say that it will be staged as the audience requested. It's not necessary to waste the fuel and go for publicity. You will go and repair all the microphones that aren't working.

After he left Bitcha said-'Rascal! Old monkey !' He doesn't let me sit peacefully even for a day.

Binod lit another cigarette and said-'The situation is very critical. What will we do now?'

Kamal Mishra said-'I am also thinking about it. Please don't worry. We will try to find out a way.'

Binod threw the cigarette down and crushed it. He walked towards the main stage.

The audience saw him on the runway and started clapping.

These people are strange.

21

Benu Ustad returned from Chana babu's house which was in a remote village. He was looking tired and exhausted. Once upon a time like Dhira babu, Chana babu was also very proficient in writing historical plays. When Benu Ustad came to know about Dhira babu's illness he left in the morning to meet Chana babu. Did he eat anything or not?

It is more painful to return with incomplete work.

How much does Bholi babu pay Benu Ustad? He was dressed in a dirty kurta which was mended in two places and was wearing an old used slipper. His lips were dry.

Binod called Nanda and ordered two cups of tea and two plates of snacks. Benu Ustad sat on the chair and lifted his left leg and said in a feeble voice-' Chana babu has expired three years back.' Before his death, he suffered a lot. Neither he had money with him to purchase medicine nor was anyone there to look after him. As he joined the theatrical company his brothers left him. His wife expired two years before. After leaving the theatre he was writing folklore. A person in the nearby village who sings folklore took care of him. He was the person who was present during his death and somehow managed to perform his last rituals. Where will he get the money from? What is his earning as a singer of folklore? Who is listening to folklore now a days? During our childhood , the folklore singer Niranjan Kar took booking amount in advance before six months.

Nanda brought tea and snacks.

Binod said-' You traveled such a long distance but it was in vain. If we would have known before..'

Benu Ustad interrupted him and said-' Why is it unnecessary?' Chana babu liked me as his brother. He suffered for two years but I didn't know that. He died three years back. If I wouldn't have been there today, I would have never known. Someday I will also die in a similar way without treatment and no one will come to know. All my friends are leaving me one by one. Let's see!'

Benu babu's words made the atmosphere gloomy. His breath was sounding deep and he was frustrated.

If 'Neela Saila' play is staged then which role will Kamal Mishra give him? There is only one character that is old in the play. Kunja Gadanayak of Brahmapur village other than that is there any other role of an old man in the play ' Neela Saila' ? Binod was puzzled.

Kamal Mishra came to know that Benu Ustad had returned. He came and asked inquisitively-'What happened?' Did Chana babu agree?

Benu Ustad couldn't give a reply to his question. He hesitated to give this bad news.

Binod said-'Chana babu had passed away before three years .' Binod sounded strange. Kamal Mishra was also surprised to hear the way he spoke. He sat silently with them.

They sat there for a long time. Bholi babu came there in search of Kamal Mishra and said-' Are you not supposed to go to Haripur today?'

Kamal Mishra said-' Yes, but I completely forgot about it.'

-' God knows! Why are you people thinking so much about 'Neela Saila'? You forget to do other things. Whom will I say? An old and experienced person like Benu Ustad is also unable to understand it. If not Jitu Mohanty or Shankar Bhola, is there any scarcity of playwrights? Can't we approach Kulamani babu? Last year his play got the first place in Dhauli competition.'

-' Who is Kulamani babu?' Binod asked.

-' It's strange! Have you not heard the name of Kulamani babu?'

-' Is his name mentioned in the G K book?' Kamal Mishra said irritatingly.

-' Last year his play got the first place in Dhauli competition. His name was published in the newspaper. Didn't you read?'

-' Bholi babu, Do you ever read the newspaper?' Benu Ustad said jokingly.

Bholi babu looked at him sternly and said-'If I don't read the newspaper then how come I give advertisements in the newspaper?'

-' Why are you talking rubbish? If Binod babu and Mishra Sir agree then I will speak to Kulamani babu about the play.'

To stop the discussion Kamal Mishra said-' We will discuss it later.'

-' Ok. As you wish! Does my word have any value? What about going to Haripur?'

-'It's already evening. We will think about it later on.'

Bholi babu left that place hastily.

Binod looked worried and asked-' Who is this Kulamani babu?' Shall we speak to him to write 'Neela Saila?'

-'Don't you know about the competency of the

playwrights those who approach the party manager with the paper cutting? In that way, Srikant is very enthusiastic about writing 'Neela Saila'. What is the necessity to go so far?'

-' Did Srikant say that he will write 'Neela Saila'?' Binod smiled and asked.

-' He won't dare to say me that. He was saying it to Malini or Muna Panda.'

Bitcha was returning from the publicity campaign with a polythene bag in his hand. He heard Kamal Mishra and said-' Is it about writing the play 'Neela Saila'? Why don't you ask Srikant Bina bhai?

Binod asked-' Did he tell you anything?'

-' Yes. He was requesting me to tell you. Yesterday I scolded him a lot.' He remembered about something. He paused and said-' Leave that!

. Today I got good prawns. I have told Dhadiya nana to prepare curry with coconut milk. Bina bhai won't eat paratha otherwise it would have been good.

Binod said-' It's ok. Tell Dhadiya nana to prepare parathas for everyone. Will my health get spoiled if I eat paratha for a day?'

Bitcha said-' If Malini comes to know then she won't spare. She will eat half of the fried prawns like a cat.

Binod said-' Go and call Dhadiya nana. I will tell him.'

Bitcha left to call Dhadiya nana.

Binod Ustad said-' Binod babu, Please don't worry so much. If Lord Jagannath wants then 'Neela Saila' play will be staged.'

Binod asked-' But how?'

Benu Ustad said-' I don't know how but my heart says that this play will be staged.'

Kamal Mishra said-' I have a solution.'

Binod was inquisitive and asked-' What?'

-' It will be good if you write this play.' Kamal Mishra said in a calm and soft voice.

-' I?'

-' Yes, you. I know you can. Please don't ask me how. I don't have an answer to those questions. My inner voice says- You can write.'

- ' Mishra sir, Lord Jagannath who is within you is making you speak in this way. God bless you! Bina babu , Please don't say 'No'. If there is any value in the blessings of this old man then I bless you! Write the play and get name and fame.

-' My best wishes! Binod. My best wishes are with you.' Madam came from behind.

All of them stood up seeing her at this time.

Madam said-' Why did you all stand up? She pulled a chair and sat down.

Bitcha came and said -'Dhaniya nana is saying that there are no coconuts in the mess. I will go and get two coconuts from the market.

He became silent when he saw madam.

-' Bitcha, why do you need coconut?' Madam smiled and asked.

Bitcha didn't reply. He stood there silently as if he has done a mistake.

Bina said-' While returning from the publicity campaign, he bought prawns. He was saying to cook prawn with coconut milk.'

-' Why are you hiding it from me? Do you think that I will eat more? But why will he go to the market to bring the coconuts? Where are the mess helpers?'

-' Bholi babu has told them not to do anyone's personal work.' Binod said.

-' What is this rubbish rule by Bholi babu? I have heard that they wash the clothes of Malini Baral and Muna Panda.

Madam called Bholi babu in a loud voice.

Bholi babu came and stood in front of madam. Madam asked-' Why did you say that the mess helpers won't do anyone's personal work?'

Bholi babu said-' If they start doing everyone's personal work then how will the mess be managed?'

-' They are washing the clothes of Malini and Muna Panda.'

-' They are senior artists. Will they do their work themselves?'

-' Who gave them the promotion to seniority? Is that you?'

Bholi babu didn't find words to give an explanation. He stood silently.

-' Do you know how difficult is it for a person to travel fifty miles in a jeep and to scream in front of the microphone for publicity? And after that to purchase two coconuts will he go to the market?

-' I would have never said 'No' if Mishra sir or Binod babu would have told me.'

-' Then what is the problem in the case of Bitcha?'

-' Is Bitcha an artist?' Bholi babu said in a feeble voice.

-' Bholi babu, Is it so that one who climbs on the stage becomes an artist? Are you running the theatrical company with this concept? Publicity is the best art of this age. In big cities, there are so many advertising agencies which are opened for publicity. Many good companies form a queue in front of these agencies for advertisement. Bitcha is an asset of Dasabhuja. Did you understand? Madam said firmly as if she was warning him. Bholi babu to make madam understand said-' Bitcha is a valuable asset for Dasabhuja." Don't I know this? But where are the people in the party to do the work of everyone?'

-' These are all unnecessary arguments. To know whose

work to be done and not done is your work. A good manager manages the work in such a way that there wouldn't be anything to make others understand. Everything goes on smoothly. Otherwise how such big industries and companies are running?

-' It's a different thing for them and for the theatrical company it's different. Here to do the work of Malini and Muna Panda we need five to ten people.

-' They are not different. They aren't special. They are paid for their talent.'

-' Do you have any doubt? Binod said with a smile to save Bholi babu from the insult.

-' Of course.' Madam laughed and replied. Then she looked at Bholi babu and said-' Tell Dhadiya nana that Benu babu will have dinner with us. There are two packets of Rasagolla in the car. Tell someone to get it. It's an auspicious day for Dasabhuja.'

-' Auspicious day? Kamal Mishra asked as he didn't understand .

-' Binod babu has agreed to write 'Neela Saila'. What can be better news than this?'

-' When did I agree? Binod said worriedly. No one could hear him among the applaud and glee.

22

There is no scarcity of dialogues and dramatic sequence in 'Neela Saila'. It's necessary to make it stage- friendly.

Kamal Mishra created this perception in his mind to boost his morale. Binod thought about it and analyzed that what he is saying is correct. 'Neela Saila' is well equipped with dialogues and dramatic sequences. He has to work on the presentation part and limit it to twenty to twenty five scenes.

But he never knew writing a play is so difficult and intricate. If people like Jitu Mohanty and Shankar Bhola can write and complete a play in a week or a fortnight then why can't he complete it?

But there is a major problem. It is easy to find faults and weaknesses of the dialogues and planning of a staged play and on the contrary, it's too difficult to write the dialogues of a new play.

In the beginning, he thought that it's difficult to capture all the details of 'Neela Saila' within twenty to twenty five scenes. Many episodes of 'Neela Saila' are written in a style that includes flash back or memory. If he arranges them in a sequence then it will be easy for him to write. But after that was done, Binod was again in a conflict- How to begin the play?

Will it begin from Saradei's mother- in- law's house in Malakuda village?

From the background will be heard the screaming and coaxing of her mother- in- law.

-' Water, water. give water . Ramachandra Deva who is thirsty and tired will enter. At the end of the scene, Ramachandra Deva will be imprisoned and sent to Barabati fort.

It won't be bad. Binod remembered the last part of Fakir Mohan Senapati's ' novel 'Rebati'.

Kamal Mishra liked the scene, and said' Wonderful!'

After that everything seemed to be easy till Lord Jagannath was taken to Gurubai Island in Chilika.

Now to connect each word is so difficult. Sometimes they are unfamiliar and sometimes difficult to comprehend. They play hide and seek with the thoughts and imagination. Is that the reason why a word is called 'Brahma?' How did Vyasa Deva compose the epic Mahabharata? From where did he get so many characters and so many stories? Were the words playing hide and seek with him?

Oh! There is no comparison between him and Vyasa Deva. It's a preposterous comparison. This isn't his primary composition. He has to search for the story and characters. It is so difficult to compose.

Do all the writers go through this? While composing to they go through the mental agony?

It's so difficult to compose. It's like a mystery.

Why was the creator stupefied and inexorable to give a shape to *Daru Brahma* floating during the doomsday? Is it because of that there was an incomplete eternity?

How can the essence of the play be realized?

'Neela Saila' is neither history nor a historical play; it's the essence of life that is limitless. How will he present it?

Who can say it?

Kamal Mishra or Benu Ustad? Both of them aren't there.

This is a solitary battle.

Hey! Jagannath! You are omnipotent, omniscient, omnipresent, and omnibenevolent.

Why did you ignite such a flame in me? Why did you show me this dream and broke my dream like an innocent child? I am left with regret and remorse.

What is the use of thinking all those now? There is no way to return.

Now I am left with piles of scribbled blocks and on that the words play hide and seek.

-' Bina bhai did you read the newspaper today?' Bitcha asked.

Binod looked at him innocently and asked-' Why? What happened?

-' Indradhanu theatrical company will stage Shankar Bhola's play ' Murder-Rape- Gang rape in Bali Yatra competition. They have published in an advertisement that it is a revolutionary play.' Bitcha said mockingly.

-' If you pay the money then anything can be published not only as a 'revolutionary play' but also as 'an advent of a new epoch'. What is there in that? Binod didn't pay any attention to what Bitcha said and was busy in his own thoughts. But why did Mini Apa (sister) left Indradhanu in between the season?'

-' Did Saudamini leave Indradhanu?'

-' Yes that's the news in 'Jatra Jagat'.

Binod took the magazine from Bitcha and started turning the pages absentmindedly. He has heard earlier that there are two or three magazines which publish the news about the theatrical companies like the film magazines. But he had never seen it before. There was a passport size photograph of Saudamini in the magazine and below that was mentioned' Saudamini left in between the innings.'

When he met her in Puri Mini was very sad. But she never told me that she will leave the party.

Why did she take such a sudden decision?

What will be she doing after leaving the party? Where is she now? Is she at home? Who is there in her house?

She said that she will feel lonely in the hotel room so want to sit near the seashore. What will be she doing sitting alone at home?

A theatre artist can never sit alone at home as it's very difficult for them to pass their time. They are used to the noisy party camp. That's why whenever Bishnu babu comes to the camp he stays there for four to five days despite Bholi babu's rebuke.

Binod called Saudamini.

Switch off! Amazing!

What has happened to Saudamini?

If there is no such serious problem then an artist never leaves in between the season. There is no news that Saudamini is joining some other party. The director of 'Indradhanu',Gora Rout is a rogue. He loses his mind once he is drunk. The owner of 'Indradhanu' is a special class contractor. He doesn't have time to think about the party. The manager is a crook. He can manipulate things very well. Binod told Saudamini not to join 'Indradhanu' but as Saudamini was very firm with her decision so he didn't say anything much. At that time Bholi babu was spreading the rumor that Saudamini is leaving the party as there was no hike in her salary.

Binod knows very well that it's not true. The reason for leaving Dasabhuja is the contradiction of thoughts that was between Saudamini and madam. At that time madam also didn't say anything about it.

If Saudamini could be convinced and brought back to Dasabhuja then it will be good. She can perfectly act the character of Rajia Begum in 'Neela Saila'. Saudamini is like Rajia Begum.

And Rajia Begum…?

Rajia Begum is like the moonlight through the fog. Mysterious... Agonized...Poignant.

Binod was excited. The trait of a composer which was dormant in him revealed its identity and he was overwhelmed.

He felt as if the scenes of 'Neela Saila' are hovering over his eyes and saying- Write Binod ! Write! Give us a shape and word.

Will you...Will you...

Neither Saudamini nor Rajia Begum was there.

Who was there? Who knows?

Binod began composing expeditiously.

23

The second stage will have a backdrop of the boughs of a banyan tree. Under it in a stony platform will be the idols of Lord Jagannath, Balabhadra, and Subhadra. Lakshmi Paramguru will be sitting and reciting gently- Neela Jamuta sankasaha takshyana..

Jaguni will enter like Hanuman with a branch on his shoulder and a creeper in hand.

Binod visualized this scene in Puri's Bada Danda. There is no technique required to incorporate this scene. Everything is predefined. He is just writing it down on a piece of paper.

The screen will close with the recitation of the sloka 'Om Madhubatha Rutyatae, Madhu Khyaranti Sidhbaha... Om Madhu, Madhu, Madhu by Paramguru. Jaguni will ring the gong continuously and repeat-Jai Jagannath!

But Ramachandra Deva being a little upset will say-' Hey Lord! You are so close to my heart but far to reach, but the day you come near me, I wouldn't have anything to offer other than washing your lotus feet with my tears.'

Is it only the feeling of Ramachandra Deva. Is it not the feeling of Binod?

The heart which is filled with the devotion

and reverence for the Lord can that be revealed in any language?

Ramachndra Deva's agony is reflected in the composition of Surendra Mohanty. This can only be felt in the heart. How can it be sequenced in a play?

It is fine till Ramachandra Deva comes to the second stage in agony after being reproved by Daitas. But is it possible to project this agony without any dialogues? Binod was confused.

Kamal Mishra would have given him his valuable suggestion but he is there at his home after the Bhadrak camp and it's almost a week now.

Will Kamal Mishra deceive him?

With whose help will he stage the play ' Neela Saila'? Who will give the direction? Where did he go?

There is no news about madam. Where did all go leaving him alone?

Binod felt as if he is away from others for a long time. It seemed as if madam, Kamal Mishra were known to him in the past.

Writing is an addiction. It's a lonesome affair like the battle fought alone by Ramachandra Deva.

Professor Samsuddin said it right but he doesn't know where he is now. At that time he said repeatedly-' Binod, you can try to write. You can do if you have the determination. You have the potential. Once you get yourself involved in writing, you will feel that other things won't worry you. The politics on the university campus, the stress of examination, and the worry about the future can't touch you. Life is like a mirage of incompleteness and regret; creativity is like an oasis in the desert. Once you are addicted to it life will be richly-watered, richly-fruitful, and bestowed with the crops of harvest.

At that time the words of the professor sounded like the words in a book but now he can feel it in his heart.

He felt as if he was swirling in the whirlpool of apprehension and conflict before he began writing 'Neela Saila'. But he couldn't realize when he completed it.

All of them have appreciated the creativity of Sarala Das and Kabi Samrat and think that it's god-gifted. Binod thought that these are deceitful blessings. But now he feels that it's the ultimate truth. Did he write the play himself? He took so much time to arrange each word. After so many tries, he wasn't able to write a proper dialogue. But how could he write? He feels as if someone made him write.

Now he feels as if he was in deep meditation for years. Today while concluding 'Neela Saila' he feels as if he is blessed.

But the play didn't have a conclusion. He couldn't express the sweet sadness of Ramachandra Deva and that dissatisfaction will linger in his mind forever.

Life is incomplete. Creativity is also incomplete like life. Lord Jagannath is incomplete. Among the incompleteness, if the play 'Neela Saila ' is incomplete then what's the worry?

That will be realized in the heart.

' There is an unquenchable thirst inside, which can't be satisfied.'

A gentle smile of satisfaction came on his face and faded away.

Madam was walking towards him with a smile on her face.

Binod said-' Madam, I have completed writing 'Neela Saila'. Now you will take the responsibility of staging it.

-' Binod, Do you think that you will get rid of this responsibility so soon?

Binod asked-' Then?'

-' You have to give the direction for this play.'

-'Me?'

-' Yes, you Binod Das. You are the playwright of the play 'Neela Saila'.'

-' How can I give the direction as Kamal babu is the director?'

-' He has taken a break from this responsibility.'

-' But why?'

-' He wants that 'Neela Saila ' should be solely your achievement.'

-' Do I have any experience in the field of direction?'

-' Did you have the experience of writing a play before?' Experience isn't earned beforehand. It comes with the experience of reality and also prospers with that.

-'But?'

-' There is no time to say 'But'. You may begin the rehearsal today. I will make the necessary arrangements to worship the book.'

- What worship will you do with these scattered papers? At least let me arrange it properly like a manuscript.'

-' I have never got a chance to read the novel 'Neela Saila'. I have heard from you that it is like the raindrops from the dark clouds over Chilika. How can you arrange it? To be scattered is its beauty and dereliction is its freedom. Why will you try to arrange it and destroy its beauty?

Binod remembered a dialogue from 'Neela Saila'- 'The sea is its yearning, the wind is its veil, and the sky is its regalia.'

Binod said-' It would have been better if instead of me you would have written the play.'

-' Are my words like the dialogues of the play?'

-' No, No. It was more marvelous.'

- 'Good!..' Madam smiled casually listening to Binod's praise. Binod also laughed along with her.

24

-' Why did you suddenly show your interest in a historical play?'

The reporters asked him on the first day at Phulnakhara camp.

Is it an interest or an obsession, or a thought?

Binod was in a conflict.

He was never interested in press, autographs, CDs, or the publicity. What is acting for him? Is it a source of earning a livelihood or a way to live? In between, he was obstinate for 'Neela Saila'. He becomes astonished when he thinks about it.

Who dragged his attention towards the Neela Chakra? Was it all predestined? Is it predetermined? Is it the wish of the All mighty?

The novel 'Neela Saila' was also written because of a small incident. Surendra babu was inspired by what an old widow told him in Radhabalabha Matha. He took her words seriously and 'Neela Saila' was the result of that.

These reporters won't understand if he says that. They have never seen the light in the eyes of Benu Ustad for a historical or mythological play as all of them are in the labyrinth of plays like ' Murder-Rape-Gang rape'. Did they understand the pain of Rasaraj Nayak who takes care of the mess? Do they have the news of Chana babu's death, who died because of nonavailability of proper treatment? They have never heard the names of Dhira Mohnaty and Bishnu Rath.

The reporter repeated the question as he was silent.

-' Who knows why there is a self will or not? Why does the rain want to drop, why does the flower want to bloom, why does the butterfly moves from one flower to another, who can say? Is there a reason for all will?' Binod asked them in return.

-' Do you think that you will succeed in this experiment?'

-' The success of an experiment is not certain. If there is a certainty then can that be called as an experiment? Other than that why do you say it as an experiment? Odisha's theatrical companies were hosting these historical plays for a long time but in past few years, there is change in the trend. You can say that to initiate that 'Neela Saila' is Dasabhuja's sincere effort.'

-' Can you say how will the audience accept it?'

-' Like the change in the social norms, the taste of the audience also changes. You can say that it's like a vicious circle. The embroidery technique which prevailed long back is back, there is a repetition of the old hairstyle. There is a saying in English' Third generation repeats'. If the audience doesn't have interest in historical plays then why would they have taken out the colour print of Mugal-E-Ajam?'

-' But in the case of theatre?'

-' Why are you thinking that theatre is different? Like and dislike of the audience is the same everywhere.'

-' I have heard that 'Neela Saila' will be your achievement. You have written it in the form of a play and also directing it.'

-' A play isn't anyone's sole achievement. There is a contribution of the sponsor, playwright, director, artists, technician etc for the play. All of them are responsible for the success and failure of the play.'

-' How did you motivate madam who is sponsoring this project? He was a little displeased. He lit the cigarette and said –' It is better if you ask her.'

-' You have got a MA degree in English. You also have a good career. You could have been a lecturer or an officer but instead of that why are you so inclined towards the theatre?

Binod suddenly remembered an uninteresting scene from' Sandha Matichi Garae'(Name of a play). He was angry. He threw the cigarette down and trampled it with his feet and asked- What's the problem in that? What is wrong in that? The reporter was baffled when he saw Binod in anger. What will he answer to his question? He said in a stunted voice- 'One more question.'

-' No more questions, please. Thank you.' Binod left the place. Malini was dressed up and was standing outside. Next to her was Muna Panda with a neck tie. Maybe they were waiting for the reporter.

Baban babu called him and said-' Bina babu you have spoiled everything.'

Binod couldn't understand and asked-' What happened?'

Baban babu said-' Didn't you see both of them standing there? You were so annoyed with the reporter. Will he publish the photograph of these two?'

-'Oh!' Binod understood and laughed.

Baban babu came closer to him and said- ' Why did Shankar Bhola come today? He was talking with Malini in the market square.'

-'I think Indradhanu is staging his play at present. Why did he come here leaving the play?'

-' That's the matter. Saudamini refused to act in his play and left the party. Who will do that type of role? Even in cinema, no one will dare to act in a scene like that. I think now he is trying to take Malini from here.'

-' Ok. Madam or Bholi babu will take care of that matter.'

-' Is it so that she would have played the role of the queen in the new play?'

-' Who told you?'

-' Who else will say? She was saying it herself. She will be the queen and Muna Panda will play the role of Taki Khan.'

-' Rubbish! Those are all wrong notions. Leave that matter. Let's go and have a cup of tea outside.'

Baban babu said-' Wait a minute. Let me call Bitcha as he was also saying to go outside and have tea.'

Binod asked-' Didn't Bitcha go for the publicity today? Today is the first day here.'

-' What's the necessity of publicity in Phulnakhara camp? It's always houseful.'

' That's why Bholi babu cancelled Patamundai camp.'

-' He is an idiot. Those people returned with disappointment.'

Bitcha came and said-' Bina bhai ,let's go and have food in the dhaba. Bholi babu has been to Chatara Bazaar. After he brings the vegetables, food will be cooked in the mess.'

-'What's Bholi babu doing? He wants to somehow manage today's lunch.' Binod knows that Benu Ustad, Raghu babu, and those who are paid less will starve till night.

He told Bitcha-'Go and call Raghu babu and Benu Ustad.'

25

Binod tried to sleep in the afternoon but he couldn't sleep. He couldn't sleep in the morning after the show. Though he was feeling tired as he didn't sleep at night but still wasn't able to sleep. He was feeling very uncomfortable. Binod knows very well about his habits. Tiil 'Neela Saila' isn't staged in Bali Yatra ground he will be tensed.

From 3 pm till 7.30 pm time is fixed for the rehearsal. Now it going to be 4 pm. Only Lata is present whereas others didn't come yet. In between, he came twice to check. Who respects time here? This is after all a theatrical company. In this country, many learned people take the pride in being late.

Lata is a new artist. She will make her debut in the play 'Neela Saila'. After few days she will also start following the trend of Malini and Muna Panda.

There is also an addiction to the profession. Experiments are done on it but they don't want to realize it. Acting is a routine job for them. Somehow they have to dress up, apply the makeup, and stand on the stage and that's the end of their work. Muna Panda thinks of himself as a professional trainer. He has mastered everything and there is nothing more to learn. His work is to teach others. He has adorned himself with unnecessary arguments and examples. Medium- grade artists like Sukanta blindly follow what he says.

He thought Taki Khan is like the Naga hooligan of the play ' Damara Rabi Dela rae'. According to Muna Panda a villain means a street loafer or a gangster. A gangster means a thick chain in the neck and brass jewelry or bracelet in hand. Jitu Mohanty and Shankar Bhola have taught him this. They don't know that each artist has his individuality, has his own sense of dressing and the way he carries himself. Kamal Mishra didn't consider him for the role of Taki Khan. He is also not able to do justice to the role of King Amichand.

Babita's acting as Suna Mahari is also not up to the mark. Suna Mahari is a wencher and is not fond of dance. King Amichand isn't attracted to her beauty. He tried to make convince them but they couldn't. In the diplomatic strategies of Amichand, Suna Mahari is like a queen of the chess board for an irresolute person like Bhagirathi Kumar. They are unable to understand the intricacies of diplomacy. Muna Panda sits leaning on the round pillow with Srikant who plays the role of Bhagirathi Kumar as if he is watching the courtesan performing in the Rang Mahal. Binu Ustad tried his best but wasn't able to teach Babita the essence of the classical dance performed by a *Devadasi*. Her gestures had the reflection of Babu Rao's record dance. Lord Jagannath's Seba Dasi Suna Mahari's dance is austerity and surrendering. How will Babita who does record dance will understand this? Does Muna Panda understand the intricacies of diplomacy other than the petty politics of the theatre?

Madam saw their performance and consoled Binod. She said- 'Is there any time to focus more on these small characters? Even though there is time but from where will we get the artist?' Suna Mahari's character is one of Surendra Mohanty's marvelous creations. There is an attraction in her gestures and devotion to get emerged in the lotus feet of the Lord like the streams of Ganga and Jamuna. Is it so easy to perceive it?

If I wouldn't have read 'Neela Saila'... Madam paused. After some time she said in a helpless tone- 'It's true that I am not a litterateur, I can't explain what is there in my heart.'

-' Who told you that a litterateur can only make others understand what he thinks? They aren't able to make others understand that's why they are called litterateur. If they would have been able to make others understand then they would have been called as cunning.'

-' Is it so? I heard this for the first time.' Madam laughed and said.

-' It's absolutely true. The day the litterateur will be able to make others understand that day it will be regarded as highly creative.'

-' Why?'

- The dissatisfaction of not able to make others understand troubles the writer. He keeps on searching for different ways and means to make others understand. That search is called as literature.'

-' Is it so that after writing the play 'Neela Saila' you are thinking that you won't write anything.'

-' Yes. I am not a litterateur.' He replied madam cleverly and both of them laughed.

Binod stopped laughing and said-'The real beauty of 'Neela Saila' lies in these small characters.'

-' But what can be done?' The trend of historical play is no more there. After all, we aren't accustomed to that trend 'Neela Saila. We have to be satisfied with what we can do. Rest is the wish of Lord Jagannath.'

That day, madam spoke the thing easily but it wasn't that easy to compromise with the situation. This is a classical novel.

It may not be Suna Mahari, Amichand ,or Bhagirathi

Kumar characters, at least Malini should try to project the character of Lalita Mahadei.

Binod didn't expect more from Lata as she was a new artist. Saradei's character is depicted properly in her voice and looks as if god has gifted her with those brimming dark eyes and the plaintive voice to do the character of Saradei.

There is no need to worry for the characters like Bakshi Benu Bhramarabara and Padmanabha. Raghu babu and Baban Biswal are experienced artists. Binod thought of assigning the character of Kantha Mekap to Baban Biswal. But if he includes the characters like Kantini and Kantha Mekap then the number of scenes in the play will be more. Now a day's artists aren't willing to work for more than three hours and the audience doesn't have the patience to sit for a longer time. If the play isn't like ' Kancha mausa' or ' Damara Rabi Dela Rae' then after the record dance the audience gallery is half empty. To caste twenty five scenes excluding the record dance, it takes almost four and half hours. Binod thought it's not wise to take the risk. That's why for the character of the king of Patia Padnabha Deva he selected the comedian Baban Biswal. Baban Biswal is hefty and large and can fit exactly in that role.

While assigning Jaguni role to Bitcha, madam was a little hesitant and said- 'Jaguni and Saradei are the two prominent characters in 'Neela Saila'. Can you manage with two new artists for those characters?'

But after she saw the performance of both of them she was satisfied and said-' Binod, your insight is very sharp otherwise Kamal babu wouldn't have entrusted the responsibility of direction on you.

The absence of Kamal Mishra had troubled Binod a lot. He couldn't take things lightly. Direction is Kamal Mishra's profession. Did he leave the party and stayed back at home so that he gets the fame? Or is it so that he didn't want to take the risk of historical play and stayed away? During the play'

Radha Hajigala Gopa Dandarae' he took the charge of directing it hesitatingly. But after the play was a flop he behaved as if nothing has happened. Kamal Mishra may be a good director but he is shrewd which Binod never liked.

There is no use in thinking all these now. The role of Rajia Begum and Taki Khan has created a problem for him.

-' Bina, are you waiting for the tea? Binod opened his eyes as Bishnu babu called him. Bishnu babu has reached the camp yesterday. He is a little moody person. He was roaming around and wasn't seen for a long time. Binod didn't find time to speak to him.

Bishu babu said-' Today they have made black tea in the mess.'

-' Why black tea?'

-' It seems the price of 1 kg sugar is Rs 40 in Malgodown and vegetable is very expensive for Kartik month. Bholi babu is in trouble now. He ordered lemon tea in the mess but Dahniya says that there is no lemon in the mess. Bholi babu came from the mess and said-' If lemon isn't available in the mess then can't it be bought from the market? Will the world come to an end if the tea is served late?'

-' The world won't come to an end but no one will go for the rehearsal if they don't drink tea.'

Binod understood why others didn't come for the rehearsal. He was annoyed and said-' There is hardly a fortnight left for Bali Yatra competition. Why are you troubling the artists at this time?

Bholi babu said-'Is it mentioned anywhere that without tea there won't be any rehearsal? One kg of sugar costs forty rupees. Five Kgs of sugar are required for morning and evening tea and other than that many people visit the camp. Does anyone have any idea about the expenditure in the mess?

Bitcha got up and asked-' Your brother in law is in the party for the past two months. What is he is doing here?'

-' Who are you to ask that question?'

- Who are you to order for the black tea? Did you take the permission of the mess committee?'

-' What is that rubbish mess committee? Why will I ask? I am the manager. I will look at the expenditures and order accordingly.'

Malin came out and said-' Did you become the manager to cut our throat? If you are so efficient then why don't you stop people coming here unnecessarily?'

She said unnecessary people referring to Bishnu babu and all of them understood it. Lata tried to ignore it and Bishu babu was standing there in that chaos.

Does the situation make people like this? Binod was surprised. Bholi babu went near Malini and said-' Am I not saying anything? Am I silent? How can I look into all the matters alone? Who listens to me?

Malini said enthusiastically-' Yes, that's the thing. If there is no head of the family then there is chaos in the family and a similar thing is going on here in the party. Here all of them do things according to their wish. Who will say whom?' Muna Panda said-' If it's not so then did Kamal babu leave the party without any reason?'

This farce was preplanned otherwise for a small thing like tea why would they fight without any reason? Why did Muna Panda say that Kamal Mishra left the party and sitting at home? Is he criticizing Binod's direction and commenting on him?

No no. These people are fools. They will be discussing the same topic again and again. They don't want to look beyond it. Why did he take such a big risk by trusting them? Kamal Mishra has done the right thing.

Bishnu babu could understand what is in his mind and said-' Bina, what are you thinking so much? It's a regular thing in the party. Have you not heard about 'Too many cooks spoil the broth?' Please don't worry. Leave everything to Lord Jagannath. 'Neela Saila' play will be staged. Let's go outside and have tea.

Binod said- 'Bitcha, you can come with us. Go and call Benu babu.'

Bitcha said-' He is discussing a song with Ramani babu for the new play. If I call him he won't came.'

After they left the place, Muna Panda said-' To have cup of tea the old man was giving a lot of speech.'

-' Binod said, You bloody rough and was going to slap Muna Panda. Bishnu babu stopped him and said-' No,Bina.'

Bitcha said-' Leave it Bina bhai. Don't spoil your hand by hitting this mean person.'

-' You scoundrel! What did you say?' Muna Pand was ready to hit Bitcha.

Binod caught hold of his T-Shirt collar and said-'Mole rat! Anything wrong?'

Bhola babu ran to stop the fight and said-' Muna Panda leave the place immediately. Unnecessarily there is a fight for a small thing. Will there be any respect left for the party if people come to know about this?'

-' Behuda, Badtamij! Do you know that there is something called prestige in the world?' Bishnu babu roared
.

Whose voice is it? Is it the voice of Bishnu babu? Binod couldn't believe his ears.

He caught hold of his hand and walked towards the tea stall taking a breath of contentment.

26

-Lord Jagganath has solved so many problems. Will the play not be staged because of an artist? Did anyone remember about Bishnu babu? Benu Ustad said.

That's right.

Binod never thought that Bishnu babu can do the role of Taki khan so perfectly.

He has his style and walks like an emperor. He delivers his dialogue so fluently. His voice which sounds carefree and philosophical sounds very deep filled with hatred and anger during the play.

-' He solves everyone's trouble and fulfills all desires.' Leave everything on him. Benu Ustad said.

What did he cling into which he will leave? Right from envisage of the play 'Neela Saila' till Bishnu babu's Taki Khan's role everything is controlled by a will. Is that the will of Lord Jagannath?

But how will I leave everything on him? How does he understand the helplessness of a human being? In which scripture it's written the way to surrender everything to him?

Has he not lost his hope many times when he decided to stage 'Neela Saila'?

Rajia Begum is the central character of 'Neela Saila'. Saradei is calm and quiet . According to the taste of the present audience, not only Saradei, Lalit Mahadai , Suna Mahari but also Rajia Begum can quench the thirst of them. Leaving aside Malini and Babita, Tanushree is left. Nothing more can be expected from her other than the role of an illiterate village woman. She can't be given the role of Rajia Begum. There is hardly any time left. Who did Kamal Mishra think of giving the role of Rajia Begum in 'Neela Saila?'

As Binod was in trepidation. Benu Ustad said-'There is only one way.' He paused in between.

Bishu babu said-' Is there any artist to perform the role?'

Raghu babu said-' If you know then tell us. Is there any time to think about it?'

-' If Saudamini could be brought back...' He was thoughtful and paused.

Raghu babu said-'Yes, you are right. Saudamini has left Indradhanu and there at home. If you speak to her, she won't deny.'

Binod thought about Saudamini long back. He has imagined her in the role of Rajia Begum. But who will say madam to bring her back? He knows very well about the indifference between both of them though he doesn't know the exact reason for indifference. Bholi babu can raise this proposal as the Manager but Bholi babu doesn't like Saudamini. Who knows if Saudamini will come back to Dasabhuja again or not? If she bluntly says 'No'?

Benu Ustad said-' Madam is going to come today. I will put this proposal in front of her. Then he indicated Binod and said-' You can find out about Saudamini's before that.'

Saudamini's mobile was switched off. Binod couldn't tell them that though he tried but he couldn't contact Saudamini.

Raghu babu saw Binod sitting quietly and said-' If required ,I will go in person and will make Saudamini understand but before that kindly convince madam.'

-' Why are you discussing convincing madam? If sir says then won't madam agree?' Malini said.

Raghu babu said-'The discussion is about bringing Saudamini back to the party.'

Malini was startled and said-' What did you say? She brought disrepute to Indradhanu and left in between the season. How can you bring her here?'

-'Disrepute ?' Raghu babu asked as he couldn't understand.

-'Didn't you hear about it? She was involved with Prabhat Sarangi so his wife came to Balasore camp along with her children. She said if they don't remove that woman from the party then she will commit suicide along with her children.'

Benu Ustad asked-'Who told you? Shankar Bhola?'

-'Why will Bhola babu tell me? There is a discussion about it everywhere. Ustad , how don't you know that?' If you don't know then ask Muna Panda.

Raghu babu asked-' How does Panda babu know about it?'

-' Don't interrogate me. I can't answer to so many questions like-Who said, when, where.'

Bishu babu said-' Are there scarcity of people to spread rumors?'

Malini said in an irritated way-' Will there be smoke without fire? She is carrying someone's child and also egoistic.

Benu Ustad said-' I don't believe in this. A girl like Saudamini will never do this. There are lot of gossips in the theatrical companies after the girls started joining. There is no scarcity of people to make big issues.'

Raghu babu said-' Is there any necessity to discuss such useless things? Is Saudamini bad and Prabhat Sarangi a good person? Why didn't they throw him out from the party?

Bishnu babu said-'Scandals are a part of the life of the actors and actresses. Did aspersions ever left art?'

Benu Ustad took a deep breath and said' That's true but what's the other way out?' Malini said-'Why are you worried so much? Can't our Tanushree do the role of Rajia? She is doing the role of Roshani Begum in the play 'Kancha Maunsa'. Isn't there Hindi dialogue in that?'

Bishnu babu tried to control his laughter and said-' Not Roshani, Roshnara.'

-' Yes,it's the same thing. I can't pronounce the Muslim names otherwise I could have done the role of Rajia.'

Binod left that place to get rid of the meaningless gossip.

The rays of the sun were soft and it was a little cool. Cuttack –Bhubaneswar Highway was busy. The busy highway indicates that life has pace. People are moving ahead in their way. Nothing has stopped.

Where do they go in such a hurry? Is life a race? Where will that race end?

Anirudh Pattanaik is working in a Multinational Company in Delhi. He completed his MA in Economics and did a management course. He was in Calcutta, Hyderabad, and Bombay and finally joined as the Regional Manager of a Multinational company. Now he is in the post of Joint Director in the Head Quarters at Delhi. He gets an annual salary of fourteen lakhs excluding perks. Two months back he was saying that he will go to the United States of America to do a Super specialty course in Marketing.

Then… Then?

Where is the end to it?

Anirudh's mobile is always busy. Sometimes he calls him at night 11 O'Clock. At that time Binod would be washing his face to go for the makeup.

Was life supposed to be like this? Or like D. Ray Choudhary's life? Books and only books. D. Roy Choudhary emerges himself in the piles of books like a hungry serpent in the jungle.

Binod sometimes compares him with Professor Samsuddin. D. Ray Choudhry is a living encyclopedia in Philosophy. Professor Samsuddin is a critic of Thete. One of them is trying to understand philosophy through books and the other one tries to analyze the new aspect of it in life.

-' Binod , can you understand life if you limit it to the books?' Professor Samsuddin asks. Doesn't' the beauty and color of the flowers, the greenery, star-clad sky, darkness, or the chirping sound of the birds have any value in life?

Binod, life is like a river. On its bank, there are many temples, towns, and cremation grounds. Sometimes there is an evergreen forest and sometimes the rocky land. It is the same for everyone. Everything is immersed here. Let it be the discard of the maternity home, or the ashes from the rituals, or the ashes after the funeral.   It accepts everything. That is the reality of life. It can't be confined to the books or the library. It will lose its essence.

Life is outside Dasabhuja camp. It is among the noisy street of Phunakhara, among the noise of day to day life, in the honking of the horn, in overtaking, in the flame burning in the roadside dhaba, and also in the greenery of the fields. Life is waiting for him but why did he spoil such a beautiful day in the dirty politics of the party?

Life also lies in Malini Baral's ugly envy, in Bishnu babu's nonchalant life, and in the hopeful eyes of Benu Ustad. Where did Saudamini disappear in this life? Where did Professor Samsuddin go?

'You commit the sin, become pregnant..'

I can't remember the next line.

Who wrote this poem? Is it Guru Prasad Mohanty?

He was trying his best but unable to recollect. He remembers only one line time and again.

Did Saudamini commit any sin? Is pregnancy a sin?

Or do people commit sin and become pregnant?

Professor Samsuddin could have answered this question.

Those who don't commit any sin and become pregnant are virtuous.

Those who commit sin and become pregnant are sinful.

Malini Baral is virtuous as she didn't commit a sin to become pregnant.

Is it a sin to be pregnant?

Hence commit sin or don't commit sin, to be pregnant is sinful.

So all the pregnant women in the world are a sinner.

Try to find out the fallacy in Philosophy.

Binod laughed to himself.

Bloody Bitcha !- Malini Baral.

He heard the car horn honking and he turned back.

Madam!

Madam gave him the driver seat and moved to the left.

'Sometimes we feel good to give the responsibility to others.'

Who said this? Saudamini? She couldn't tell about it. Maybe she might have thought to say but her thoughts were blown with the wind.

Binod thinks that maybe Saudamini tried to tell him or thought of telling him.

All women in the world is the same. He knows it well.

Is also Kalyani?

Suddenly the question came to his mind.

Can Kalyani be called a woman? She has inclination towards committing sin but hesitates to do it as she doesn't want to lose her beauty and become pregnant.

She thought to depend on Binod for anything is to lose her independence. She is just like Malini Baral.

Binod smiled but was a little upset.

Again the same logic and fallacy?

Where is he going with madam? Is he like a puppet in

her hands? As soon as madam opens the car door he will drive and go? Madam saw him driving silently and asked-' Were you going to Pahal Rasagola market in search of Rajia Begum?'

Binod wasn't in a mood to answer her question. He asked-'Are you returning from Cuttack?'

-' No. I went to the camp in search of you.'

-' Me? But why?'

-' Today we were supposed to go to Haripur.'

-' What will I do at Haripur? What idea do I have about dresses? It's better if take Bishnu babu or Benu Ustad.'

-' I heard that Cuttack's Padma Chitralaya has brought good craftsmen from Haripur and is making the costumes. Isn't it good to purchase directly from there?'

-' Till now we couldn't select the artists.' Binod said with displeasure. He thought that madam will speak to him regarding Saudamini. As she was returning from the camp so Benu Ustad must have told her.

-' There won't be any scarcity of artists for the role of Rajia Begum. An experienced artist will take only four days to understand the role. It's only a matter of four to five scenes.'

Experienced artist? Whom is Madam is talking about? Did she decide to bring Saudamini back? Binod was happy.

He asked-' Did Benu babu say you anything?'

Madam became serious and asked-'About what?'

Binod was disheartened. He could understand madam's attitude towards Saudamini. To change the topic, he said-' If you want to go to Cuttack then why this way?'

-' I will purchase some Rasagola from Pahal market. I came to know that Dhira babu has recovered. Benu Ustad was saying that he loves sweets. We will go to meet him after completing our work in Chitralaya. Anyways your rehearsal is at 3.30 pm.'

In Pahala's market shops are extended for almost two

kilometers. Big bowls of aluminum on the roadside shop are the identity of Pahala market. Where will she stop the vehicle?

Madam understood what he thought and said-' Binod, stop the car near the next shop.'

27

- 'Malini was very scared and she performed her role properly.' Why was she showing so much attitude?' Bitcha asked derided.

Malini and Muna Panda's performance was somewhat ok today. Binod laughed silently. Yesterday Malini and Muna Panda returned from Bhubaneswar around 7 pm. Charan Das isn't well for the past three days. He isn't able to eat. Malini isn't bothered about him. She bought a house almost two years back near Aeginia . She went to see the house in the morning and came back late in the evening and forgot to bring medicine and electral powder for Charan Das. Charan Das was angry and scolded her in front of others. All of them know that to go and see the house was just an excuse. It hardly takes half an hour to reach Phulnakhara from Bhubaneswar. She sometimes went with Muna Panda from Balugao and Chandikhol camp to Bhubaneswar to see the house which was just an excuse.

She entered the room hurriedly and saw madam sitting there. Madam heard about the bad performance of the artists from Binod and had come to see the rehearsal. Binod noticed that madam wasn't in a good mood after looking at the way Malini's dressed up. Malini was wearing bangles till half of her arms, she had a long bindi on her forehead, and wore four- inch Stilettos which was making a loud sound as she entered the room. Madam controlled her anger. Malini had applied lipstick on her lips and nail paint on her fingers which she bought from the street hawker. Bini madam never tolerates this but, to see their performance she sat quietly.

Muna Panda reached half an hour late. He was wearing a Doria T- Shirt and a faded jeans jacket. He either didn't see madam or pretended as if he didn't see her and said unabashed- 'On the way suddenly I met Mahapatra babu. He was after me to cast me in his previous film and at that time I denied it. But now he wants to cast me in his new film so he made me sit in a hotel and narrated the story of the film. That's why I am late.'

Is he explaining or trying to boast? It couldn't be made out from his gestures. All of them knew that he was telling a lie. No one can compete with Muna Panda in bragging. Madam was still sitting silently.

Is it the calmness before the storm? Binod was perturbed. There were only ten days left for Bali Yatra competition. If madam suddenly bursts out in anger then what will happen?

But madam sat quietly and observed their performance. Binod was a little bit relaxed. Thank god nothing happened!

-' Binod babu?' Madam called him seriously.'

Binod was startled. Why did she address it in this way? Why did she say Binod babu instead of Binod?

-' Do you want to present the play in Bali Yatra camp with this type of performance?'

Is madam going to blame him as a director and a playwright?

Madam paused for a while and said-'It's better not to perform rather than performing it so imperfectly. This rule is applicable to everything in this world. You are going to present 'Neela Saila' which is a classic creation. It will be a disgrace to

'Neela Saila'. No one has the right to dishonor such a classic. As a director you should have made them understand the substance of the characters of Lalita Mahadae and King Amirchand.'

-'Whom are you saying it, madam? Are you saying it to Malini or me?' Muna Panda asked in a little high pitch as if he isn't bothered about madam's comment.

Madam said confidently-'To both of you.'

-'Then exclude us from this play. We weren't ready from the beginning to act in this historical play.'

-'There is no value of your willingness or unwillingness as far as the party's decision is concerned. Dasabhuja's fate won't be based on your wish. You are a highly paid artist at the party. You aren't doing a favour by performing rather you are bound to do that. You are paid for it. Did you understand?'

Madam was too angry. She has never been so much angry anytime before.

No one could make out whether Muna Panda understood what madam said. He wanted to speak something but madam interrupted in between and said-'Try to improve your performance in two days. It should be satisfactory. If you don't do that then I will cancel the bond between you and the party giving the reason that you broke the rules of the party. After that, you can join Mahapatra babu's cine group or any other dance group.'

-'This is a new type of play madam...,' Malini was trying to convince. Madam interrupted her in between and said-'No more arguments. If you want you may also leave the party but if you want to be in the party then you are bound to follow the rules of the party. With whose permission did you give a photo pose to the journalist hanging ten rupees worth necklace on your neck?' All of them looked at Malini. Malini was wearing the same necklace so that everyone can notice it.

-' Do you know what people are thinking about the party after your half- naked photograph was published in the magazine?'

-'He requested us for the photo.' Muna Panda said softly.

Madam ignored his explanation and said-'This isn't Shankar Bhola's play and I am not like an ignorant audience sitting in the audience gallery who will be impressed by listening to the stupid words in English used by you in between the dialogue. Did you not request the journalist to publish that photograph? Did you not purchase fifty copies of it to show it to others?'

-' I swear madam. I didn't know about so many things. I swear madam.' Malini said.

-'Stop that unnecessary drama. If you want to be in the party then follow the rules of the party otherwise you may leave with your husband.' Charan Das stood up, folded his hands and said-'I don't have any mistake, madam. I won't leave Dasabhuja and go anywhere.' Ramani babu tried to make him sit down.

Madam cooled down a little. She said-'Ok, Ok. I am not forcing anyone to leave. I am forced by the circumstances. Every institution runs with regimentation. If that regimentation isn't followed then it's evident that the institution will collapse. There is no scarcity of people to act if money is offered. In Bali Yatra competition the play 'Neela Saila' will be staged at any cost. I hope that it's clear to everyone present here.'

Madam left the place stormingly.After some time the honking of her car could be heard near the turning.

Today Muna Panda reached for the rehearsal before fifteen minutes, Malini is trying to impress him and today Bholi babu has given sugar, ginger .and cardamom to add to tea.

There is a lot of change in the atmosphere. Binod laughed to himself.

Bitcha said-' Bina bhai why are you laughing? Why are you not saying anything?'

-' What will I say? Binod said.

-' You don't have a role in this play with Malini. It would have been fun if it would have been.'

-' We are both like the streams flowing in opposite direction. How will we meet? Binod said taking a deep breath. He remembered Kalyani's Katyayeni look.

- ' How is it so? Even though there was indifference between them as husband and wife but still why are they not meeting?

- ' Bitcha, It not only happens in the play but also happens in the real life. Some of them are born with that fate. Leave that topic. Did Bholi babu give you money to repair the microphone?'

-' How did you know? He gave me before I asked him with the breakfast expenditure amount.'

-' This morning breakfast expenditure amount rule has to be changed. What for there is a distinction in this?'

-' That will be good. How do Benu Ustad and others manage with only three rupees for breakfast? It's difficult to believe unless you see it.'

Binod said-'You discuss this in the mess committee. I will put a word to madam.'

-' Madam won't deny if you say. I know that.'

Binod laughed and said-'As if you know everything.'

Bitcha said-'Let's go and have breakfast in the dhaba. They have prepared cabbage curry in the mess. Dhadia nana has mixed water in that as the cabbage was less.'

Binod said-' I lay a condition. I will pay the money today. You have paid many times. I don't want to be indebted.'

Binod never thought that Bitcha will become emotional. He controlled his emotions and said-' Bina bhai, How could you think about me in this way?'

Binod was unprepared for this. He stroked on Bitcha's back and said affectionately-' Are you mad? You are crying like a small child for such small things. Ok, you may go and call Bishnu babu and Benu Ustad. Raghu babu won't eat non-vegetarian today otherwise we all would have eaten together. But before Bitcha could go and call Bishu babu there was a call from madam. She said-' Binod, is today an off day for you? If so then you may come to my place. We will go together for dinner. Be ready. I will send the car.'

Madam disconnected the phone and Binod couldn't say anything.

28

Madam was wearing a zari kurta and a payjama and was waiting for Binod on the balcony. Binod couldn't recognize her but after he recognized he was astonished. Why she is suddenly interested in this type of attire? Binod has never seen her wearing salwar kameez. Why this Nabakalebar? He remembered that the salesman of Chitralaya was showing two to three pairs of dresses like this for Rajia Begum.

Wealthy people think differently. What they do is unpredictable.

After Binod stepped down from the car, the driver stood there waiting for the instruction from madam. Madam ordered him from the balcony-' Pran, Leave the car keys and you may go.'

-' Pran?'

The name is of course not peculiar but the name doesn't fit his personality. The man was middle-aged and was simple. His clothes were clean but not ironed properly. The sandals on his feet weren't polished and were shabby and he had a little grey beard on his face and his name is Pran. Amazing! Is this also a conviction of a rich person like madam?

-' Binod, come upstairs. We will have tea and leave.' Madam said.

There was no one in the ground floor. There was no one upstairs. Does madam stay alone in such a huge double-storied building? Last time he didn't see anyone there but when he looked at the house and the garden he felt that almost four people are required to take care of it.

Binod didn't hesitate the way he hesitated last time but he was a little uncomfortable to enter the drawing room. He could hear some noise from the kitchen. Maybe madam is cooking. She called him from there and said-' Binod, come to the dining space.

Binod went and sat down on a chair. The dining space was in between the kitchen and the drawing room and was quite big. On the double door refrigerator was kept a vase and on that was a fresh rose bud which will bloom tomorrow.

There was a calendar hanging on the wall. It seems the pages weren't turned for many days. On the page was the picture of Golden Oriole. Maybe the page displays the month of March.

In his village, the Golden Oriole comes and sits on the drumstick trees in the backyard. At that time the tree was laden with drumsticks. The call of the Golden Oriole gives the signal of the arrival of Spring. After his marriage the tree was chopped because of the fear of catterpiller.

Madam brought cauliflower pakodas and two cups of tea in a tray. She sat on a chair in front of him and said-' Fresh cauliflower is available in the market and I bought two cauliflowers today. Dinner won't be cooked tonight so I chopped one and fried pakodas. The other one is in the fridge. I will give it to Pran tomorrow.'

Binod laughed as he heard the name Pran again from madam. Madam asked-' What happened? Is there more salt in pakodas?'

Binod said-'Not at all. It's good. It's better than the pokodas in Bihari's shop in Puri seashore.

-' Is it true?'

- 'I swear' Binod said

-' Why did you laugh?'

-' I heard the name Pran and laughed.'

-'Oh! Madam also laughed and said- 'His name is Pranath but that name is only heard in the mythological play and historical play. What should I call him? Should I call him Pranath?

She gets dimple on her cheeks when she laughs. The dimple on her cheeks is attractive. She looked like a bouquet of Tubor Rose in her dress. He remembered about the last incident. Madam was wearing a thin nightgown but today she is dressed up differently.

Is it the attraction of a lady towards adornment?

Madam looked down and asked-'What are you looking at?'

Binod realized. He was looking at madam like an innocent child for a long time. He looked down.

Madam said-' We will go to 'Bansal Jewelers'. I will purchase an earring and you will select it for me.'

Binod said-'I don't have any idea about it.'

-' Did you have any idea while writing the play? You could write so beautifully. You can select whatever looks good to you or is it so that you don't have an idea about beautiful and ugly?

Binod didn't say anything and got up from his place.

' Bansal Jewelers' is a treasure trove. He had never an idea that a city like Bhubaneswar has such valuable stuff as gold, silver, and gemstones. There was completely one section which had only earrings. There were so many varieties of earrings like Jhumka, cluster earrings, studs, danglers, drops, and ear cuffs. Binod thought that if the person who has said ' Dazzling eyes' have never seen anything in life then this is the place where one will lose his mind.

The world is amazing. He suddenly remembered about Dr. Ray Choudhary. When you enter his personal library you lose your mind. It's a different world of books, magazines, and journals. But this is a world of sparkling diamonds and other gemstones. In the library Rr. Ray Chaudhary sits among the books wearing spectacles with thick lens but here Mr. Bansal is sitting in the cash counter wearing a thick, long gold chain.

The color of the drink may be different but the impatience of a thirsty person is the same.

An attendant came with two cool drinks. Binod sent him back saying-' No Thanks'. A salesman left the counter and ran towards them. He asked very softly-' Sir, shall I get tea or coffee?'

-' Tea' Binod said softly and walked towards a showcase. Madam was looking at one after other showcases. Women are always attracted towards jewelry let it be Malini Baral or madam. Kalyani will never forgive him as he couldn't earn money and because of that she never forced him to purchase any jewelry. Once he purchased a pair of anklets for her which she impassively hung on the hook attached to the wall. After Kalyani left for many days the pair of anklets was hanging on the wall mocking Binod's inability.

What he imagined for his wife is just an emotion that actually doesn't happen in the real life. Kalyani wore a pair of slippers in the house so that the dust in the mud floor doesn't touch her feet. He never liked her wearing the slippers but there is no value of his like or dislike.

-' Hey! What are you doing here? Won't you select the earrings for me?'

-' Madam I don't have any idea about hangings and drops. What will I select?'

Madam caught his hand and pulled him towards a showcase. She said-'In these three showcases there are only hangings. You can select any one of them.'

-' Are you going to test my likes and dislikes?'

-' I never doubted your likes and dislikes. She said softly-
' But you selected Malini Baral for the Lalita Mahadae's role.
She added this as a parenthetic clause to her sentence.

Binod said jokingly-' You should have used the
parenthetic clause in the middle of a sentence.'

The salesman had kept four pairs of hangings separately
which madam had selected. Binod imagined madam wearing
those hangings one by one. He selected two pairs but was
confused. He took them in his hand and looked at them.

Madam laughed. She asked-'Are you confused? While
making the final selection it happens. It's ok if I take both the
hangings.'

Madam went to the cash counter to make the payment
and the salesman followed her with the earrings.

The attendant came with a cup of tea.

While drinking tea Binod suddenly remembered-
'Opulent!'

29

Binod drank a little more whisky, not beer. When he said about beer, madam said-' Who drinks beer in the month of November? Stomach bulges if you drink beer. Do you want to have a bulging stomach like Baban babu?'

They returned to madam's house from 'Bansal Jewelers'. Binod thought that if they eat outside today then he will make the payment. Madam said-'Do you want to give a treat? After your play is staged and appreciated you will give me a treat.'

Binod completely forgot about the play among the dazzle of the 'Bansal Jewelers' and the noise in the market building. When madam made him remember this he said-' Till now I didn't get a good artist for a prominent character like Rajia Begum. How will the play be staged?'

-' Forget about the play now. There won't be any scarcity of artists for the character of Rajia Begum. Near Jaydev Vihar over bridge, there is a dhaba. We will take the tandoori chicken from there.'

-' I thought that I will go to the camp.' Binod said hesitatingly.

-' Today is an off day for you. What will you do in the camp?'

Binod couldn't say anything.

Drinking is also an amazing experience. The intoxication of whiskey was gradually advancing its fangs like the tender evening of the month of Kartik.

Everything seems to be chaotic and indefinite. Definite is lost in indefinite. The memory was evoked.

Poetry ? Yes, Poetry. Each word is turning into a poem. Binod felt like reciting a poem in front of the beautiful lady sitting in front of him. Why did he write a play instead of poetry? There are so much of confusion and problem in the play. Poetry is like a stream. It flows on its own.

Madam sat with down casted eyes. There were dreams in her eyes.

No, no. Why did he think of her like a bouquet of Tuber rose or sharp dagger? She is soft and smooth like Charu Chandralekha.

Madam got up from the chair. She took the whisky glass in her hand and walked towards the mirror.

Ah! Is there so much of insobriety in the gesture of a woman? As if the ripples are created in the lake.

The color of the sky is blue, so is water and dreams. If a woman has any colour then that is blue.

The color of the mirage is also blue.

What is a woman?

Is she the sky, water, or the mirage?

No,No a woman is nothing like that. She is an enigma.

Binod laughed loudly.

Madam kept the whisky glass on the mirror stand and was trying to open the backside clip of the hanging to wear it but wasn't able to do that. She was startled by Binod's laughter. The clip fell from her hand on the ground. She bent down to search for it and that revealed the curvature of her body. Binod was excited.

Madam took the clip from the ground and requested Binod-'Please'.

Binod pulled the clip and again laughed loudly.

-'Hey! Is it your historical play? Madam said and showed her other ear.

She wore the hangings, smiled, and asked Binod-' How does it look?'

Binod said-' Am I a poet that I will immediately find words to appreciate it?'

-' Even though you aren't a poet but you are a playwright. All the litterateur are poets. Try once.'

-'Professor Samsuddin says-'Similes and imagery comes with deep feelings. But this isn't a meteor but a flame. Where can he find a simile for this from his experience?

-' You cheat'. Madam was a little disheartened.

Binod knows very well about the anger of a woman. But it was his first experience with the resentment. He knows many ways to fight anger but how to face resentment?

Krishna makes his ultimate supplication to Radha to shed her anger and said- ' Smara Garal khandanam Mama Sirisha Mandanam Dehi Pada- PallavaM Udaram.'

What will he do? Binod was again confused.

-'Whom do I look like? Try to remember.' Madam encouraged him.

Like whom? Binod tried to recollect. Is she looking like Mama Mishra or Saudamini? Like Kalyani or Suna Bhauja? Not like anyone.

-' Why will you look like someone? You look like yourself. You don't have any comparison. You are incomparable.'

-' Binod, which plays dialogue are you repeating and trying to elude me? I am wearing this kameez and the salwar and hangings on my ears. Don't I look like someone?'

Who was wearing this type of clothes? No one. Tanushree takes this getup in the play 'Kancha Maunsa'. But how can she be compared to Tanushree? No... Binod didn't like the comparison.

-' What happened? Did you remember? Madam asked curiously. Binod said helplessly-' Why will you look like someone? This attire and the hangings from 'Bansal Jewelers' can never be compared with your beauty rather you have enhanced their beauty. Believe me.'

There was discontentment in her eyes. What did she expect to hear?

She went to the bedroom and said-' Go and freshen up. We will have dinner. If the tandoori chicken gets cool it won't taste good.'

There was an urge in her quite from sometime and it suddenly dropped down. She had an insistence right from dressing up in the attire, purchasing the hangings from 'Bansal Jewelers', standing in front of the mirror to wear the hangings and the inquisitiveness to know whom does she look like. Everything was in smithereens.

Imagery cropped up in Binod's mind as if in the deep forest the musk deer is in search of the musk. To break the resentment he entered the bedroom.

Ah! Is it an ocean of beauty or is it a conspiracy to make him insensate? Binod was dumbfounded. He came back and sat on the chair.

After some time, madam came draped in a saree. She asked-' Why didn't you freshen up and sitting here?'

Neither there was any excitement in her voice as before nor she was sad because she didn't get an answer from Binod. She wasn't shy as Binod saw her while changing the saree or wasn't angry as Binod was sitting there.

Everything was calm and quiet.

After taking bath he was feeling fresh but there was something that was tweaking his heart. What was it? Is it the sweet tremor of a song? It's a note of which vocal music? Ramani babu can say. Sometimes Ramani babu plays this type of plaintive music during the afternoon. Binod tries to find the meaning of the music and tries to give it a lingo. He tries to compare it with sadness but he doesn't succeed. He says Ramani babu-'You didn't let me sleep during afternoon. Why do you play such heart piercing music? It pierces my heart.

Ramani babu tells in a sad voice-' Binod babu,is there music without sadness? Malini gets angry because I do the practice in the afternoon.'

Binod didn't notice that there was an open terrace adjacent to the dining room. The city looks beautiful from here. It seems Bhubaneswar is decorated with lamps.

On the evening of Diwali, Lata decorated the second stage with lamps. Instead of brake dance, a play was staged. Mena arranged the electric firecrackers. Tanushree acted as Maa Kali with a sword and a skull cap. Ramani babu played Mangalacharan in his violin. According to Benu babu's direction, Santosh performed Siva Tandav.

The audience clapped sitting in the audience gallery. At that time Binod had a strong notion-'The interest of the audience is just a plea.' It will move ahead of the way the sponsor and the director want to. On that day no one demanded the brake dance of Babu Rao.'

-' Binod, What are you thinking ? Madam asked. There was a little sadness in her voice.

Binod said-'Throughout the year it's Diwali in Bhubaneswar. The topography of the city is that. I looked at this view from the hostel terrace when I was in the university.'

-' Alone?' Madam asked jokingly.

-' By 10 O'clock the hostel gate of Mama Mishra and Alka Chaudhary was locked. Who will come to give me company?' Binod answered.

-' After listening to you I remembered the song' Tum Sath Ho to Har Din Diwali,Har Din Holi' that's why I thought that may not be personally but someone may be there in your thoughts.'

Sometimes Binod thinks that he is like a thirsty traveler in the world of seductress. He is chasing an illusion. Sometimes he imagines Mama Mishra, Alka Chaudhary, or the bride in the village or Saudamini and sometimes he visualizes Suna bahuja or madam. He is trying to create the woman of his imagination who is an assemblage of all these beauties. The day he can catch hold of that illusion he will be free from insobriety. He will be broken. Life will become difficult.

Bloody, my foot!

The daughter of the businessman thought that Binod will be attracted by seeing her beauty. How will the stubborn daughter of the contractor understand the difference between attraction and temptation?

Madam was arranging tandoori chicken on the table in the terrace. What will he do after eating? If he could get a folding cot he can spend his night on the terrace comfortably.

What is today according to the calendar? It is a waxing Crescent moon. Madam has knowingly switched off the light on the terrace. The shadow of the Bakul tree camouflaged the terrace. In that darkness, madam was going to and fro the kitchen. She said only tandoori chicken but what other things is she bringing? There is no more place on the table.

-' Binod, will you have some beer?' Madam asked from the kitchen.

- ' After drinking whiskey, beer will taste like coconut water.'

- 'Would you like to have some more whisky?' Madam brought a whisky bottle and came to the terrace.

She kept the whisky bottle on the table, opened the casserole and checked the tandoori chicken and said-'These aren't in a condition to be eaten.' I will make four to five parathas.'

-' Why will you prepare food so late at night?' We will manage.

-' No issue. The dough is already there in the fridge. How much time it will take to prepare parathas?'

Madam took out dough from the refrigerator and went to the kitchen. Binod came back to the terrace and sat on a chair. He could hear the sound made by the goods truck plying on the National Highway. On the sky was the crescent moon. There is exhilaration in the night sky. Before he joined the theatrical company he had a habit of wandering outside till late night. Kalyani never waited for him rather she said -' You are stinking. Move aside and sleep.'

Binod use to take the pillow and go outside the room. Kalyani use to say-'You have all the bad habits of a villager. Does any gentleman wander outside till late night?' Binod felt like giving a tight slap on her face to make her understand the meaning of courtesy. But he refrained from it .

He could see madam in the kitchen. She was preparing parathas and side by side she is cutting vegetables for the salad. There is sweat over her face. She is busy with her work. Though it's the month of November still it's hot in Bhubaneswar. Binod walked towards the kitchen door and said-'What was the necessity of doing so much of hard work? You are drenched in sweat.'

-' Hard work? It's not hard work. Who would have eaten that cold tandoori chicken?' She kept some fried cashew nuts and salad on a plate and gave it to Binod and said-' You can go and have your drink. I will finish my work, freshen up and come.'

She switched on the gas stove and asked- 'Didn't you bring your trouser and kurta?'

-' I didn't think of staying back at night.'

-' How long will you sit wearing the same shirt and trouser. Change into this towel.' While taking the towel from her hand Binod felt like wiping her sweat. Madam pulled a saree from the wardrobe and entered the bathroom. Binod took the parathas, salad, and water bottle from the kitchen and kept it on the table.

Madam came out from the bathroom and said-'' Who told you to do all these things?' She brought the plate which had fried cashew nuts and salad.

While opening the cap of the whisky bottle Binod said-' I troubled you unnecessarily in the night.'

-' Why are you thinking that you troubled me? I thought of preparing chilli chicken but as we had to go to 'Bansal Jewelers' I couldn't. What gives more happiness to a woman other than preparing food and serving to the near and dear ones?'

Dear ones? People in Dasabhuja are discussing it for a long time. Why is he so happy listening to it from madam just like the Ramani babu's raga ' Kalyan Bahar'? Binod looked at her in fascination. She looked charming in the brightness of the moon.

Madam took the whisky glass and asked-' Are you feeling bad about me?'

Binod was startled by this question and asked-'Why'?

-' Because I drink and make you stay back at night. Are you thinking me as unconventional?'

' Madam, I have seen different guise of woman. But I have never seen anyone who is so virtuous and humble as you.'

Binod emptied whisky from the glass and said in a loud vice-'I hate people those who are pretentious. It is wrong to say that a woman is a 'gate to hell' rather she should have been addressed as pretentious. In this world woman is the most beautiful creation of God. The world will be losing its majesty if a woman is excluded from it. But a pretentious woman is worse than hell.'

-' It would have been better if you would have become a philosopher rather than a playwright.'

-' Why are you saying it as philosophy? This is the truth of life and it's my experience. Philosophy without experience is just like the words in a book. I never believe in that and don't want to believe it.

-' It would have been better if you would have been a teacher.'

Binod laughed and asked-'Think and say what I would have been. Do you hate my profession?'

Madam said-' Please don't misunderstand me. My intention wasn't that. If you would have been a teacher then the next generation wouldn't have been rote learners rather they would have understood the exact meaning of life and what's the difference between a philosopher and a teacher? Can a teacher be a good teacher if he isn't a philosopher?'

-' Every profession has a goal even the job of a clerk. It is necessary to understand it and to make it fruitful.'

-' Let's stop the discussion. What will you give me if your play is staged and appreciated?'

Did Binod listen to such a question before? Who told this to him? Binod tried to recollect. He was slowly getting intoxicated after drinking whisky. Everything seems to be unclear and vague. He wasn't able to recollect.

Binod stood up in excitement and said-' I am just a theatre artist. What do I have to give you? If the play'Neela Saila 'is appreciated then will it be only my achievement? You, Benu Ustad, Ramani babu, and even Bitcha are a part of the achievement.'

Binod paused for a while and again said-' Hey ! What am I saying? It will be the triumph of only Lord Jagannath.

Madam said-' I knew that litterateurs are very good at speaking but I never knew that they are imposters. Don't try to mislead me. With the blessings of Lord Jagannath the day

'Neela Saila' becomes successful; will you give me what I ask for? Do you promise me?'

Before Binod could promise his mobile rang.

Bholi babu was on the other side and he asked worriedly-'Where are you Binod babu?' Binod wanted to answer but he stopped.

He asked-'What happened?'

-' Panda babu has gone somewhere and he didn't return till now. As the show is late, people are shouting. Who knows what will happen after some time?

Binod pulled madam's hand and said-'Madam, Let's go immediately.'

Madam asked- 'What happened?'

Binod didn't reply to her question and hurriedly went down the stairs.

30

Today there is no rehearsal. It isn't necessary to think about the scenes. It's not necessary to look for an artist for the character of Rajia Begum. It's no more necessary to count the number of days.

He has got rid of the responsibility of 'Neela Saila.'

If Lord Jagannath wants that then what can he do?

His heart is still filled with sadness from the melancholic music of yesternight. He can hear the melody, but unable to understand its meaning. It seems as if a stormy dark cloud which was about to rain has become still in the sky.

Imagery is upraised deep in his heart.

What was madam trying to make him understand? The soft leaf which was sprouting in her heart in the attire suddenly withered. He thought of not thinking about it anymore. He removed his makeup and tried to sleep but couldn't. Sleep is more deceiving than Muna Panda.

No one thought that Binod will manage the proxy role so wonderfully. Bholi babu who sleeps during the show was also awake and was watching him acting sitting in the music circle. Sometimes he came and offered him tea. From the audience gallery was heard the clapping and Nija Khan- Jindabad !.

He can't escape from the identity of Nija Khan. Yesternight he performed Muna Panda's villain role. Does he look like a villain? Why is the audience so enthusiastic to see him in the role of a villain than a hero?

Ramani babu has started his practice in the morning. Why does he play such heart touching melody? Heart is filled with lamentation listening to it. The world seems like a desolate island where a lonely man's heart- bursting outcry could be heard.

He could hear Benu Ustad. He said-'The man is born with Gandharba Kala. I have been in the theatre company for many years but Bholi babu, I have never seen an artist like him. If he does the role of King Ramachandra Deva in 'Neela Saila' people will be astonished.'

-' Do you think that 'Neela Saila' can ever be staged?' Where will we get the artists for those two main roles? Who knew that Muna Panda is such a big traitor?

-Do you think that he is only a scoundrel? What about that obstreperous lady? Malini came running to fight with Bholi babu and said-'What are you saying Bholi babu?' What Bholi babu mumbled couldn't be heard. Malini again repeated- 'She is a sneaky woman.' I don't know when I will die but the day I saw her I understood that she will do something like this. Her father is eating here free. Didn't he see or hear? He has done it purposely to get rid of his daughter's responsibility. Why didn't he kill such a daughter?

Yesternight Lata eloped with Muna Panda. Binod came to know after he reached the camp. Where did they go? Why did she elope with a man like Muna Panda who is a drunkard and shrewd?

Binod remembered about the ugly scene in hotel Madhulika- A man behaving like an animal and licking the floor.

Bholi babu said-' Binod babu managed yesternight but

who will do the role of Muna Panda now? Where will we get an artist now?' He has troubled us a lot.

-'There is no one other than Santosh who is available now.' Benu Ustad said.

-' He is a new guy. Can he manage the roles of Muna Panda?'

- Bholi babu, don't think about new and old now. The main thing is experience. Whoever has that will never fail. Didn't you see how did he perform Siva Tandav on Diwali night? Inexperienced artists can't do it.'

Santosh is a new artist. He came to the party in search of a job during Bhadrak camp. He looked tired and was dressed up shabbily. He didn't have much experience in acting but he has a lot of enthusiasm to act. When Bholi babu saw him he said-' Is this a 'C' Class party? Experienced artists are waiting eagerly to join Dasabhuja. Where do we have a vacancy to fit new people?

Santosh was going back disappointed.

-' Listen !'. Binod called him from behind. He remembered about his old days when he was going from one party to another party in search of a job.

Santosh turned back hesitatingly, walked towards him, and stood silently. What did Binod see in him? Ownself? He thought that the boy is capable. Santosh had the enthusiasm to work and he decided to keep him. That's why Santosh isn't in the good books of Bholi babu. On Diwali night when he thought about performing Siva Tandav instead of breakdance, Bholi babu didn't appreciate it. Siva Tandav was appreciated by the audience so he couldn't say anything.

Benu Ustad said-' Santosh can perform the role of Amichand in 'Neela Saila' but what about the role of Saradei...? He paused. He couldn't gather his courage to say about Saudamini. Two days back he suggested madam to bring Saudamni for the role of Rajia. But as soon as madam heard the name of Saudamini she became silent and serious. Binod wasn't there at that time and later on, he heard it from Bitcha.

-' But? Malini asked- Didn't you see Ustad how madam was annoyed as she heard the name of Saudamini? Why are you talking about her? These two have already dishonoured the party. What will she do if she comes here?

Bholi babu said-' Why are you worried about it? What will happen if she comes? Who will play the role of Taki Khan? Do you think that Bishnu Rath can ever show his face here? Does he have the guts to do so?'

That's right. Binod hasn't seen Bishnu babu since yesternight. Did he also leave the party out of shame and humiliation?

Binod got up from the cot.

31

'Why are you unnecessarily worried? What can you do if you are worried?'

Who said this?

It's neither a question nor a challenge. Who said these comforting words? Is it Lord Jagannath?

He didn't see Lord Jagannath in his dream. He didn't appear in front of him with conch-shell trumpet shankh, discus whirring around his index finger or chakra, a mace or gada, and a lotus or padma. There was no fragrance of sandal and musk in his room nor was the fragrance of *Dayana* leaves There is an inkling that Lord Jagganath had come. Is he amorphous and come stealthily and leaves his hazy footprints to create an allusion?

Who knows?

He feels as if he has got rid of the burden. He is free from anxiety and tiredness. The cool breeze blowing outside is soothing. What's the time now? He could hear the noise outside.

Binod was roaming around like a vagabond throughout the day. He crossed Phulnakhara square and went to an unknown village. On the other side of the village was a vast field. In the vast field, the ripe corns looked like gold. He didn't feel like returning to the camp. What will he do in the camp?

By the time he returned it was twilight. Dhadia

nana was going to the mess to prepare tea. He asked-'Sir, where did you go? I prepared paneer curry today.'

Bitcha asked-' Bina bhai where did you go? Madam asked about you. Your mobile was also switched off.'

Binod didn't give a reply to anyone. He lied down on the cot.

If Suresh Bhanja would have been there he would have analyzed and said-'Alas! 'Neela Saila' couldn't be staged so he is disheartened.'

But whom did he see in his dream? If he had favored him he could have appeared in front of him. His thirst would have been quenched! He is beyond his reach and far away.

Binod's heart was filled with emotions.

Dhadia nana came and stood near the door with tea and a mug filled with water. He asked-' Sir, Are you not well? Why are you sleeping in the evening?'

Binod took the mug from his hand and washed his face. He drank tea and said-'Did you finish cooking?'

Dhadia nana said-'How can I finish cooking in the evening? You were sleeping so you are thinking that it's already late at night. Are you hungry?' He didn't wait for his reply and said-' I have kept paneer curry separately for you. If you are hungry then I will make some puris and bring them. Why are you roaming around here and there without having food? It doesn't matter if the new play isn't staged. Neither madam nor the manager is worried about it. Why are you so worried?'

Dhadia nana would have continued but Bitcha came running breathlessly and interrupted in between. He said-' Bina bhai come and have a look. Mini apa has come.'

Saudamini ? How did Saudamini come here? What is the use of coming now? Saudamini, you have come very late. Everything is over.

Benu babu came there hastily. He was filled with

happiness and said-' Finally, Saudamini has come. There is nothing to worry about now.'

Nanda came and said-' Sir, madam is calling you.'

Is it the consequence of his dream? But no one has indicated to him – 'Neela Saila ' play will be staged.

Maybe it's just a coincidence. Maybe his sixth sense worked. Suresh Bhanja says-' At many times the sixth sense of a human indicates the future.'

But, he had not thought about Saudamini today in this conscious or subconscious mind. It's just like a puzzle.

Madam stopped as the room was dark. She asked-' Binod, are you not feeling well? Why are you sleeping in this darkness?'

Binod got up and switched on the lights.

Madam said-'I heard that you were roaming around without food today. Where did you go? I came in the morning but couldn't find you.'

Binod didn't reply but smiled a little.

Madam said-'I brought Saudamini back. Now you will take the responsibility of 'Neela Saila'. Don't blame me afterward.'

Binod asked-' What about the role of Saradei?'

Madam's enthusiasm faded. Her expression changed.

She asked in a feeble voice-'Won't Saudamini do the role of Saradei?'

-' Then, who will do the role of Rajia Begum?'

Madam didn't reply anything and sat on a chair. Binod said-'If you have thought about any artist to play the role of Rajia Begum then kindly call her to attend the rehearsal. We have only a week in hand. There is also a problem regarding the role of Taki Khan.'

Madam said-'Today is the last day of the camp. After the show is over come to my house tomorrow morning. We will discuss it.'

Madam left the camp suddenly. Binod couldn't understand anything and looked at her innocently.

Bholi babu came and asked-'Shall we repeat the play tomorrow? There is a public demand.'

Binod was a little irritated and said-'Why are you asking me?'

32

There are two sides of a coin. Every human being shows only the brighter side of him.

Who said this? Mark Twain?

Maybe Mark Twain didn't come across people like Muna Panda.

Professor Samsuddin said it rightly. All famous proverbs are hypothetical. That is said in a particular situation. To consider it as gospel isn't substantially real.

If he wouldn't have seen Muna Panda in 'Arogyam' Binod would have never understood the truth in what Professor Samsuddin said.

After the show, in the morning, Binod heard the voice of Bishu babu in Muna Panda's mobile. He was surprised. He requested him to come to 'Arogyam' Nursing Home which surprised him. He was anxious and instead of going to Trishulia camp and to madam's house to discuss about ' Neela Saila' he went to 'Arogyam'. Bishnu babu narrated everything in front of him.

He was indebted to Muna Panda and wanted to speak about it in front of someone.

' He is helping us so much since that night..' Bishnu babu paused. I don't have words to express my gratefulness.

Muna Panda was sleeping on the floor. Bishnu babu looked at him and said-'The road wasn't good.

It was full of mud and it was difficult to drive. I was shivering. Lata was not in her senses looking at the condition of her mother. She was sitting with her mother in her arms. I thought that we won't be able to reach the hospital.'

' I couldn't give her anything in life. Will she die without treatment...?' He became very emotional and couldn't speak.

Is he the same person? Is he the man who stays in the camp despite of Bholi babu's rebuke? Is he the same man who asks others for tea and cigarette and roams here and there aimlessly? Is he the same Bishnu babu who does the role of Taki Khan and mesmerizes everyone by his dialogue-Kambakhat, Kafir! Now he is crying like an innocent child.

He was a lovable father. Otherwise, after being continuously rebuked by Bholi babu why did he come to the camp after every ten days? But Binod never understood that a person like Bishnu babu who is so careless has the heart of a father.

Binod never found words to console anyone. Today also he couldn't. He tried to change the topic of the conversation and asked-'How is she now?'

-' She is fine now.' The doctor has told me to take her home tomorrow.

-' Lata? Binod asked. He didn't see Lata after he reached the hospital.

-' She has gone to her uncle's house. After she brings some money we will pay the hospital bill.'

-' How much money you have to pay?'

-' Muna is taking care of all those things. Still, I think we have to pay two thousand rupees. Binod took out four thousand rupees note from his purse. He gave it to Bishnu babu and said-'Don't worry about money. If you need more, you can call me.' Bishnu babu took the money hesitatingly and said-' I wouldn't be able to repay it... ,' He was trying to find words to convey his gratefulness.

Binod hurriedly left the Nursing Home.

33

There was a sudden change in the weather. It was stormy. There was a power cut due to the storm so the show was cancelled. This is a problem in the coastal belt.

The generator was switched on and the rehearsal was going on but that was also over. Others have already gone to sleep. Only Bholi babu along with Nanda and Bagula was arranging the things. Binod was trying to sleep but he couldn't.

He lit a cigarette and came outside. At a distance was the river Kuakhai. The river water was dazzling like a brass plate.

Bishnu babu left his wife in her mother's place and has come back to the camp to make the necessary preparation for the play 'Neela Saila'. Lata and Muna Panda have also come along with him. More effort isn't needed for Saudamini.

'Neela Saila can be staged now.

But he feels as if he has lost something among these which he can't get even though he searches for it. But what is that thing? He isn't able to make it out.

Human mind is really amazing and mysterious! What goes on in the mind is incomprehensible. Suresh Bhanja says-'The subconscious mind is like a riddle. Memories of the past are captured in that. A man dreams to fly in the sky, that is the memory of his previous life as a bird.' He tries to make it understand by giving examples. It may be true.

Suddenly he remembered about an incident in his childhood and recalled someone's face whom he has seen long back. He never paid any attention to it and never tried to understand. Sometimes he remembers his past memory but it has never disturbed Binod's consciousness. He remembers about the black plum tree in the village, the Moringa tree at the back yard, Mama Mishra's blue saree, the yellow petals of the flower, and the old book under the pillow of Suresh Bhanja . Sometimes he remembers the Banyan tree growing on the wall of an overbridge of a city and below that the slum dwellers and many more things from his memories. There is no way to differentiate between memory and imagination. He tried to recollect few things but he couldn't and they seem to him more realistic than the present.

Which incident of the past will peep out of the memory in a subconscious mind is unknown. Who knows that? It may be something like that which Binod can't understand now. Time flows at its own pace. It's difficult to understand it.

Binod lit another cigarette and came down the porch. He tried to hide from Bholi babu's sharp eyes and took the other way to the road. There was a dhaba but it was closed because there was a power cut. Two stray dogs barked, he stopped and again started walking.

It's an amazing scene of Mahanadi. The river Kuakhai begins flowing from Naraj and then the stream of Kuakhai begins from Katahjodi. River Mahanadi is bifurcated into many branches. It is difficult to remember which river starts from where and where it merges with another river. But in this complicated network of the river Mahanadi, there is the greenery of the fields and villages on its bank. The cyclonic storm causes havoc here and on the contrary there is luxuriance.

He has seen the river Mahanadi in various places. Right

from Chattisgarh's Dhamtari till Hirakud, Sambalpur, Cuttack, and Bhutmundai. Where could he have got this experience if he wouldn't have joined the theatrical company? Different places, different types of audience, and a different experience every day. There's a thrill in this profession. Professor Samsuddin was right. Here there are people like Malini and Saudamini, people like Benu Ustad and Muna Panda.

Muna Panda is a difficult character to understand. He was a different man in 'Arogyam Nursing Home' and he behaves differently in Dasabhuja. It's difficult to understand which one is true and which is just acting. Today he told Saudamini to come and play Ludo with him and also took Malini Baral to the dhaba.

Why can't Binod look at people and trust them easily like Benu Ustad?

When he saw Muna Panda in the hospital he remembered the disgusting scene in the hotel. He tries to find his gain in everything. The false smile on Saudamini's lips look like the moon covered by clouds in the sky and he looked for the hero of Indradhanu,Prabhat Sarangi in his imagination.

Was Malini telling the truth? In which nursing home did Saudamini go for an abortion? If not so, then why is she looking so pale? She has changed a lot after he met her in Puri. She has become more stubborn and proud. Madam made a mistake by bringing her back. She thinks that it's madam's defeat. Malini was asking Binod in the morning-' How do you adjust with these people?'

Are there not people like Malini Baral in this world? But it's of no use to make Saudamini understand that. Saudamini thinks that she is very special in the theatrical company. She is different from Malini, Tanushree, Babita, and Lata. She thinks that she is the only girl who has done her BA and brings glory to the party. People like Muna Panda and Prabhat

Sarangi who are shrewd tell her that she is beautiful and praise her. It's difficult for her to look at reality.

Binod smiled a little and avoided that topic.

The tent of Dasabhuja was drenched in rain and in the moo light looked like a paper bag filled with envy and criticism from a distance. He could hear the whistle of a long-distance train. From the trees which are on the other side of the river is heard the screeching of the birds. Breaking the silence of the night is heard the sound made by the goods carriers plying on the highway. There was a puddle of water underneath the over bridge which has become a play area for the tiny toads. There is silence on the riverside which seems to be asleep. The night is mystical. Mr.BadaJena who is a lecturer said rightly. This is a beautiful place that looks like a landscape in between Cuttack and Bhubaneswar and that's the reason why he bought a piece of land here and constructed a house. It's quite a large piece of land in which he has constructed the house. Though the house is not so big but it's beautiful. On the ground floor, there is a drawing, dining, kitchen, and a guest room. From the outside porch, there is a staircase that leads to the master bedroom and the study room. From the balcony, one can see the river Kuakhai and on the other side of it is a mountain. On the mountain, there is a temple. It looks like a northern star from a distance and the lights in CDA Bidanishi's looks like a necklace at night.

The study room is well maintained. It doesn't have many books like the library of D. Ray Chaudhary nor is cluttered but there are many good books on the bookshelf. Mr. Bada Jena has good taste. He is different from Professor Ray Chaudhary. He is neither crazy like Professor Ray Chaudhary nor is interested in writing books for the coaching center and other small books like Madhu Samal. He does what is required. He has good knowledge of various aspects of life. His son is there in one of the boarding schools in Delhi and he has been transferred to one of the colleges in Cuttack.

Binod gave a second thought whether he will go to his house or not as he had invited him. He has this bad habit since his childhood. After he joined the theatrical company he has developed that complex in him. Benu Ustad once said- ' Now a days no one appreciates art and artist. During our time people like Bholi babu never managed the mess. It was taken care of by the villagers. They invited us to their house. According to their capability, they fed us.' Then he took a deep breath and said-'That was a different time but you must go Binu. The gentleman has invited you. If you don't go he may feel bad.'

Like the lecturer, his wife was also aesthetic. She looks young. There is no artificiality in her dressing but she takes care of herself. She draped a Sambalpuri Pasapalli saree , wore glass and gold bangles in her hands, and a gold chain on her neck. There was a pair of earrings in her ears and she adored her hair with the Mogra flowers. She covered her head with the saree and looked like a beautiful woman of a dignified family. There were many Mogra shrubs in Mr. Bada Jena's garden. There were also Marigold plants in which the buds were in a blooming stage.

Binod thinks that the veil on a woman's head covers her imperfection. Kalyani never appreciated covering her head with saree pallu. She thought that it is done only by villagers. To keep the woman under the veil is a proposition of male dominating society. Kalyani couldn't get admission to any of the colleges in Cuttack. She stayed in her maternal uncle's house in a village and went to the nearby college. Where was it written about the male dominating society in the Sociology books of that college?

After listening to her immature arguments Binod couldn't understand whether he will laugh at it or get angry. While serving Mrs. Bada Jena said- 'I watched your play two years back at Dhenkanal. At that time my husband was working in a college at Dhenkanal.'

Mr. Bada Jena said-' Dhenkanal is a good place. It is surrounded by mountains.' Binod remembered that two years back his party went to Dhenkanal during Gaja Lakshmi Puja. He couldn't ask Mrs. Bada Jena which play did she watch as he was still hesitating as it's a part of his nature.

Mr. Bada Jena said-' We will go to Bali Yatra competition to watch the play 'Neela Saila'. I appreciate the taste of Bini madam. When she was in the Bhadrak College she dramatized 'Paraja' and staged it during the college annual function. She also acted in the play. She acted the character of Jili and was so lively. She was dressed up traditionally like a Paraja girl and no one could recognize her. All of them thought that the person who is playing the role is a professional artist. For many days I teased her as Jili.'

'Was Bini madam a lecturer?' Binod was astonished.

Mrs. Bada Jena said-' She is very affectionate. She was after me all the time. She is from a wealthy family but she left her job and formed a theatrical company as she was interested in that. Otherwise, the students and the staff of the college liked her a lot.'

Mrs. Bada Jena brought the sweets from the kitchen and suddenly asked-' Is she doing a role in the play 'Neela Saila'?'

Binod couldn't give an answer to her question.

He recollected the way madam dressed up in the zari salwar suit and wore the hangings on that day.

He is such an idiot!

He returned to the camp immediately from there.

Where did Bini madam go?

He didn't see her since yesterday.

-'Binod ? Binod looked back.

Bini madam had stopped her car.

But from where is she returning so late at night?

34

The first draft of the play 'Neela Saila' looks like a complicated entanglement. It's difficult to arrange it. Bitcha has prepared the manuscript. He copied down the content with his big round handwriting. After Bitcha copied down the content Binod thought that he will make two photocopies of it and throw the first draft. There are so many corrections in the first draft. Something is written at the bottom of the page with an asterisk mark, somewhere there is an arrow mark pointing at the points, and somewhere it is written to turn to the next page. In the beginning, Binod sometimes couldn't understand it properly during rehearsal and was in trouble.

He should appreciate Bitcha.

But now after the manuscript and the photocopy have been made he doesn't feel like throwing the first draft. When he turns the pages of the first draft he feels that, it not the dialogue composition of 'Neela Saila' but a thing that is very close to his heart, his aspiration, and his imagination.

Binod was very choosy. Whenever he didn't like the dialogue, he thought over it, changed it, and worked diligently to make it better. So how can he throw it now?

He moved his palm over the pages tenderly and became emotional. Who knows whether this devotion, emotion, and enthusiasm will ever come in life again or not? But whenever he goes through it he will remember how he was motivated looking at the Shree Mandir, Lord Jagannath, Sudarshan Chakra, and the flag while sitting in a tea stall in Puri Bada Danda. To give it the form of a play he worked day and night.

Let it be in the briefcase. He will keep it at home when he goes there during the holidays. He will keep it in the same box where he has kept his old books, a love letter from his classmate Reba Kanungo when he was in class nine, his father's spectacles, professor Samsuddin's letters, and a rejected headscarf of Kalyani.

Whenever Kalyani tied that headscarf she looked beautiful. When Kalyani left the house she left it behind as she thought that it's not useful.

Others may say that those are insignificant and useless sentiments but Binod has preserved all those as a part of his memory. He will be left with nothing if he throws them away.

In his path of life, these are small milestones. They have made him what he is now. These are the evidence for the making of the man and his identity of life. How can they be unnecessary sentiments?

Is there life without sentiments? What the worth of life without sentiments?

-' Did you know that madam went to Haripur yesterday?' Saudamini entered the room and asked. There was a crooked smile on her face.

What does Saudamini want to know? She has asked the same question so many times. He feels that these aren't questions but mockery. He pretended as if he didn't hear and started arranging the first draft.

Saudamini didn't get an answer from him and asked-'

Is it so that you are drinking along with madam and staying in her house at night?'

He tried to smile and politely asked-'Who said? Is it Malini or Muna Panda?'

'Why will only those two people say? Everyone in the party is discussing it.'

Binod laughed. It wasn't only a loud laugh but a laugh mixed with hatred and mockery. He suddenly stopped laughing and said dramatically-' Hey ! They don't know anything. To go to her house and to drink is a simple thing. We sleep together on the same bed. Go and tell them. Do you want to know anything more?'

Saudamini was startled by this sudden outburst. She couldn't understand what to say.

Binod said-'I thought that you are an educated person so you must be thinking rationally. But you are also like them those who never think something good.'

-'They were talking...' Saudamini tried to explain him.

-'You couldn't tolerate.. ' Binod asked sarcastically.

-'You must be knowing how they gossip here.' Saudamini said.

Binod didn't allow her to speak and said-'Is this theatrical company is like International diplomacy or like Bombay's stock exchange that I have to keep minute details of it? All of them have come here to earn their livelihood. It's not a place to gossip or criticism. Did you understand?'

He doesn't know whether Saudamini understood or not. She stood there silently.

Binod kept the first draft of 'Neela Saila' in the briefcase and came outside. He was very angry.

Srikant asked-'What happened sir?'

Benu Ustad was calling him.

Malini was standing there as an innocent child. Binod didn't say anyone anything and went outside.

He was on the Kuakhai Bridge. Yesternight he met madam there. She stopped the car seeing him there so late at night. Madam knows his habit therefore she wasn't at all surprised. She went to Haripur because she didn't like a few costumes provided by Padma Chitralaya.

She doesn't have any vested interest in the play 'Neela Saila'. There is no certainty that it will be a success. It's just an experiment. An overwhelming desire or it can be said as fervor. As a sponsorer, she could have liked Jitu Mohanty's spicy play. Maybe she had a little desire for this play which she destroyed by bringing Saudamini back.

But, she is working for this play with devotion and sincerity.

She had ordered a big painting on a canvas from Raghurajpur. She has told an artist from Patnagad to come and draw a backdrop in Pattachitra style. Any painter from Cuttack or Bhubaneswar could have drawn a screen for the second stage for five thousand rupees. But Bholi babu didn't like the proposal and said Binod-' In an auspicious moment in life Lord Jagannath appeared in front of your eyes while looking at the Shree Mandir, Sudarshan, and the flag on it and that is the fruit of the constant meditation in the previous birth. He is Omnipresent, Omnipotent, Omniscient , and shapeless. Is it possible for any artist or painter to give him a proper shape?'

Binod was overwhelmed. Bholi babu was trying to give words to his eternal feeling.

' It's a phenomenal, intangible, and elixir. What can be said about it? Is it a notion? What can be said other than notion? We have not seen the Himalaya. But when we hear the name Himalaya a picture is formed in our mind which has snow clad mountains and Pine trees. What can that be said? Is it so that as we have seen the picture of Himalaya because of that we have framed this picture in our mind?

Suppose you haven't seen the picture of Himalaya, then? In that case to draw a picture is difficult. Everyone can't draw that picture. But he can do. The picture of Bhima Bhoi or the statue that we see now represents a blind man who is already there in our mind. There was no photo of Bhima Bhoi. After reading his poetry whatever notion the artists framed in their mind they gave it a form with paint and brush.Now it has become a convention.'

He became emotional saying this. He said –'Once I wrote in a poem -'A distrustful artist promises that he will draw the city of my imagination. He ridiculed it.'

From the horizon of the sea, with the first ray of the sun, there was a gleam and that gleam was reflected on his face. He has never seen him so engrossed. It's difficult to describe that aura. But it looked heavenly.

He was engrossed in his thoughts about the artist.

When the woman is fascinated, there is nothing more expressive than her silent eyes. Binod was envious of that artist.

That artist is busy now drawing the Pattachitra on madam's terrace as madam had asked him to come. Madam also told that she will send the vehicle in the morning but Binod refused to go. Tomorrow the camp will be set in the Bali Yatra ground and he was busy arranging the manuscript of 'Neela Saila' and as Saudamini came to him so he wasn't in a proper frame of mind.

How will he go to Bhubaneswar now? When will he get the bus from Trishulia square to Bhubaneswar?

Before he could reach Trishulia square Suna bhauja rang him and said-' Bina, Please come quickly. I have to give you two good news.'

35

Suna bhauja was very happy to see Dahi Vada and Alu dum as if she has never eaten it in her life. In Trishulia square a vendor sells Dahi Vada and Alu dum in his bicycle. Binod eats two to three plates every day not caring about his acidity issue as it's very tasty. Suna bhauja likes Dahi Vada. Today after receiving her call and before boarding the bus he bought two plates of Dahi Vada and Alu dum for her. He also bought some sweets but Suna bhauja was more interested in Dahi Vada and Alu dum.

She kept tea on the stove and said-'Sura had come to the University for some work. In the university, during the lecture one of your Professor gave him the phone number and told him to inform you to call him immediately.'

-' Who? Is he Professor Samsuddin? Binod was excited. Where is he now? Is he in the university campus?

Suna bhauja smiled and said-' How do I know? You can call him; You will come to know.' She kept the Dahi Vada plate aside and took out a paper that was under the fridge cover and gave it to Binod.

While Binod was dialing the number his hands were shaking in excitement.

-' Hello ! Professor Samsuddin speaking.' Binod couldn't answer after listening to his voice. Professor

Samsuddin again said- Hello! Hello!. Binod said in a faint voice-' Sir, Binod here.'

It seems as if he was eagerly waiting for a call from Binod. He was overwhelmed with joy. He said-' Why did you take so much time to get my contact number? Any how you reach Delhi by the twentieth. I will SMS you my address.

-' Delhi?' Binod couldn't understand anything and asked him.

Professor Samsuddin said-'There are so many things to tell you. When you come to Delhi you will come to know. This is a new university. It is not exactly in Delhi but ten kilometers away from Delhi. It is constructed in a vast area on Noida road. There is a dream to construct it as Shanti Niketan in the natural environment at least till the hustle and bustle of Delhi don't destroy it. Let's see what happens. There is a vacancy to teach American Literature. Where will we get a better scholar than you to teach American Literature? I had suggested your name and the selection committee has approved it. You have to come as soon as possible.'

-' Sir, I... Sir,I don't remember American Literature now.' Binod fumbled.

Professor laughed loudly and said-' Binod, after working in the theatre for such a long time still you couldn't get rid of that complex? I have also contributed a little to mold you. Am I calling you to sing the folklore here? Why will you mug up American Literature and come here? I think you have a good idea about the way I teach. You will come here to mold a new generation, not to show your mastery. Come without any hesitation. I am waiting for you.'

Professor Samsuddin disconnected the phone. Maybe he was busy. He could hear the voice of some students over the phone.

Binod felt as if he has reached an unknown world. He felt as if everything is unknown to him. The people around him looked unknown to him as if he is a newborn child looking innocently and crying.

Twentieth? What's today's date?

He didn't know what Suna bhauja understood but she looked very happy and said-' It will be good. Sura has been transferred to Delhi. You will again have a good time together.'

-' Is Suresh in Delhi now? He completely forgot about Suresh. He asked-' Why didn't he call me when he was here?'

-' He came here on some urgent work. He took your number from me and tried to contact you over the phone but your phone was switched off.'

After drinking tea, Binod felt a little better and asked-' What's the second news?'

Suna bhauja was a little shy. There was a glow on her face and she looked down.

She was trying to make Binod understand.

Binod asked-'What happened? You have told me that there is two good news.'

Suna bhauja pulled her plaits on her chest and said-' What else will happen? Whatever has to happen has happened.'

-' What do you mean?'

-' You have left the family and are always busy with the theatre. If you don't understand then how can I make you understand?' She pretended as if she is annoyed and went to the kitchen.

She walked lazily like a swan. Binod could now understand the mystery of the untold secret.

He laughed loudly and said-' Such a piece of good news. Why did you hide it from me?'

-' I tried calling you many times but your phone was always switched off.' Bhauja replied from the kitchen.

-' But how did it happen? You said that Bira bhai is after someone in Dubai.'

- ' If he is after someone how does it matter? Is there any scarcity of men?' Bhauja brought two cups of tea from the kitchen and said-'There is chicken in the fridge. Let me cook that for you. You will have your lunch and go.'

- 'No, don't worry. At this stage why will you work?'

-' Is it so difficult to cook? I will also eat along with you.'

Binod asked-' How will you stay here alone in this stage?'

Suna Bhauja said-' Your brother has joined at Delhi. He said will money take us to heaven? He doesn't want to stay there alone without me. He is looking for a house in Delhi. He will take me there.'

-' What about this house?'

-' We will think about it later on. People are ready to take it on rent but will the tenants take care of the house?'

-' If no one stays here then the thieves will take away even the grills and windows.'

-' That's true.'

Suna bhauja wanted to say something but at that time madam called. She asked-' Binod, Did you get the bus? Shall I send the car?'

Binod said-' No, I am here at Bhubaneswar. I will reach immediately.'

36

It's a path to the celebration. He had this feeling in his mind while going. The month of Ashwin (October) is already over. The sky is clear and the bright rays of the sun are scattered all over. Kasatandi flowers, the beauty of autumn ....The sweeping expanses of this feathery, long-stalked, white broom like blossoms under the azure sky isn't gracing the landscape but still, he could experience it.

During his childhood when Binod went on a bicycle along with his father his heart was filled with joy. After crossing the river and covering seven kilometers there was a town. In that town, they kept the bicycle in a known person's house and boarded the bus to Cuttack. From Cuttack, they took a train to Puri. At that time Puri wasn't a place of pilgrimage for him but a place that is different from this world. Whenever he left the village and his friends in the village school and went to Puri he felt as if he is at the top of the world. He was more attracted towards the people dressed in colourful clothes and several shops on both sides of Bada Danda.

He didn't know about the train that they took to Puri. By the time they reached Malatipatapur it was almost dawn. He looked outside and saw the night receding and the sun blooming on the horizon, golden petals stretching ever outwards into the rich blue sky. It is the brilliant flower of the sky that warms the day and an invitation to a new day. Whenever he heard about going to Puri he was always excited. He felt as if Lord Jagannath is waiting for him. At that age, Binod never understood the things like Shree Mandir, Neela Chakra, Ratna Bedi, Garuda Stanbha, and Singh Dwara. Lord Jagannath seemed very close to him and he could feel that intimacy in his heart.

His father pointed outside the window of the train and said-' Look, You can see Shree Mandir from here.' But, Binod was still engrossed in his thoughts. He thought that Lord Jagannath must be like his father.

When he was in the university he told Suresh Bhanja many times to go to Puri by the night train. But Suresh denied his proposal and said-' Who will look for a hotel in Puri to take bath in the morning? We will go now and spend the evening near the seashore and come back by the night train.'

-' What are you thinking so much? Is it about your play?' Madam asked.

Binod was still engrossed in his thoughts. He didn't answer anything.

Madam said-' Don't worry. With the blessings of Lord Jagannath, the play will be a success.'

Binod looked at her. She was draped in a yellow silk saree and had washed her hair as they were going for Lord Jagannath Darshan. Her wet hair was scattered on her back. There was a small red bindi on her forehead and the hangings on her ears that she bought from Bansal Jewelers. She was looking beautiful.

Why can't he control his feeling though he is going for Jagannath Darshan? Madam looked down and asked –' What are you looking at?'

-'Nothing'.

-' Liar'. She said.

What was she expecting to hear? Did she expect that I should appreciate her?

Do all women want to be appreciated by men?

Malini Baral also wears an imitation silk saree and before going to the stage she asks-' Sir, how do I look in this saree?'

Saudamini also wore the dress which was ordered for the play and asked-' How do I look in this dress?'

When I appreciated Kalyani for her beauty she always got irritated and said-' Do you know anything other than a woman's body?'

Kalyani isn't a woman- She is like a dictionary that has the words like abuse, taunt, disdain, and scorn.

Binod laughed loudly.

-' What happened? Madam asked curiously.

-' Nothing happened.' Binod replied.

-' Did you decide that you will tell me lies and go for Jagannath darshan?'

Binod left way for the lorry which was behind to overtake their vehicle and said-' Lie is a beautiful and safe way to escape.' 'Does anyone speak the truth in life? To run after false promise and possibility is life. Death is the biggest truth! But human beings think that is a lie and ignore it. If I ask you about what were you thinking, will you tell me the truth?' Binod asked in a challenging way.

Madam smiled silently. Binod said-'Someone has said, language conveys the feelings but it also hides feelings. He has told the truth."

-' I don't want to listen to your Tattva (Element of reality). Tell me what will you ask Lord Jagannath for?'

Binod answered very softly-' To ask and to give is immaterialist for him. He is omniscient. What is the necessity to ask him? He is the king of the kings. What will anyone give him? Whenever I stand in front of Lord Jagganath I couldn't understand what to ask him for. Is there any perfection in life?' Binod sounded a little serious.

-' You too dangle between perfection and imperfection is life. Is there life without imperfection or life without perfection?'

He said in a lighter note-' I was talking about the element of reality but now it has turned to Philosophy.'

-' This is Shreekshetra'. Here a fool becomes wise and I am just a mere human being. How much time will I take to become a philosopher?' Madam said and smiled.

The car was crossing the bridge at Atharnala. As the road was under construction so there was a diversion.

Which way is Bada Danda?

Binod took the vehicle on the south side diversion.

37

On the Puri –Konark Marine drive there was a multi-storied building. Binod was surprised to see the well- planned house. There was a big hall on each floor and a wide porch in the front. In front of it was the Marine drive. There were bushes on both sides and a few cashew nut trees. From the porch, the sea looked like a vast landscape. Very far, near the horizon, a fishing boat looked like a silhouette. A flock of birds was flying towards the south.

Binod suddenly remembered that it's migration season. During this time thousands of birds migrate from Siberia to Chilika.

Whenever he remembers Chilika he remembers the small fishing boats and the swans. He remembers about Saradei and her little thatched house. While traveling from Balugao to Rambha he remembered Saradei's husband who left her. Where Saradei would have been sitting waiting for him? Though he knows that these are the characters conceived in the novel, still he finds them real. Even though he knows the reality but still he searches for it as if,if he finds Saradei he will feel a little relaxed.

They were on their way for a picnic. Suresh Bhanja got irritated by his thoughts and said-' You sentimental fool. You could have collected Saradei's address from the novelist.'

Lata is doing the role of Saradei. She can manage though not so well. Still, something is lacking somewhere. Binod isn't able to make out. He can find flaws in Muna Panda and Malini's acting but he isn't able to make out the imperfection when Lata acts as Saradei.

He couldn't completely cover 'Neela Saila' in detail. Few stories couldn't be completed like the last dialogue of Ramachandra Deva. What can he do? He is just an artist. There are many things that aren't feasible.

He could understand that the house belongs to madam. But he couldn't understand her intention. He has seen many lands on the way which were surrounded by a fence. Real estate owners purchase these lands either to do the plotting and sell it or to construct apartments. Maybe madam is interested in real estate or construction.

They are rich people and they can do anything.

What will be the dimension of this land? Is it thirty acres or more than that? There is a boundary wall in the front and on the other three sides, there are concrete pillars with a wire fence. How much property does madam have? She must have spent three to four crores for making an 'A' class party like Dasabhuja.

She left the government teaching job and he is dreaming about such a job. In the mystery of that dream the enthusiasm for 'Neela Saila' is slowly fading. Now he feels as if 'Neela Saila' is a burden for him. He will go to Delhi as soon as it's over. Where did madam go leaving him alone? The watchman also went along with her. Maybe any of her relatives is there in the nearby village.

Puri is crowded now because of *Panchuka*. People have to take the ticket and go in a line under the supervision of two to three security guards. In between if the people in the line stopped moving the security guards like the bus conductors say- Move ahead! Move ahead. It 's difficult to see Lord

Jagannath and pray the Lord in that huge crowd. It is too disheartening to go to Puri and not being able to see Lord Jagannath properly. He had no interest to go to the sea beach in the sun. Bihari's snacks stall is also closed during the daytime and it will open in the evening. They drank two cool drinks and went to the Marine drive. They thought that after the darshan of Lord Jagannath they will eat something so they didn't have their breakfast in the morning. Now they were hungry. There were no shops nearby. Where did madam go?

In the Bali Yatra competition, Dasabhuja's performance will be showcased on the last day. There was a good collection in Trishula camp and because of that Bholi babu extended the show for two more days.

Today is an off day for Binod. During the rehearsal of 'Neela Saila' already the rule of Economics' Law of demising returns' is into practice. There are no new prospects in the imagination. There is nothing more to expect from Malini, Muna Panda, and Babita regarding their acting. There is no point in rehearsing for namesake. It would have been better if 'Neela Saila' would have got a chance to be staged at the beginning of the competition so that he could have made the necessary preparation to go to Delhi. He doesn't know whether he will get a reservation on the train or not. It will be better if he books his tickets today while returning. He isn't able to gather his courage to say madam regarding his Delhi trip as she is very keen and is taking a lot of interest in the play.

The watchman came with four coconuts and madam was walking behind him.

While drinking coconut water she asked-' How is this place?'

-' The place is on the Marine drive so what is there to ask about it? Are you going to the plotting of this land and sell or are you planning to begin any type of construction here?'

-' I don't have any plans to go ahead with real estate or construction agency. I have taken this land from the government on a lease for ninety nine years. I have a plan to construct a studio here like Kalinga Studio and have taken the lease based on that condition. Isn't it a good place for a studio?' Madam asked and looked at his face eagerly.

-' I don't have much idea about it. I haven't got an opportunity to see Kalinga Studio. How can I give my opinion?'

-' I have thought that after Bali Yatra competition gets over we will go to Hyderabad to see Ramoji Film City. I will get some basic idea.'

-' What's the use if I go? Rather it's better to take a technical person along with you.'

The watchman came and said-' Prasad from the temple has come. Shall I serve? Madam said-' We will discuss it later. You may go and wash your hands. We will have lunch.'

The watch served the food on the porch in banana leaves. There were few things like rice, dal, paneer curry, cauliflower fry, coconut chutney, and some sweet dishes. Binod ate such tasty Prasad after so many days. He ate to his heart content.

After having his lunch he asked-' Where did you get his tasty Prasad? It is like embrosia.'

The watchman said- 'The Prasad prepared here is very good. People come from different places to have Prasad here. It's the grace of the goddesses. Even if only rice and dal is cooked then also people like it.'

It was like his childhood memory to eat in the banana leaf. At that time during marriages and other ceremonies, food was served in banana leaf. Kaeya Jena use to arrange for the banana leaves. It tastes different when hot food is served on a banana leaf. Where is banana leaf available now a days?

Madam said-' There is no electricity connection till now. The transformer is in the village. A separate transformer is necessary for the studio and to begin with the construction. After Bali Yatra competition is over something can be done.'

The watchman was spreading the bed in a hall. Binod picked up a mat and said-' I will sleep on the porch.'

Madam said-' There is no fan here. Can you sleep?' She was giving a wicked smile.

Binod said-' Wind is blowing from the seashore. Is there any necessity of fan here?

The watchman brought a pillow and gave him.

Binod was feeling sleepy. He didn't get time to take a rest after the show and he immediately fell asleep.

38

Saudamini bought a red silk saree for the wedding night scene of Ramachandra Deva and Rajia Begum. She was constantly giving instructions to the makeup artist Mohan on how to do her makeup. There is no information in 'Neela Saila' regarding the attire on wedding night but Binod has imagined it differently, with a glittering kurta and salwar. Ramachandra Deva might have also never thought of Rajia wearing a saree. Of course, he was startled to see Rajia in *Baise Pahacha* dressed in the Muslim attire. But that was a different situation. That is the story of another novel. There is no room for such self enjoyment in 'Neela Saila'.

Attire refers to the conception in our mind like when we think about a teacher, we imagine him in dhoti , kurta, and glasses with an innocent face or a lawyer in a black coat and white pants. Similarly wedding night creates an image of a gorgeous silk saree, red vermilion on the forehead, alta on feet, and mehendi on hands. There is no connection of wedding night with the attire like a glittering kurta and a salwar. It's a thought of the preoccupied mind that can't be argued.

Rajia Begum was a victim of state politics. Ramachandra Deva's union with her wasn't because of self interest or conspiracy. But Ramachandra Deva introspected himself in isolation and concluded that- If required he will renounce his religion for the sake of Rajia Begum and he won't regret it.

Is it simply an attraction? It may not be. It's an emotion of a man shown in return for the selfless love of a woman. The arguments and conflicts which are between men and women are based on affection and ego. Literacy, culture, heritage, and progress are just empty slogans of man's subconscious mind.

He has a conflict in his mind to go to Delhi as he is emotionally bonded to Dasbhuja. Isn't there an attraction of unconditional love?

He suddenly remembered the incident that happened three days back.

The day he went with madam, he slept in her house on Puri Konark Marine drive for a long time. Madam was waiting eagerly for him to wake up from his sleep. She told the watchman to prepare tea and explained to him her next plan.

She said that she will settle the retired artists there. To make Binod understand clearly she said-' Do you remember Dhira babu's face on that day? He can make his living, unlike Chana babu. He has his wife to take care of him but he looked as if he is rejected by everyone. He is living in an unfriendly atmosphere waiting for his last.'

Binod thought that it's absolutely true. Though Dhira babu is self confident and friendly, he looked colorless and subdued on that day like a barren tree.

Madam said-' You must have heard about the ill fate of Chana babu. When I think about the future of Bishnu babu, Benu Ustad, and Raghu babu ,I feel sad. The tent of the theatrical company is a colorful world. After they retire from there, no one thinks about them. Those who confine them to the materialistic world are not true artists. A person who has spent his life as an artist and in old age when returns to the materialistic world, he is like a fish out of water. At least they can spend their time along with the friends and other retired artists. If I construct an auditorium they can stage play there. As in the school, the play is performed by students in a similar way plays will be performed here by the old artists. It will be fun. It will help them to spend their time. You will write plays for them and I will go to Haripur to arrange costumes for them.'

Where is the time to fulfill these dreams? After 'Neela Saila' is staged he will go to Delhi. Binod was thinking absent mindedly. He visualized the study room of Mr. Bada Jena. Books, magazines, class notes, lectures in the class, and research.

That is a different world. There won't be any need for makeup at night. There won't be a woman like Malini Baral , a stubborn girl like Saudamini, a man like Muna Panda, or a cheap playwright like Shankar Bhola. He will also guide an enthusiastic student and give him knowledge of life.

-' This house will be a holiday home only for the artists those who worked in a theatre. Whenever they visit Puri and Konark they will stay here.' Madam had many plans.

Binod interrupted her in between and said-' I think… He couldn't gather his courage to tell anything to madam.

-' What are you thinking?' Madam asked curiously.

-' I will go to Delhi.'

-' Do you have any work at Delhi?'

-' Professor Samsuddin has invited me and after that Binod spoke to her about his dream, his regret, and his weakness towards teaching. He wanted to say everything and feel lighter.

He thought that after listening to him madam will become serious. But nothing like that happened. After listening to it madam became very happy and said-' It's good. Why didn't you tell me this good news yesterday? She said- 'Today I had a notion that something good will happen.'

What is the relationship between her notion and going to Delhi? Is he so dear to her?

How different is she? Just a few minutes back she was planning to go to Hyderabad and about writing a play and now she is motivating him to go to Delhi. Doesn't the shattering of dreams have any effect on her? Or is she far away from all the emotions?

-' When are you planning to go?'

- 'I have to reach by the twentieth of this month. On seventienth, we have the competition so I will leave on eighteenth.'

- 'So you will leave on the eighteenth but till now you haven't booked the ticket. Will you get the tickets or not? Let's go back to Bhubaneswar immediately and book the ticket before the reservation counter is closed.'

It seems as if madam was waiting eagerly to send him to Delhi. But what's the point in thinking about it when it's certain that he has to go to Delhi. He has to leave everything and go. Why is he becoming emotional as it's time to leave? Where were so much of his emotions buried? He has spent a long time in Dasabhuja. He has come across happiness, sadness, envy, criticism, and praise under this tent. Dasabhuja has given him a place when he was jobless, has given him recognition. Just because Professor Samsuddin called him, he is leaving all these behind. He will leave behind Bitcha, Ramani babu, and their selfless love. He can speak to them sometimes in his busy schedule but what about the folding cot, the table fan, and the porcelain bowl in which he mixes color for his makeup? He doesn't know if he can meet them again or not. They will go into the custody of someone else. All these memories will slowly fade. If by chance he takes out the manuscript of 'Neela Saila' it will be like an old album for him.

It will be a new life. How will it be? Will it be engrossing like American Literature or will be grizzly like the sky of the month of October? No one can say.

He wants to go around and say goodbye to all of them. He wants to say them- All of you remain hale and hearty. I don't know whether all of you will remember me or not but I will miss you all.

Binod went and looked at everything as he will be busy with the preparation of 'Neela Saila' and in winding up things. He showed his love and affection for everyone.

Bholi babu said-' I am also giving a thought to leave the theatrical company and to go back to the village. How much will I work at this age? What will be the condition of the party after you leave? The people of my village are insisting on me to be the Sarapancha. I am here only because of the attachment to this party.

Benu Ustad said-' I knew Binu, you will one day touch the pinnacle. Take care of yourself in an unknown place.'

Malini Baral said-' Will sir remember us after going to Delhi?'

Muna Panda said-' The thrill in theatre is different Binod babu. I would have got another job. Why are you so much interested in the teaching profession? Now madam will burden me with all the responsibilities. As you were there I was free from the burden.'

Bitcha said-' Bina bhai I will go to the station to bid you farewell. Both of us will eat together for the last time. It's not possible to meet you again. He became emotional. He tried to ease himself and said-' I will not request them to give money.' Bitcha turned his face and left. He was trying to hide his tears. What will Binod answer? How will he make Bitcha understand? He doesn't know how to console others. He stood still under the tent of Dasabhuja as if he was waiting for someone.

39

Where was so much excitement? There were so much of emotions for the play 'Neela Saila'

After getting a phone call from Professor Samsuddin his anxiety for the play came to an end. While going to Puri along with madam to perform the rituals for the manuscript he wasn't so enthusiastic. He was engrossed in his thoughts, in dreams, in reminiscence, and in melancholy.

Does it happen often? When a human being waits for the ultimate and when it comes, it evanesces. He envisaged so many things before bringing back Saudamini to the party but after she came back he feels that it would have been better if she wouldn't have come back.

He thought that like other plays, 'Neela Saila' will also lose its charm after it has been staged. That was most pathetic. Professor Samsuddin could have called him a little late. The passion that he had for 'Neela Saila' was the cause of his agony. Though he was trying his best still he wasn't able to concentrate as he was captivated by his thoughts about going to Delhi. But that passion was concealed somewhere in the Bali Yatra ground and as soon as he reached there they predominated.

Who publicized about 'Neela Saila'? There was no advertisement from the party in the newspaper regarding this play. Neither there were posters nor the jeep went around for publicity. Maybe whatever was done was done by the Natya Mahotsava committee. People thronged around 10 O' Clock in the morning to purchase the tickets. The committee inevitability discussed with Bholi babu and opened the counter around 2 O' Clock in the afternoon. By 5 O' Clock all the tickets were sold and a House Full board was hung on the counter.

Kamal Mishra had already reached Trishulia camp and today Dhira babu came. After watching two to three scenes during stage rehearsal he hugged him and said-' Binod you have written a wonderful script. I feel blessed.'

Binod said-' Sir,You must be knowing that most of the dialogues in this isn't my composition. I have included many dialogues directly from 'Neela Saila'. I thought that it's not required to change those. Surendra babu was not only a litterateur but also a dramatist. ' Prithiva Balabha', ' Madhu Singdha' 'Kandhai Ghara' are some of his famous stories. He had a lot of interest in writing novels during his youth. He spent the money from his pocket,took Annapurna Theatre on rent ,and staged ' Mahakhyudha' drama.

Dhira babu patted on his back and said-' I know.' But I think you don't know the problem with the new dramatists. They think that the audience is naïve so they prolong the dialogues which becomes difficult for the actors and the actresses to remember and also become incomprehensible to the audience. It's good that your play doesn't have that problem. I couldn't have written a better play than this and if you sincerely want then you can also become a good playwright.'

Kamal Mishra said-' Binod babu has planned to leave the theatre and to become a lecturer. Where does he have time to write a play?'

Dhira babu touched him affectionately and said-'It's good, very good. If he becomes a lecturer of course he can't act, but what's the problem in writing a play? To become a good teacher you need to be a good actor.'

-' It will be good if Binod babu will write the play and send it. I will give the direction. Of course, there will be a difference between my direction and his direction. He is more focused.' Kamal Mishra Said.

Binod interrupted him and said-' Kamal babu, Please don't say like that. If you would have been there then the play 'Neela Saila 'would have been better. You didn't want to take a risk for a historical play and that's why you kept yourself away from it.'

Kamal Mishra stood up and held his hand. He said-' Who said this to you? After spending so many years in the theatre don't I know about the psychology of the audience? Any play based on Lord Jagganath has neither flopped nor will flop in the future. I wanted that this play should be your sole achievement. I can't be at par with you but can't I be a well wisher of yours?'

He became emotional.

-' Binod was about to say- Excuse me, but he couldn't. He hugged Kamal Mishra affectionately.

Ramani babu suddenly started playing the tune of the Hindi song-' Dost –Dost- Na raha'.

Baban babu suddenly got up and said loudly-'Stop ! Ramani babu, stop!. Now play the tune of new music- Dost-Dost-Dost- Kanha Nahi gaya, Yaha raha-raha' The rehearsal hall burst with laughter.

He danced with joy and said-' Bolo Anadae Ake bar. Haribol!.' But is it possible? Binod knows that it's a momentary excitement. After the play 'Neela Saila' is staged gradually everything will become normal and all of them will again go back to their shell and by that time the time given by Professor Samsuddin will be over. If he will miss this chance once he can get it again.

Saudamini came to him and asked-' What are you thinking?'

Bitcha made an announcement-' Binod bhai will take the final decision after the play. Let's rehearse now. Anshupa and Indradhnu didn't stage their plays well but Indrani opera has staged a good play on the first day. Anyhow we have to bag the first prize and that will be the greatest gift to Bina bhai during his departure.'

Baban babu said-' Are you a bad omen? You say both good and bad. You said just now that Bina babu will rethink his decision. Why are you again saying that he will go?

Kamal Mishra stood up and said-' Baban babu ,just wait for a minute. Benu babu and Ramani babu have prepared a classical dance for the *Devdasi* dance. I think that after that dance is over the focus on the screen will be minimized and in the close up will only be on Lord Jagannath , Balabhadra, and Subhadra and finally, it will focus on Lord Jagannath. Jagannath will be on his chariot. The sound of the bell, conch, and clarinet will be heard in the second stage. On the chariot Jaguni will shout like the Dahuka- Bolo Ananda Akebar !-' The audience will say-' Haribol'! The chariot will move forward and will slowly become invisible. Lord Jagannath will be visible and Ramachandra Deva will enter the stage.

Binod shouted in excitement- 'Marvelous idea friend, marvelous!'

40

Where did Binod see this scene?

Was it in his dream or imagination?

Is it in Puri's Bada Dana or while writing the dialogues of 'Neela Saila'?

But this scene is very close to his heart. In front of eyes, neither was the second stage of Dasabhuja nor was the artificially created *Ratna Bedi* .

His imagination was unearthly illuminated in front of his eyes. He felt as if he lost his consciousness. He became still. He was enchanted and looked at that heavenly sight. Tears dropped down from his eyes. The sound of Omkar reverberated and he said-' Jai Jagannath !'. There was utter silence in the audience gallery and suddenly the silence broke with the utterance of – Jai Jagannath ! The plateau of Mahanadi reverberated with the sound.

He was speechless, motionless, and enthralled and was standing on the main stage. He felt as if he was in deep meditation for a long time to listen to the huzzah. Today it has become fruitful and he has been blessed.

He could hear the sound of the conch, bells, and clarinet. Bitcha zestfully shouted- ' Jai Jagannath, Jai Jagannath.'

Bali Yatra ground reverberated with the sound of Hari Bol, and *Hulahuli* .*Nandighosa* started rolling.

"Jagannath Swami Nayana-Patha-Gami Bhavatu me" Ramani babu sang the devotional song dedicated to Lord Jagannath fervently.

But is it Bada Danda? Is it Lord Jagannath's *Ghosayatra*?

This is attainment of Nirvan and *Koili Baikuntha* of all the human desires. Thirst and satisfaction are both same here. Binod was overwhelmed as if he has attained enlightenment.

After the scene was over and the lights were switched off Kamal Mishra came running and lifted Binod and went towards the green room.

Dhira babu was waiting outside the green room. He hugged Binod and said-' I have seen Lord Jagannath with this mortal eyes but today I experienced his existence in my heart. My life is blessed.'

Benu Ustad who was performing the role of Lakshmi Paramaguru came down from the second stage. Binod didn't get a chance to touch his feet before going to the stage. He kneeled to touch Benu Ustad's feet. Benu Ustad said- ' What will I bless you? A person who is blessed by Lord Jagannath doesn't need anyone's blessings. You are like my son. I will not touch your feet but I will salute your expertise in acting.' He folded his hands.

Binod said-' Why are you saying like this? You aren't only respectable for me but also venerable. Is my acting worth it? I don't know what happened to me today. I forgot my dialogues when I looked at Lord Jagannath.' Dhira babu said- ' Is it possible for a human being to answer this question? Only Lord Jagannath can answer to it but he is quiet. Try to understand his silence.'

Raghu babu came outside the green room and said- 'When I was learning acting at that time I heard about aesthetic acting. I have done the role of Jagannath, Balabhadra, and Subhadra in many plays but today I understood the meaning of aesthetic acting.'

-Hey ! Raghu babu why are you discussing so many things? Look at Bholi babu how is he sitting in the second stage.' Baban babu pointed at the second stage and said.

Bholi babu was laying down on the stage and was praying. Today he completely forgot about the collection, calculation, and his sleep.

Kamal Mishra came back with tea and water. He made Binod sit on a chair and said-' Binod, today you have astounded everyone with your performance. I was thrilled. This play will be a turning point in the history of Odia theatre.'

Binod interrupted him and said-' You are wrong my dear friend. Your scenography made me powerless. I forgot my dialogues and acting.'

Kamal Mishra said-' I shouldn't boast about it. What experience do I have about historical plays? It is the sublimity of the play. In Shreekshetra a donkey becomes learned but in the play 'Neela Saila' a mere record dancer turned into a classical dancer. Did you ever notice Babita dancing so perfectly during the rehearsal?'

Babita danced tirelessly on the main stage as Suna Mahuri. She danced perfectly today without any hesitation. Benu Ustad was giving her instructions sitting in the musical circle but Babita didn't pay any attention to it. Binod thought that she will keep on dancing continuously and will lose her consciousness on the stage.

-' Ramachandra Deva , now be prepared for the war.' Said Benu babu and laughed loudly. Binod turned back and looked at him. Bishu babu gave him a cigarette and said-' Bina, do you know what do I wish for after seeing you acting today? I feel if Lord Jagannath could make me young I will act as a villain opposite you.'

Binod said-' Today in this makeup who can make out your age? You look like a thirty years old young man.'

Bishnu babu took out the sword from the scabbard and pointing at the chest of Baban babu said-' Stupid Padmanavha Deva, have you ever seen a villain turning old?'

Baban babu bowed his head like a courtier in front of the king and said-' Gustakhi mafah, Jahapanna.'

Kamal Mishra laughed and looked at Bishnu babu and said-' Mohan Singh is a magician.'

Before going for the makeup Binod saw that Bali Yatra ground was overcrowded. As many of them couldn't get the tickets they were trying to sneak into the tent. The authority requested madam to take out the barricade.

Madam asked Binod-' Will there be any problem with the second stage? Binod didn't have any plan for the second stage. He thought that right from the beginning till the end of the play, a screen will be hanging there. So he answered-' There is no problem.'

Kamal Mishra would have objected but he kept quiet looking at the situation. Binod saw that people were gathered on Mahanadi Ring Road and were pushing each other as if they have come to see Ratha Yatra.

But where is madam? He didn't see her for a long time. If he has acted so wonderfully in the play then madam would have been the first person to congratulate him.

Lata came outside the green room with a pitcher under her arm. Before going to the stage she kept the pitcher down and touched the feet of Binod and Bishnu babu. Today she is going to act for the first time on the stage. Binod wished her and said-' What are you doing Lata? Why did you touch my feet? I am just a mere human being, a mere artist. You should bow down before the Lord.'

Lata looked at the screen on the second stage and bowed down her head.

-' Sara, Hey! You ill-fated woman.'

Who is giving the voice-over today? Shrikant is in the green room. Who is imitating the voice of an old lady so flawlessly?

From a distance was heard the sound of the horse trotting. Binod remembered that it was interval and the stage lights were switched off. Lata went ahead towards the stage slowly and he climbed the second stage hastily.

While pouring water in his hands Binod noticed that her innocent face was looking more innocent. Her eyes were filled with sadness. Her eyes were brimming like the water of Chilika. Did the water from the pitcher fall on her saree and she got wet or was it Kamal Mishra's direction? Her youthfulness was revealed through her wet saree. There was no artificiality in that. Her face was shining like the still water of a lake.

Lata said shyly like a village bride-'Please, give me the way.'

But as Lata was inexperienced and there was no microphone near her so she couldn't be heard. Lata stepped back and again repeated the dialogue-'Please, give me the way.'

This time she was heard but her voice was very feeble like the tone of a helpless woman.

The audience clapped in the audience gallery.

Before the scene of the wedding night Saudamini wore the red silk saree and asked- 'How do I look?' Binod couldn't understand what she asked. What does Saudamini want to know? Does she want to know how does she look like in that saree?

Malini sometimes asks in a similar way. The only difference is between the silk and the imitation silk saree but the intention behind asking the question is the same. He turned his face as he was irritated. Saudamini came closer to him and asked –' Won't it be good if I don't wear a Burkha? Binod couldn't understand whether to laugh or to be annoyed at her as she was talking foolishly.

To control the situation Kamal Mishra said-' What is the necessity of wearing a Burkha on a wedding night?'

Saudamini was happy and acted as if she knows everything and said-'I was saying the same thing to Mohan Singh but he compelled me to wear a Burkha.'

- 'In the previous scene, it was necessary. In that scene, Rajia Begum was meeting an unknown man but the next scene is the scene of the wedding night. What is the necessity of wearing Burkha?'

Saudamini was again trying to argue. Kamal Mishra said firmly-' Why do you argue all the time?'

Saudamini said-' Am I arguing? In the last scene, he told me to wear a Burkha and in this scene, he is telling me to wrap a shawl.'

Binod wanted to say-' People aren't able to see your silk saree that's the reason why you are arguing'. But he didn't say anything to her and went to the green room to change his dress.

After the scene was over he thought that it was the worst scene of the play.

Scenes of 'Neela Saila 'were staged one after another. There was a lot of appreciation from the audience. But,Bishnu babu suddenly noticed that someone from the audience threw a sandal on the stage. Then there was a scream and he used abusive language and said-' Pull that Muslim fellow from the stage.'

Bishnu babu announced in the voice of Taki Khan-' Then let Jagannath temple be demolished.'

Binod was in the green room at that time to change his dress from Hafis Kaddar to Ramachandra Deva. He was agitated and was ready to go to the stage to protest.

Bishnu babu came down from the stage. He laughed

and said-' That sandal which was thrown is like an appreciation for my acting. If they wouldn't have thrown the sandal and would have given the slogan- Taki Khan Jindabad, would you have been happy?'

The audience was calm and quiet. There was pin-drop silence. He has never seen the audience sitting so quietly and watching the performance.

But, where did madam go? Of course, she is never available during the show but today she should watch the play.

It's right that he conceived the thought of staging 'Neela Saila' but madam is the whole and sole of it. She took so much interest and was enthusiastic about the play and finally she went to a stubborn girl like Saudamini to bring her back. Maybe no one knows about it but the Almighty and Binod know that she was very much interested for the role of Rajia Begum. Saudamini has a smiling face and her acting has a resemblance with Rajia Begum but Rajia Begum's selfless dedication wasn't there in Saudamini's nature or behavior. She is like Kalyani who always thinks about her freedom and is filled with ego. Ego spoils the beauty of a woman and Saudamini doesn't know that. It's worthless to make her understand.

Bitcha called him and handed him over a broomstick covered with golden paper and said-' It's time for **Chera Panhara** scene.'

They named the scene in this way during rehearsal. Binod walked towards the stage like a king and he heard-' The king represents Lord Jagannath.'The sound reverberated from the audience gallery- Jai King of Khurdha Ramachandra Deva!

Who taught them this huzza? The preparation which was made before was different. From a distance was heard a huzza.

On the microphone was heard a devotional song of Dina Krushna Das. Ramani babu was singing the song which touched his heart. Today he is singing a song in praise of Lord Jagannath. Binod was filled with emotions and at that time Benu Ustad came down from the second stage and welcomed him to do the rituals of Chera Panhara .

Binod had an apprehension that by the time the play gets over it will be dawn. During the day the actors and actresses of the theatre in their makeup will not look good. But Kamal Mishra managed the things well and the last scene of the play was staged before sunrise.

Where did madam go? The play will be over after one more scene. The announcement of the result of the competition is a process but they should get the prize. Where will he search for her? Whom will he ask? Bitcha is on the stage.

He could hear Benu Ustad chanting the mantra- 'Om Madhuvaata ritayate madhuksharanti sindhavah.

Maadhveernah-santvoshadheeh. Madhunaktamutoshasi madhumat-parthivam rajah. Madhu dyaurastu nah pita

Madhumaanno vanaspatir-madhumaam astu sooryah. Madhveergaavo bhavantu nah. Om shantih, shantih, shantih.

Binod was waiting for the audience to be silent. Ramani babu announced in the microphone- Shantih, Shantih, Shantih but the audience didn't become silent. Binod was looking at the devotion of the audience. He has to go to the main stage and from there he has to come to the second stage again. He would have gone back to the first stage but that wasn't possible.

'Neela Saila' was incomplete. Was it the wish of God?

Is it a call for 'Niladri Bijaya'?

What is this new drama Lord Jagannath?

What is your wish Lord?

The judges and the chief guest got up from their place.

The result of the competition was announced but on the backdrop was still hanging the painting of Lord Jagannath with a mysterious smile.

Binod looked at the eyes of Lord Jagannath and asked in a disturbed voice-'Madam?'

Before his voice could be unheard in that huzza he heard her voice. She called-'Binod !'

Binod turned back and held her hands.

■■

BLACK EAGLE BOOKS

www.blackeaglebooks.org
info@blackeaglebooks.org

Black Eagle Books, an independent publisher, was founded as a nonprofit organization in April, 2019. It is our mission to connect and engage the Indian diaspora and the world at large with the best of works of world literature published on a collaborative platform, with special emphasis on foregrounding Contemporary Classics and New Writing.